LOVE IS BLIND

By Peter J. Murgio

ISBNs:
eBook 978-1-960346-77-3
Paperback 978-1-960346-78-0
Hardback 978-1-960346-79-7

Published by Authors Unite Publishing

Dedication

———— ❦ ————

Love Is Blind is dedicated to the most beautiful woman in my world, my loving wife. For fifty-four years, she has been the inspiration that enlightens me, the spark that keeps me going, and the wind that propels my journey...not only as a writer, but as a husband, a father, and a better man. Her love, patience, and quiet strength have carried me through every chapter of life.

She is the one who steps up without hesitation, offering her heart, her wisdom, her courage, and above all, her unconditional love. I have seen beauty around the world, but none like the woman who stands beside me through sunlit days and storm-dark skies.

Thank you, dear Kathy, for showing me what true beauty is. My gratitude also extends to my family, to my readers, and to my editor, Erica, whose rare blend of talent, insight, and generosity helped shape this book and refine my voice.

To my wonderful wife, and to all who inspire, uplift, and believe in love.

Chapter 1

Bursting with Pride

Bernie jolted awake, his mind still racing from last night. Today wasn't just another morning. It was a page-turner.

Not just for him, but for Joy Nordstrom, his latest and greatest client.

To Bernie, his job was his wife, and his clients were his children. Joy wasn't just a client, she was his newest newborn. And he had raised plenty over the years. No matter their age or accomplishments, they were all his "babies." It was his charge, no, his duty, to nurture them into stardom, fame, and fortune.

Of course, altruism was part of it. But so was his 10 percent. The 1980s and 1990s had been good to him.

That 10 percent had bought Bernie a very comfortable life: penthouse views, designer suits, and a reputation that could open just about any door in New York.

He threw back the covers and strode to the window, peering down at Fifth Avenue. The usual hum of traffic rolled by, indifferent, predictable, oblivious.

But Bernie wasn't indifferent.

He was charged. Restless. Waiting.

His eyes flicked to the door.

Where the hell was Julian?

At last, the knock.

"Good morning, Mr. Rubin. Here are the papers."

Bernie snatched them up as if they were bars of gold from Fort Knox, his chest buzzing with anticipation. This was it, the whole enchilada.

He told himself, *it's just business,* but it never was; every deal, every headline, any of his "babies" had the potential to crown him ... or crush him and his reputation.

Fate was knocking. And Bernie? He was setting the table, pouring the coffee, and pulling out the chairs, ready to welcome his old friend.

It was his morning ritual, reading every paper, furiously. It was his lifeline to what was happening in the world and often the inspiration for his next big move. So, Julian was charged with collecting *The New York Times, The New York Post, The Daily News,* and *The Wall Street Journal.*

Realizing Julian was still standing there, Bernie patted his pajama pockets, searching for his usual tip, only to remember he wasn't even dressed.

"Wait a minute, Julian, I'll be right back."

He scurried back to the bedroom and fished out a crisp fiver, a habit he never skipped. Delivering papers wasn't part of Julian's job, but for Bernie, he made an exception.

Bernie "took care of him," which, in New York terms, meant only one thing: he was a generous tipper.

Bernie returned with the bill, handing it over.

"Here you go, bud, have a cup of coffee on me."

Julian smiled. Bernie said the same thing every day, and Julian always responded with the same heartfelt reply.

"Thank you, sir. It's most kind of you."

"You're welcome, Julian. And good morning to you too."

Julian was the longtime and dedicated night doorman of Trenton Towers, an upscale Fifth Avenue residential building. Designed by Emery Roth, one of the city's most prestigious architects, Trenton Towers stood at the corner of Fifth Avenue and 64th Street, gazing over Central Park like an unshakable grande dame.

Living at the "Towers" wasn't something to be taken lightly. Not that long ago, someone like Bernie wouldn't have stood a chance. The well-heeled neighbors had made that clear, especially Mrs. Cornelius Van Zile, whose blue hair matched her blue blood.

Mrs. Van Zile saw herself as the gatekeeper of old wealth, determined to keep the "undesirables" out. To her, anyone outside the inner circle was a mere social climber. And those who weren't Anglo-Saxon, or worse, were part of "the tribe" with their silly Saturday services, were persona non grata.

Historically, many prestigious Fifth Avenue co-ops discreetly enforced antisemitic and racially restrictive policies. In New York's social circles, it was an open secret: prospective buyers who didn't "fit" were quietly marked "NOK" (Not Our Kind) by gatekeeping co-op boards, ensuring rejection before an application was even considered.

But things changed. By the 1980s, wealthy "NOKs" leveraged new anti-discrimination laws and the fading fortunes of old money to crack open doors that had once been bolted shut.

Bernie's new money bought a lot: the finest clothing, personal drivers inexpensive cars, and, of course, his crowning acquisition, the penthouse at Trenton Towers.

Unlike most mornings, Bernie didn't wait for coffee before reading the papers. He usually saved *The New York Times* for last, out of habit. But today, the *Times* being the most influential paper, he needed to see what they had to say about last night's gala.

Bernie wondered if all his bets would pay off, or if Lady Luck would give him the finger.

His fingers flipped through the pages, faster now. Where was it? He scanned, heart pounding. And then, there it was! Lifestyle section. Boldface type, just above the fold.

He swallowed hard, forcing himself to move forward despite the possibility of being panned.

Diamonds, Couture, and a Rising Star: Joy Nordstrom Steals the Show By Jo Jo Littlejohn

Last night, New York witnessed three L'incomparables: the priceless Mouawad necklace, the most extraordinary haute couture, and the breathtaking face of the most beautiful woman in the world, Joy Nordstrom.

At the risk of being trite, a new star was born on the runway at De Beers's spectacular international event at Javits Center's Upper Exhibition Hall, previewing $600 million worth of exquisite jewelry. The star was not Joy Nordstrom, already the world's most celebrated beauty, but a fashion star: her newly launched design house, World Couture.

The hall had been transformed into a fantasy land by Broadway and Las Vegas set designer Chip Duncan.

As the lights dimmed, mist rose carrying the scent of fresh rain. Storm clouds churned, lightning flickered, thunder clashed. From the ceiling, an orchestra began Ravel's Boléro—softly at first, then swelling until the vast room shook with sound.

Suddenly, sunlight pierced the storm. The music shifted to something lighter, romantic. The first model stepped out, walking through the storm into the sunlight.

Bernie, swelling with pride, took a deep breath and continued reading.

But it was the grand finale no one will ever forget. Princes and moguls, presidents, and playboys leaned forward as silence fell, broken only by a fanfare of trumpets. The lights blazed white-hot. Verdi's Aida Grand March thundered as the most beautiful woman in the world appeared: Miss Joy Nordstrom, dazzling in Mouawad's L'incomparable necklace.

Bernie broke into a sweat as he read. Christ, this is powerful.

The crowd rose, not in applause, but in stunned astonishment, as she glided down the runway in the most elegant of all her gowns. A single spotlight caught the 407-carat diamond—though in this editor's opinion, the gem paled beside its wearer.

When he finished reading, Bernie put the paper down and gazed up at the ceiling.

God had sent him a gift: Joy.

And *The New York Times* was telling the world about her.

It took a few minutes for Bernie to regain his composure.

Weak-kneed and *verklempt*, Bernie reached for his mobile phone.

He punched in the all-too-familiar number, his thoughts consumed by his number-one client.

"Good morning, Joy," he purred, his voice dripping with pride. "It's your Bernie."

At that moment, he realized he wasn't just holding a client. He was holding lightning in a bottle, and the world had no idea what was about to hit it, nor did Joy.

CHAPTER 2

❧

"For unto us a child is born..."

Braga, Portugal. Christmas Eve, 1975

Jonathan Nordstrom rushed through the crowded streets of Braga, one of Portugal's most historical and picturesque towns. The streets were teeming with people, all ready for the holidays. He smiled as he passed the roundabout, seeing the live Presépios with locals dressed as characters from the nativity story.

This rich tradition prevailed throughout the country and vividly displayed the Portuguese people's love of their Catholic faith and the birth of their Savior. Entire families strolled the streets, visiting the different neighborhoods, each with its own tableaux, one more elaborate than the next. Street entertainers wandered about singing *Janeiras*, some of the carols centuries old. Ladies and young girls donned traditional garb and danced gaily to the music.

Even in haste, Jonathan paused for a second. He admired the long bouffant skirts in richly vibrant patterned fabrics, some checked, others striped, ballooning as the women twirled in joyful circles. The outfits were completed with kerchiefs covering dark and silky hair, some tresses so long they passed the dancers' cinched-in waists.

A toddler, dressed as an angel and no more than two years old, pulled on Jonathan's hand, smiled, and whispered, "*Feliz Natal, Senhor.*"

"*Feliz Natal* to you, my little angel," he mouthed back and blew a kiss.

This night felt magical. He was about to become a father.

He arrived at the Saint Miguel de Carvalho Hospital, breathless and flushed with anticipation and nerves. The nun at the ward's desk rose immediately.

"Senhor Nordstrom, come with me. She is in labor."

He was ushered into the delivery room. It was large and softly lit, arranged Lamaze-style. The scent of disinfectant filled the still air and clung to everything, sharp, sterile, and oddly comforting. Nestled in the clutter of lights and equipment, his eyes met Carmella's, lying in bed, her face pale but determined. Monitors beeped softly. A nurse nodded at him gently.

"Come, you may stay. Here, on the side, and hold her hand."

Jonathan stepped to the bedside, grasping Carmella's hand in his.

"Where were you?" she whispered.

"I was out on the boat. The housekeeper couldn't reach me. You weren't due until after New Year's."

Carmella smiled faintly. "Well, I'm sorry, but this little bundle just didn't want to miss Christmas."

Jonathan smiled, leaned in, and kissed her forehead.

Then came a contraction. She squeezed his hand, holding back a scream as best she could. Jonathan grimaced, wishing the pain were his, not hers. Several more contractions followed in rapid succession, each appeared more excruciating than the last. The staff moved into position as the obstetrician coached her through the breathing exercises. The baby was almost here. Jonathan looked on, sharing in the room's rising anticipation, the miracle of birth. A blur of movement. Nurses shifting. A soft whimper, barely audible.

"It's a girl," a nurse exclaimed.

Then ... nothing.

No cries. No chatter. Just silence, dead silence.

The mood shifted in an instant. The nurse's smile vanished. A quiet urgency settled over the room and concerned looks flickered across every face. Machines beeped, then fell silent. Voices dropped. Glances were exchanged.

"She's not breathing."

The obstetrician's tone sharpened.

"No pulse."

"Apgar's still zero. No response," a nurse reported quietly.

He hesitated, then spoke even lower.

"If no change by six ... we call it."

The doctor motioned to one of the nurses. "Get him out of here, stat."

Jonathan froze.

A nurse took his arm and led him quickly out of the room. The door closed behind him with a solid thud.

He stood in the corridor, stunned. His ears rang. He turned to see the nun who had escorted him earlier. She motioned to a wooden bench nearby. He sat, unable to speak.

Through the door, he could hear it, just barely. The soft squeak of shoes, the muted beeping of a machine. Then came the words that shattered him: "She's not responding, doctor. We've lost her."

Jonathan's heart seized. He leaned forward, elbows on his knees, head in his hands.

He couldn't bear it. Not after everything.

The memory came rushing back, all these years. And then his mind drifted to Tuscany, the second honeymoon they saved for and savored, and probably when this long-awaited child was conceived.

They were in a modest but charming hotel set against the rolling hills. Carmella sat on the terrace, a glass of Chianti in her hand, watching the sun melt into the Mediterranean. Her long chestnut hair cascaded to her waist and her dark eyes sparkled with a mix of innocence and allure. He had tiptoed up behind her, covering her eyes.

"Guess who?"

She laughed. "The waiter with the dreamy eyes?"

"Nope. Just that old soldier who still thinks he has the hottest wife in Europe."

Carmella turned and smiled.

That night in Tuscany, they had made love slowly, reverently, not with urgency, but with deep affection, as if honoring something already lost. Parenthood, once a shared dream, had quietly slipped beyond their reach now that they were in their forties. They had accepted that they would never be parents. But they still had each other. And in that quiet knowing, their intimacy had evolved. What had once been a mission, filled with hope and pressure, was now simply an act of love, tender, grounding, and unburdened. Lovemaking had become a sacred ritual, no longer about creating life, but about celebrating the life they had built together.

They thought that chapter had closed, that some dreams were not meant to be. But life, with all its mysteries, wasn't finished surprising them.

Jonathan recalled months later when Carmella stood in their kitchen in Braga, holding a letter from Dr. Angelo.

"I just came from the church," she had said, breathless. "I went to thank God."

"For what?" he asked.

"For our miracle," she whispered. "I'm pregnant."

"Are you sure?"

She nodded. "Tests. Two of them. A baby, Jonathan. We're going to have a baby."

A cry, then another, brought Jonathan back to reality of the cold, dreary hall, just outside the delivery room.

The door opened. The nurse, in a starched white habit with a gold cross on the lapel, stepped out, breathless.

"She's alive," she said softly. "They brought her back. They worked on her, and she came back."

Jonathan stood, unable to speak. The nun crossed herself.

"She's a fighter."

Not long after, they brought Jonathan into the infant urgent care unit. It was dimly lit; soft beeping and the hissing of machines filled the space. A warming lamp glowed over a hospital crib.

"There she is," said the sister. "She doesn't need an incubator, just monitoring."

Jonathan stepped forward.

She was resting peacefully, wrapped in a pink blanket. Wires connected her to blinking monitors.

The nun added gently, "She's not seriously ill. The wires are for observation only."

Jonathan moved closer. His eyes filled with tears, his heart beating so fast, ready to burst. She had unusually thick blonde hair and perfect fingers and toes. Her skin glowed rosy pink, and her eyes were as blue as a July sky. Clearly, she favored his Nordic genes.

"She was born with a smile on her face," the nun said. "So help me, God."

Then Jonathan spotted something on her tiny but elegant neck.

"Look here. She's got a birthmark."

The nun leaned in, squinting over her glasses.

"Oh, *sim*. A little one. Shaped like a heart."

Carmella, now wheeled in beside him, gasped softly.

"Let me see."

The old nun studied it closely. "Indeed, a heart... but in two pieces."

"Yes, Sister, it's so cute. Don't you think?"

The nun hesitated, her eyes lingering on the mark.

"Maybe," she said softly. "But sometimes, God leaves a mark for a reason."

Her remark was quiet, nearly lost in the swirl of joy and relief. But the tone lingered, like a whisper from some deeper knowing.

The next day, as the couple lingered in the hospital room, holding their baby close, the conversation around her name circled back once more as the clock counted down to their discharge. By regulation, hospitals would not allow a baby to leave unless the infant had an official birth certificate, which required a proper name.

"Jonathan," Carmella began, her tone both gentle and determined, "it would mean so much to my family to name her Juliana. My mother has been waiting for this moment almost as long as we have."

Jonathan shifted uncomfortably, casting a wary glance at their sleeping daughter. "I know, Carmella, but … Juliana? I just can't help but think of your mom. You know how she is, a bit of a … presence, let's say. I'd love to give our daughter a fresh start, something that feels more like ours."

Carmella chuckled, sensing his hesitation. "Presence? You mean buttinsky, don't you?" she teased, her eyes twinkling.

"Okay, yes," he admitted with a sigh, "a buttinsky, but in the most loving way, of course. Don't you remember when I wanted to marry you? She did everything short of making you a nun to prevent it."

Carmella laughed, shaking her head. "Oh, believe me, I remember every detail."

"Yeah, me too. I remember when I first came to your house. I was in my uniform. Your mother almost died."

"'A soldier!' she said. 'Not only that but an American soldier. Couldn't you find anyone else?'"

"You know, my mother had been planning my life from the day I was born. According to her plan, I'd marry a nice, local boy, maybe a merchant or a city official, who'd come from a 'respectable' family. Someone like my own kind. After she met you, she said, 'There are so many other men who are dying to have you as their wife … you know, our kind, not some nefarious Americano.' She expected my husband and I would live in a house just down the road from her and produce grandchildren, one after another. But the idea of her little Carmella taking up with someone who was not only an American GI, but a 'heathen' was beyond her. A foreigner, who barely could speak our language, and who would more than likely whisk me away to America, never to be seen again, it scared her half to death."

A small laugh escaped his lips. "Heathen ... I love that part."

"If you only knew how bad it was. She'd look at me with these pleading eyes and say, 'But Carmella, he's not Catholic! Can he even say the Hail Mary? And God knows, he probably eats meat on Friday and worse!' My mother thought anyone who wasn't Catholic was just putting in time here on earth, destined to be damned to hell.

"She was convinced you would drag me into some kind of reckless adventure, a life of sin without redemption."

Jonathan raised his eyebrows, recalling his own encounters with her mother. "Reckless adventure? I wasn't exactly a lawless scoundrel. I was an educated professional, a decorated member of the military, never even got a parking ticket or ran with the wrong crowd. No, all I wanted was just to marry the woman I fell madly in love with. Was that so bad?"

Carmella's smile softened, her laughter fading into a quiet sigh. "She meant well, you know. She was terrified of losing me, she didn't understand about us."

Jonathan nodded, his gaze drifting to their newborn daughter, sleeping peacefully in her crib. "And now we have this, a reminder of endless commitment and boundless love. She's here because we believed in something no one else could see."

Carmella reached out to take his hand, her voice barely above a whisper. "She never fully understood us, did she? But she came around in her way."

"Yeah, but it was painful. I paid the price. Not only did I have to become a card-holding Catholic, I had to promise never to break your heart. And if I did, she swore she would put the 'evil eye' on me."

Carmella laughed, squeezing his hand. "I think it surprised her to see that we made each other happy without needing to fit perfectly into her idea of what our lives should be."

Jonathan nodded thoughtfully. "You know," he said, his voice quieter now, "she might have fought us at first, but deep down, I think she always knew how much I loved you. And when she finally came around, it felt like I was gaining permission to truly be happy."

Carmella's eyes softened. "I think she saw it too. She just didn't know how to say it."

They turned their attention back to their baby, whose tiny hand peeked out from her blanket.

Jonathan smiled, a new thought dawning. But before he spoke, his eyes landed once more on the faint mark at the base of her neck, shaped like a heart, but cleaved down the center.

Maybe the nun was right, he thought. *Maybe God does leave marks for a reason.*

But he decided to let that thought pass.

Carmella gazed lovingly at him. "What if ... what if we added something? A middle name, something that feels like both of us."

He thought for a moment. "Juliana Joy. What do you think? 'Joy' for Christmas Eve and for what she will bring into our lives."

Carmella's eyes brightened, and a smile broke across her face. "Brilliant! Juliana Joy Nordstrom. Yes, I love it. She'll carry a piece of my family's tradition and the joy that's ours.'"

They sat silently for a moment, the memories of their early years filling the room. Finally, Jonathan chuckled. "So, I guess 'buttinsky' is more of an affectionate title now. And maybe she'll be proud of the name we've given her granddaughter."

Carmella nodded. "I think she will. And someday, when Juliana is old enough to hear this story, we'll tell her all about the grandma who nearly turned her mother into a nun... and her father, who loved her enough to weather the storm, Hail Mary's and all."

Jonathan agreed, a warm smile spreading across his face as a sense of peace settled over him. "All right, Juliana Joy it is. She'll be her own person, full of joy, and let's just hope the buttinsky gene skips a generation."

With that, he picked up the birth certificate, carefully writing her name to make it official. Then, leaning close, he sealed the moment with a gentle kiss on Juliana Joy's tiny forehead, their perfect gift on her very first Christmas.

CHAPTER 3

⁓

The Mark

Over the years, Jonathan's wishes prevailed, and Juliana became known to all as Joy, except for her grandmother. The name was a perfect fit, given her personality and disposition. As the child grew, she became more and more beautiful, a splendid mixture of her mother's exotic Latin looks and her father's classic Norwegian features and Nordic bone structure. Joy's future was bright, and her parents awaited what destiny would bring.

Jonathan and Carmella had high expectations for their only child. From the beginning, they realized she was more than special. An exceptional student, she was fluent in three languages by the time she was twelve and a gifted artist. Joy inherited a keen work ethic from her father and a deep sense of spirituality from her mother. Overshadowing everything, though, was Joy's incredible looks, adorable as a child and even more fetching as a teenager. Yet her approachability and authentic sincerity eclipsed her obvious beauty.

Tall for her age and blonde, Joy stood out among the predominantly Portuguese population; people noticed. They whispered as she walked by. She wasn't just beautiful; she was different, a presence that made strangers turn and stare, even before they knew why.

Whether tourists in English declaring her beautiful, or fellow Portuguese declaring, "*Oh, meu Deus, que beleza!*" women would whisper. From the men came much more provocative comments, making Joy self-conscious and, at times, uncomfortable. It happened often. Older teenagers and adult men, the less honorable kind, followed Joy, making unsolicited advances.

One hot summer day, the sun high in the azure sky, thirteen-year-old Joy walked through the village. She wore her favorite pale green shorts and a Braga Portugal T-shirt, supporting her favorite football team, the fourth in the rankings in Portugal. Her long hair was pulled back into a ponytail, exposing her long, graceful neck and helping to keep her cool in the punishing summer heat.

As she strolled through the Praça dos Pássaros, the Piazza of the Birds, and she passed a gypsy Roma woman perched on the worn, discolored steps leading to the church. The woman was selling bright yellow pencils, the kind Joy loved for her sketches.

Joy studied the bent old woman, recalling a conversation she'd had with her father just a few months earlier when a similar woman had approached them begging.

"Joy, you don't have to worry about these people," he'd reassured her. "They're generally very kind and usually harmless."

"But, Papa, they look so different, and that's kind of scary," Joy had replied, stating the obvious. The gypsies did indeed stand out with their distinctive appearance. "And they talk funny, too," she had added.

Jonathan, a history enthusiast and well-read, had seized the opportunity to educate her.

"Gypsies arrived here in Portugal in the early sixteenth century," he'd explained. "Many of them are Romani, with roots extending as far as Eastern Europe, the Iberian Peninsula, and North Africa. And yes, Joy, they do sound different, at least to you. Many of them speak their own language, Caló, a blend of Romani and Portuguese with other influences accumulated over centuries. But as you've noticed, it's not too hard for us to understand what they're saying."

Now, studying the old woman on the steps, Joy couldn't help but notice her weathered appearance. Her skin resembled an elephant's hide, tough and pockmarked. The faded kerchief on her head barely concealed shabby, matted gray hair that needed washing and a trim. A faint shadow of a dark mustache lingered above her withered lips, and a large, discolored mole with wiry hairs jutted from one cheek. Several front teeth were missing, and a trace of dry spittle sparkled in the sun.

Gypsies had long been a fixture in the piazza, their colorful culture and unique traditions woven into the fabric of Braga and the Praça dos Pássaros. On holidays, the Romani would dance to *fado,* lively and expressive traditional Portuguese music reimagined in their style, captivating audiences who gladly pitched coins into a bucket.

Joy's love of drawing drew her attention to the pencils the old woman sold.

"Pardon me, but I'd like to have some of your pencils. How much are they?" Joy asked politely.

The old woman looked up and smiled, a toothless grin. Five escudos, Miss," she replied.

"Very well, I'll have two, please," Joy said, reaching into her pocket for a coin. As she did, it slipped from her hand and fell to the ground. When she stooped to retrieve it, the gypsy noticed the back of Joy's head. Just below her hairline was a small but distinct birthmark.

"Sit, my dear. I must warn you," the woman said suddenly.

"Warn me?" Joy scoffed. "Of what?"

"My beautiful child, you are lovely, so lovely, and you will always be. But your looks are like a knife that is sharp on both sides. One side brings blessings; the other brings pain. Your beauty is a gift but also a curse."

"A curse?" Joy asked, now confused and uneasy. "I don't understand."

The old woman stood and took Joy's head gently in her hands, startling her.

"What are you doing?" Joy yelped.

"It's this. The mark!"

"What mark?" But then Joy remembered. She rarely saw the birthmark high on the back of her neck because it was small and usually hidden by her hair.

The gypsy traced the birthmark with her finger. "You see, it's a heart, but it's broken, divided in two. It signifies troubles of the heart."

Joy's voice quivered. "What do you mean? I'm going to have a heart attack?"

The old woman smiled again. "No, my dear. Not that kind of trouble. Your heart is healthy. But love may elude you. What seems right may be terribly wrong."

"Stop, old woman! You're upsetting me," Joy said, her unease growing.

But the gypsy continued as if compelled. "You must be careful, very careful, in your choices. Many will love you; even more will lust after you. But you must be vigilant. Love, when it comes, may not look the way you expect. True love is blind; you'll know it when you feel it. It may be an illusion, a fantasy surrounded by temptations. Only you will know if it's true."

The old woman released her gaze and whispered, "*Você é filho de Deus, um anjo; viva a vida com Ele ao seu lado.*"

Joy stood abruptly. The mysterious woman had told her, *You are God's child, an angel. Live life with Him by your side.* It was unnerving. She took the pencils, handed the woman the coin, and rushed off into the crowd. "Thank you," she called as she hurried away.

As she walked home, the gypsy's words clung to her, refusing to let go. Cursed? Because I'm pretty? How absurd.

Her father's steady and reassuring voice echoed in her mind: "Joy, people will always have opinions, but you're the one who decides what to believe." He had a way of making everything feel manageable, even the overwhelming things.

Her mother's words followed, softer but just as certain: "Pray for clarity, my darling girl. God has a plan, even when we can't see it. Have faith and you will always see the way."

Joy tried to push the gypsy's warning aside, dismissing it as nonsense. *What could an old woman selling pencils possibly know about me?*

But as she turned onto the quiet lane leading home, an uneasy feeling crept in, unwelcome but persistent. *Your beauty is a curse. Your heart will break. You may be blind to the truth.*

She quickened her pace as she neared the front door, now shaking her head as if to clear it. "No. That's ridiculous," she reasoned. And yet, something about the old woman's eyes, pensive and knowing, made the words harder to forget than Joy wanted to admit.

CHAPTER 4

Bon Voyage, My Darling

Lisbon Airport

The spring before high school, Joy waited for the mailman each day, hoping for acceptance letters from boarding schools. It was her middle school dean who encouraged her to apply for scholarships at elite schools in England, one in Spain, and two in the United States.

Her teachers recognized that Joy's academic and artistic abilities weren't just impressive, they far surpassed those of most of her peers. They often joked that she was a rising star, destined to go far. But even more remarkable was how Joy's natural beauty seemed to blossom alongside her growing academic success. She became more and more striking, yet she remained astonishingly unaffected, almost completely unaware of the attention she drew. By the time she was a teenager, people said she should be in films.

But because of her extraordinary academic achievement and a remarkable portfolio, the dean encouraged her to apply not just in Europe, but to try for a scholarship to a prominent American boarding school, Miss Porter's. She told her parents and applied almost on a lark. Portugal was a very, very long way from the elite school nestled in the verdant green of Connecticut.

She remembered the day. "Papa, I can't believe I got in!" she had exclaimed, waving the acceptance letter in the air like a hard-won trophy.

"I knew you could do it, sweetheart. You've always been at the top of your class." Jonathan beamed.

But now the reality of going to school far, far from home was here. The two-and-a-half-hour drive to the airport felt endless. Jonathan drove in silence, gripping the wheel a little too tightly, while Carmella sat in the passenger seat, fingering her rosary beads. Every so often, she glanced at Joy, who sat in the backseat, staring out the window. She was going to the country of her father's birth, but a place she had never been before in her life.

The sky was a brilliant blue, unmarred by clouds, but the mood in the car was heavy. Joy felt it pressing on her chest. She was excited; this was the chance of a lifetime, but the thought of leaving her family behind made her heart ache. It was Jonathan who spoke first. "Joy, sweetheart, you do understand that going to this really special school ... it's the chance of a lifetime."

Joy nodded, clutching her ever-present sketchbook, the one she drew in at every opportunity. Art and fashion were her loves.

"Yes, Papa, I know. I read all about the school. It's pretty famous. A place to get a first-class education and a place known to open doors to their alumna."

Jonathan glanced in the mirror to see if Joy was listening. "You getting selected to go there makes the sacrifice worth it, being away from us, from home, from your friends ... but Mama and I know you can do this."

"I know, Papa." Joy ran her fingers through her hair, thinking for just a moment, and then blurting out an unspoken worry. "I might get a little homesick."

"You might," he said, "but you know we'll always be here for you, thinking of you ..."

Carmella added, "And praying for you."

Jonathan had so much more to say, but he just couldn't get it out. All those emotions, all those concerns, all those wishes for his beloved Joy were stuck in his throat, choked up and unspoken.

When they reached the airport, Jonathan ended his "chat". "You are Mama's and my pride and Joy." He laughed at the pun. "And we send you off with the full knowledge that you'll be perfectly safe and sound, and one day, you'll look back at this time as the most formative in your life."

He pulled the car into the airport parking lot and unloaded her bags. Joy hugged her mother tightly.

"Mama, I'm going to miss you so much," she whispered. "But I'll keep in touch, I promise. I'll write, and I can call, can't I?

"Of course, any time." Carmella kissed her daughter's forehead, holding her face in her hands. "My darling child, I will miss you too. But this is your time. God has blessed you with so many gifts. You must go and share them. Your papa and I will visit, I promise."

Joy turned to her father, who stood silently, his hands shoved deep into his pockets. "Papa, I'm a little scared," she admitted.

Jonathan pulled her into a hug, his strong arms wrapping around her. "It's okay to be scared, sweetheart. But you're ready for this. I always remember what the nun told your mama and me, the day you were born. She said you'd have an extraordinary future, and I know she was right. You'll make us proud."

His words brought tears to her eyes, but also a sense of peace. Yes, Joy remembered; her mother had told her that story a hundred times. But the mention of it brought to mind another prophecy, the one of the old gypsy: "Your beauty is a blessing and a curse. Be careful who you trust, or your heart will break." Joy shuddered, shaking the thought away.

Turning back one last time, she waved at her parents. Carmella clung to Jonathan's arm, her lips moving in silent prayer.

Jonathan stood tall, his eyes fixed on the plane as it taxied down the runway. "Bon voyage, my darling child," he whispered. The plane ascended, growing smaller and smaller until it disappeared into the brilliant Portuguese sky. For a long moment, Jonathan and Carmella stood together.

Jonathan reached out to hold her hand, giving it a firm squeeze. "Letting go isn't easy," he said softly. "But this is just the beginning."

Neither of them could know how true that was.

CHAPTER 5

Romeo, Oh Romeo, Wherefore Art Thou

Farmington, Connecticut

Joy arrived on the elite girls' school campus just a few months before her fifteenth birthday. Leaving her parents behind in Portugal to travel to the United States had been hard. She stayed connected through frequent newsy letters and occasional phone calls, but she missed them terribly and worried about them constantly. Joy had to agree, her father was quite right, Miss Porter's was an amazing school, and this opportunity was one of a kind.

Nonetheless, life at boarding school was a mixed bag. Most of her classmates came from worlds vastly different from her own, children of multi-millionaires, Hollywood stars, and even European and Middle Eastern royalty. Miss Porter's School was a sanctuary for the rich and famous, its yearbooks filled with faded likenesses of debutantes like Jackie Kennedy Onassis, Lilly Pulitzer, and Gloria Vanderbilt. There were, of course, other girls more like Joy, middle class, an international student scholarship recipient, or the occasional scholarship "townie" from the area.

Joy's enthusiasm and discipline helped her excel in everything she attempted, but her striking beauty often made her a target of jealousy. Curiously, it was the wealthier girls who envied her the most. She couldn't understand it. "How could girls who have everything in the world be jealous of me?" she wondered. One girl in particular, Cynthia Randolph, seemed unusually unkind from the very beginning.

It was a crisp October morning, the sunlight casting long shadows over the campus as Joy made her way to French class. The brick paths connecting the historic buildings glowed softly in the soft light of the gas lanterns that dotted the campus, bordered by vibrant red and yellow maple trees like a necklace of rubies and amber.

Cynthia, a sophomore, sauntered past her, her designer loafers clicking on the brick path. "Oh, it's what's-her-face ... Joy, right?" she sneered.

"Yes, Cynthia. It's Joy," she replied evenly, fully aware that Cynthia knew exactly who she was.

They both lived in Porter-Keep House, the most historic and prestigious dormitory on campus. The stately building, with its Revival-style architecture, majestic two-story portico, and massive Corinthian columns, had been home to Porter's elite for decades. Its recent renovations, funded largely by the Randolph Family Trust, had only enhanced its grandeur.

Joy's assignment to the dorm was purely accidental. She had been a last-minute replacement for a freshman from Saudi Arabia who had refused to attend after learning she'd have a roommate and no private bathroom. Her father, a wealthy oil tycoon, had offered to fund extensive renovations, including adding a private suite for his daughter, but the school declined, unwilling to set such a precedent.

"Oh, it's Joy," Cynthia said with exaggerated sweetness. "You're in P-K, aren't you? And who did you sleep with to get into that house?"

Joy froze. "Sleep with? No one!" she said, appalled.

"Maybe it was your mother who did, then," Cynthia continued, smirking. "Perhaps a little *rôle dans le foin* with the dean of admissions?"

Joy felt a surge of anger. She knew the phrase meant "roll in the hay." It was disgusting and slanderous, but she chose not to respond.

Cynthia's insults grew nastier. "Or was it your daddy's millions that got you the room? Oh, wait, you don't have millions, do you? That's *my* daddy!" She raised her arm, showing off her 14K gold heart bracelet as it glinted in the sunlight. "Like it? It's from Tiffany's and cost $4,500. I doubt you'll ever have one."

Joy quickened her pace, ignoring the jeers. She couldn't understand why Cynthia had it out for her. Cynthia was well-dressed, had a boyfriend, and was reasonably popular. Joy wondered if Cynthia's nastiness was rooted in insecurity.

"So, Joy-bitch," Cynthia called after her, "are you going to the mixer at Chatmere? I'm sure every boy on campus will want to see what you're wearing, or better yet, what you look like wearing nothing."

Her friends snickered. "Yeah, Joy," one added, "I bet they'd love to see how deep that beauty goes."

"Maybe she'll end up under the bleachers," another chimed in.

Cynthia delivered the final blow. "Yeah, probably with the whole hockey team. Slut!"

Joy ignored them, heading into the Language Arts building.

Porter's offered a wealth of extracurricular activities, from equestrian competitions to fine arts. Joy gravitated toward theater and music, as well as a fashion club. Nearby, the all-male Chatmere Academy also had a robust theater program. For decades, the two schools had collaborated on performances, which offered students a rare opportunity to mingle.

When Joy auditioned for Chatmere's production of *Romeo and Juliet*, she was cast as Juliet. Her Romeo was Travis Lynch, a devastatingly handsome junior with a reputation as a star lacrosse player. Travis had been conscripted into the play as punishment for missing two consecutive work assignments in the school's refectory.

At first, Travis resented his role, but his attitude shifted the moment he saw Joy step off the van from Miss Porter's.

"Hey, Trav," one of his friends teased, elbowing him. "Check out the blonde. She's Juliet, right? You get to kiss her!"

Travis punched the boy lightly. "Shut up, dork."

Another friend held up a pair of tights. "Wait till she sees you in these!"

Travis rolled his eyes, but he couldn't deny that he was intrigued by Joy. She was beautiful, poised, and unlike anyone he'd ever met.

For Joy, Travis was different from the other boys, confident yet kind. They quickly developed a rapport.

Rehearsals alternated between campuses, and Joy and Travis spent time together outside of practice. Their connection deepened, and Travis found himself looking forward to their walks back to her dorm. One evening, he mustered the courage to take her hand. Joy smiled, her heart racing.

The night of the final performance arrived, and the theater was packed. Joy's parents couldn't make the trip from Portugal, but the energy in the room was electric.

When Travis delivered Romeo's lines during the balcony scene, Joy was mesmerized:

> *"If I profane with my unworthiest hand*
> *This holy shrine, the gentle sin is this.*
> *My lips, two blushing pilgrims, ready to stand*
> *To smooth that rough touch with a tender kiss."*

The director had consistently cut the kiss during rehearsals, but tonight, it was real.

Travis's lips brushed hers, and for a moment, time seemed to stop. The applause erupted around them, but he barely heard it. When they finally pulled apart, their eyes met, and Joy felt a rush of warmth she couldn't explain. Was it part of the play? Or was it something more?

For Joy, the kiss felt like a fairytale moment, stirring emotions she didn't fully understand but couldn't ignore. For Travis, it awakened something new and raw, a feeling he hadn't anticipated but didn't want to end.

The applause swelled around them, and even the hoots and hollers from the lacrosse team couldn't break the magic of the moment. It was a kiss that transcended the stage, a kiss that left them both changed.

After the play, Travis and Joy became inseparable. They spent Saturdays together, exploring parks or visiting the mall, where they window-shopped and walked aimlessly, talking the whole time. Their connection deepened, but Travis found himself wrestling with emotions he didn't fully understand.

Sure, he thought one restless night, *Joy's amazing. But is wanting more ... wrong?*

He wasn't sure if his feelings were love, desire, or something else entirely. What he did know was that Joy mattered to him in a way no one ever had.

As the fall term drew to a close, Travis decided it was time to take a chance. He wouldn't rush things, but he couldn't keep holding back. He had to know if Joy felt the same way he did.

CHAPTER 6

One Size Fits All

When they were reunited after Christmas break, Travis borrowed a car from one of the day boys. It cost him $45 and an agreement to cover three dining hall work assignments. The plan was a simple one: he would pick up Joy right after Saturday classes and drive to the nearby reservoir. He had heard many guys brought girls there and "got it on." But first, he had some business to attend to in town, a visit to Rudy's on Main Street.

In preparation for the visit, he didn't want to look like a Chatmere student and devised a scheme to look older. A maintenance worker, he thought, yeah, maybe a plumber. So, he "borrowed" a pair of coveralls that one of the maintenance men had left at the door of the school's laundry. He figured he'd return it later, and no one would be the wiser. Travis squeezed into them. They were decidedly two sizes too small, but he figured they'd have to do.

His dad had given him a tool kit to take to school in case his bike needed repairs, so he grabbed the hammer and a couple of screwdrivers and jerry-rigged them to his school belt. In preparation for the masquerade, he didn't shave for three days, but it had little effect since his handsome baby face could barely produce heavy-duty peach fuzz.

As ready as he would ever be, he peered into the full mirror on the back of his dorm room door. The overalls were more than snug; his arms, calves, and other parts bulged through.

"Crap," he said out loud, looking into the mirror. "I look like one of the Village People." He gestured: "Y-M-C-A!"

Travis walked the mile to the charming village. He didn't want to take the school shuttle looking like this, too many questions and probably a lot of pointing and laughing.

It was a picture-perfect New England village, complete with a dusting of snow. The village green was at the center, and charming old homes, some dating back to pre-Revolutionary times, dotted the perimeter. At one end were the shops: Village Bakery, Farmington Hot Shop, Lux Dry Cleaners, and next to Rudy's Pharmacy was the A&P Market. A couple of doctors' offices and law firms completed the commercial offering.

Travis took a deep breath and entered Rudy's; the bells on the door announced his entrance. Heads turned, as they would in most small towns, to see who had come in. Travis blushed and moved to an out-of-the-way spot to avoid further scrutiny. A couple of old ladies were contemplating which lipstick to buy, and a mother with two kids was picking out colorful Band-Aids.

Travis was on a mission, but he needed some advice, so he patiently waited until the kids got their Band-Aids and the old ladies left without buying a thing.

Finally, he saw that the store was empty. He'd better hurry up before anybody else arrived. Ever so casually, he moved up to the counter.

The clerk was a heavy-set college kid, just a little older than he. His curly hair and lousy complexion would undoubtedly be a turn-off to girls, so he probably didn't have much experience.

"Is the druggist in?"

"Yeah, pal, but I can help you."

"No, I need to talk to the druggist."

"Well, okay, but he's in the back laughing his ass off. He just dropped a bottle of iodine, and it's all over the damn place. And guess what? Yours truly has to clean it up, and he thinks that's hysterical. He's quite the joker, this guy, seriously sarcastic. He likes making people feel like crap. You could be next. Wait here, I'll get him."

The clerk walked back and yelled, "Hey, Mr. Finny, some guy wants to talk to you." Under his breath, he muttered, "Maybe he's got the drip."

Travis was now perspiring and took one of the complimentary tissues off the counter to wipe his brow.

Mr. Finny appeared, dressed in the white coat often worn by pharmacists. He was still snickering about the counter boy having to clean up the spilled iodine.

"Good morning, young man. You're from Chatmere, right?"

Travis flinched. So much for the disguise, and after all that work.

"Good morning, Sir," Travis said in the most mature voice he could muster. As he shifted from one foot to the other, a screwdriver came off his belt and fell to the floor, clanging loudly. He bent to retrieve it and heard an audible rip.

Mr. Finny loved it. "Got a problem, boy? It looks like your tool is all over the place."

"No, no, I'm good," Travis assured him.

"So, then, what can I do for you? I need to get back to work; lots of prescriptions waiting to be filled, you know."

"Well..." Travis hesitated. "I need your advice."

"Advice? Well, maybe you're in the wrong place. Do I look like a priest?" Finny quipped sarcastically. "St. Paul's is across the green."

Travis flushed. *Oh my God, I had to get a comedian.* He continued, "No, I think you are the one who can help."

"Soooo? Out with it."

"You see, I have this friend who asked me to get him some..."

"Some what?" Finny smirked, having heard this story more than a few times. "And I'll bet this friend is you! Isn't it?"

Travis sheepishly nodded admission and continued.

"Well, he, I mean, I, need... well..." Travis finally blurted it out. "Some protection."

Mr. Finny, who already understood where this conversation was going and was enjoying himself, decided to let this baby-faced cherub sweat it out.

"Protection? We don't sell insurance, kid, and I don't know anyone in the mafia."

Travis, now totally flustered, stuttered and sputtered, "No, no, not that kind of protection. You know, *protection*, the kind you buy in drugstores. You know ... condiments."

Finny coughed to suppress his laughter. "Condiments? You don't get them here. You'd better go next door to the A&P. They have all the condiments you want: ketchup, relish, salt, pepper ... whatever."

Travis realized his malapropism and cringed.

Pretending to catch on finally, Finny said, "Oh, now I know what you want. How old are you?"

"Twenty," Travis lied.

"Twenty?" Finny nodded, smiled, and said, "Sure you are."

Travis stared blankly back and said nothing.

"Very well," Finny continued, pushing his mockery further. "So, what size do you want?"

"Size?" Travis was unprepared for that question. "They come in sizes?"

"Of course, they do. So, what size do you want?"

"I don't know," Travis squeamishly admitted as he looked down at his bulging overalls.

Mr. Finny, thoroughly enjoying himself, watched Travis turn an even deeper red and continued the farce. "Well, I don't have a ruler handy. Maybe you have one in that 'tool' belt of yours."

"No, sir, I don't," Travis said, worried about what might come next.

"I don't have one handy either," Finny confessed. "So, we'll have to use the old standby: the rule of thumb."

"Old standby?" Travis worried. *Is this guy going to measure my thumb, or worse?*

"Yeah, the old standby." Mr. Finny leaned over the counter and instructed Travis to step back. "What size shoes do you wear?"

"Thirteen. Yeah, I'm pretty sure they're size thirteen; that's what I got the last time I bought new ones."

"Hmm ... size thirteen." Mr. Finny opened a drawer behind the counter and consulted an imaginary chart. "Let's see... ten, eleven, twelve, thirteen, here we go. According to the chart, you will probably be best suited with large or maybe extra-large. What do you think?"

Travis looked down at his feet. He remembered once when his mom bought him shoes that were too small and how uncomfortable they were.

"I'm not sure, but I'd better get the extra-large," he said, quietly hoping it wouldn't fall off.

The clerk, returning from cleaning up the iodine mess, enjoyed Mr. Finny's spoof and couldn't help joining in. "Don't forget to ask him if he wants the reusable extra-strength ones."

"Good call, Harold. And how many do you want, young man?"

"Um…" Travis thought. "Two?" Yeah, he figured he'd get one as a backup. "Yeah, I'll take two."

"Two dozen?"

"No, just two."

"Well, they only come in six, twelve, or twenty-four packs."

With the painful purchase now completed, Travis walked back to the campus, enjoying the beautiful New England sunset. He opened the bag and read the large print on the box:

ONE SIZE FITS ALL: DISPOSABLE, NEVER REUSE.

"What a fool. I've been had," he muttered.

CHAPTER 7

Not All Broken Hearts Are Birthmarks

The next Saturday, the borrowed Volkswagen pulled up to the off-campus bus stop where the couple usually met. The ancient car had a foul odor, a combination of a stinky gym bag and six-month-old McDonald's French fries. The seats, well-worn from years of service, had Band-Aid-like duct tape patches covering rips and tears.

"Hey, Joy, it's me."

"Travis? Where did you get the car?"

"I borrowed it from Joey; he's a day boy."

"Couldn't you get in trouble? I don't think they allow boarding students to drive."

"Well, no one will know. Just you and me."

"And Joey."

"Yeah, Joey, but he's okay. He's a pal. He'd get into as much trouble as me if they found out. He won't say a word."

"And how about me?" Joy asked. "I'm not sure I'm allowed to get into cars with students."

"Come on. Let's be a little wild just for the day. Get in. I've got a place I want you to see."

Joy opened the door and slid in, immediately taken aback by the odor. Travis found a can of "kumquat room deodorant" discreetly tucked in the side well of the driver's side door. He gave the can a good shake and proceeded to blast the interior cabin. The car filled with a mist, and the offensive stale odor was masked by the sickly-sweet smell of fresh fruit.

The car drove down the narrow dirt path that encircled the reservoir. Travis came to a stop. "Here, look at that."

"At what?"

"The reservoir. It's so serene."

"Yeah, it's beautiful." Joy looked around. "Look how the trees are reflected in the water, like a mirror."

Travis leaned over, put his arm around Joy, and decided to make his move. He kept the car running for the heat, but the little Volkswagen was drafty! It was 28 degrees out, maybe he should have thought this through. "Look, Joy, I know we've been going out for a while, and ..."

"And what?"

"And I really like you. I mean, I *really* like you."

"And I like you too, Travis. A lot." Joy was getting the picture. This little jaunt was Travis's way of finding some privacy.

Travis pulled Joy closer. "It's cold; let me keep you warm."

Joy melded into his strong athletic arms.

They kissed, each growing more urgent. He maneuvered beneath her bulky winter coat and slipped a hand under her shirt, inching toward her breast. She knew she was about to step into uncharted territory. All her life, she'd been taught about purity and virtue, but no one had ever spoken of love. Not the kind that transcends dogma and ancient mores. Still, in the quiet certainty of her heart, she knew this moment was right, for her, for Travis.

And in that moment, she felt it: the true light of love shining deep within her, calm, clear, and unwavering. She sensed she was no longer a girl, but a young woman stepping into her own.

Suddenly, Travis said, "Maybe I should turn off the engine. What if we get carbon monoxide poisoning."

Joy nodded and noticed how steamed up the windows were. "Look, we can't even see the water anymore." She pointed out the windshield, completely fogged over.

Travis turned off the car, and they resumed their kissing and, in Travis's case, fumbling. Within a few minutes, despite their steamy make-out session, they both began to shiver and Joy's teeth chattered so much she could barely speak.

Joy looked at Travis, and Travis looked back at her. Then they both burst out laughing. Suddenly the moment was gone. Joy came to her senses; they were too young. They weren't ready. Looking at Travis's face as he laughed and they both trembled in the freezing temperatures, she thought she saw relief.

After that awkward but wonderful afternoon in Joey's VW, Joy and Travis still spent every possible hour together. Things were getting serious, and their chemistry was perfect. Every time they kissed, Joy felt her head go dizzy with fireworks.

Parents' weekend was coming up, and Travis was excited.

"Joy, I can't wait to introduce you to my parents. They're going to love you. Just wait; they're actually pretty cool for being so old, in their mid-fifties."

Joy vaguely recalled briefly meeting the Lynches, just after the *Romeo and Juliet* performance, and the kind of glare Mrs. Lynch had given her after that on-stage kiss.

"Mom and Dad, do you remember Joy? She was Juliet in our play. Joy, these are my folks."

Joy looked spectacular. She wore her hair pinned back, trimmed with a stylish black organza flower, Eva Perón–style, and a simple red mini-dress. Although Travis was one year her senior, Joy looked every bit of twenty-five or twenty-six.

"Very lovely to see you again, Mr. and Mrs. Lynch. Travis speaks of you often. I feel as though I know you well."

Proud as punch, Travis reached over, grabbed Joy's hand, and squeezed tightly. His mother couldn't help but see the glimmer in her "innocent" boy's eyes. Mrs. Lynch cast a withering look at Joy, then back at Travis. She thought, *It seemed like I was changing his diaper and nursing him just minutes ago, and now he's ... God knows ... involved?*

"So delighted to meet you, Joy," Mr. Lynch said. "My, you're breathtakingly beautiful."

Joy blushed and tried to deflect the compliment while Travis's father just gawked, something that didn't escape Mrs. Lynch's notice or disgust.

Mrs. Lynch confirmed there was a lot more going on here than "just friends." Her baby had met a siren, and not even one of their kind. A foreigner! With looks that could stop traffic and an unsettling charm that left even her husband gawking like a schoolboy.

Her mind raced. Joy was far too confident, too polished for a girl her age. This wasn't some sweet, innocent romance. It wasn't just about Travis anymore; it was about everything Mrs. Lynch had worked so hard to protect, their family's reputation, their place in Newport society, and her son's promising future.

A foreigner. That word stuck in her head like a thorn. Not our kind! What would the ladies at the Newport club think when they heard Travis was smitten with some Portuguese girl who wasn't "one of them"? They'd smile politely, of course, but behind closed doors, the whispers would begin. Questions about her background, her upbringing, her intentions. The thought made Mrs. Lynch shudder.

This relationship had to end. Not the least of which, she did not appreciate how her husband seemed to be overly impressed with this young beauty.

Later that day, back in Travis's room, Mrs. Lynch was going through the freshly delivered laundry and made a startling discovery in her darling son's sock drawer. She could not hold her tongue.

"Travis, I was putting away your laundry and found something unusual in your sock drawer."

Travis blushed and stammered. "What are you doing going through my things?"

"I'm not going through your things. I was just putting your socks away. And now this!" Mrs. Lynch held up the bright red-and-white box: Durex Extra Sensitive Condoms. "They're yours, right?"

"They're none of your business."

Travis transferred from Chatmere before the spring term ended, and before he and Joy could consummate their love. Mrs. Lynch was convinced that if her son wasn't removed from temptation, he would end up with a bigger problem than just his average grades. And then there was, of course, the unmistakable expression on Mr. Lynch's face every time he crossed paths with Joy. No, she knew this could not stand.

Travis left Chatmere at the insistence of his mother, without a single word to Joy, shattering her heart. No letter, call, or explanation ever arrived. She sensed that Travis's mother was behind the sudden transfer, leaving him no choice.

Joy would not soon forget him. She was devastated by the loss. They had met as Romeo and Juliet, and like Shakespeare's tragic lovers, Joy and Travis were destined never to be. Torn apart by family who thought they knew best, separated just as their love was beginning to bloom.

Each night, as Joy lay in bed, silent tears slipped down her cheeks, the weight of heartbreak pressing on her like a thousand pounds of earth. She had experienced love, only to lose it in the blink of an eye.

Her heart ached with a new, unfamiliar pain. This love lost stripped her of innocence and planted seeds of mistrust. She knew she would always remember Travis, that dashing, handsome, tall athlete who had captured her heart and changed her forever. He was her first love, and like every young woman with a broken heart, she couldn't help but wonder: Would she ever love again?

CHAPTER 8

Mea Culpa

Joy's time at Porter's had come to an end. She had blossomed into a stunning young woman. However, her looks were a double-edged sword. Her male contemporaries were either too intimidated to approach her, fearing rejection, or they were downright aggressive, often getting handsy and unruly. Middle-aged teachers and even the shuttle bus driver made inappropriate advances, suggesting more than a professional relationship, something Joy would never encourage.

It was Memorial Day, a bright May morning, when Miss Porter's senior class assembled in the rear of the admissions building. The hired orchestra began playing the traditional "Pomp and Circumstance" as the girls, all clad in long white dresses, ceremoniously marched toward the dais, where the headmistress and trustees awaited.

The campus was at its most beautiful. Lines of apple trees, seemingly blossoming on demand for the occasion, framed the scene, while honeysuckle bushes provided a sweet aroma that swirled in the gentle breeze, like a natural atomizer. Rows of bright white folding chairs sat on the manicured emerald-green lawn, reserved for parents and friends. The century-old New England buildings surrounding the green seemed to nod in silent approval of graduating yet another class of Miss Porter's women.

Joy's parents, bursting with pride, sat in the second row, seats assigned by the school's protocol officer.

The Nordstroms watched with wonder as the headmistress spoke.

"And it is with great pleasure that we recognize and award this year's prestigious Valedictorian Summa Cum Laude award to Miss Juliana Joy Nordstrom."

After the ceremony, Joy and her parents sipped iced tea and mingled with the faculty and guests.

"Joy, Joy! Got a minute?"

It was Cynthia.

"Sure." Joy walked over.

Cynthia had been Joy's nemesis during her first years at Porter's, until one evening when Joy had paid her a late-night visit.

It was midterms when Joy had tapped on Cynthia's door. "Hey, Cynthia, I can see you're struggling with calculus and Spanish II. How about I help you out?"

Cynthia had snorted. "YOU ... help me? Why?"

"Because you need the help, and I'm able to give it to you."

"Or because you're kissing up to me and want something ... right?"

As soon as she said it, Cynthia realized how wrong she was. The look on Joy's face told her everything. Joy wasn't there to borrow a cashmere sweater or gain favor in the clique. No, she was offering help, sincerely and unconditionally. No hidden agenda, no strings attached.

"We can study together after dinner, a couple of times a week. It could help."

"You'd do that for me? Why? I've been a bitch on wheels to you. Don't you hate me?"

Joy smiled. "That wouldn't be hard, but I don't. I don't hate anybody."

"Even me, after what I've said and done to you?"

"Even you. I think you're basically a good person but all packaged up with sarcasm and fear."

"Fear? I'm not afraid of anyone. I don't have to be."

Joy looked directly into Cynthia's eyes and said nothing, letting the silence speak volumes. Cynthia felt completely exposed.

Joy kept her word, and Cynthia miraculously passed calculus and Spanish II with solid C's, despite the hours of tutoring.

Now, at graduation, Cynthia grabbed Joy's arm. "Joy, can we talk a minute?"

"Sure."

The girls walked away from the graduation festivities toward the science building.

"Joy, you know, I was a real shithead in the beginning, but you outclassed me a hundred to one. When I acted snotty and superior, you just smiled and brushed it off. I knew it was hurtful and callous, and frankly, I didn't give a crap. But when I needed help, real help, you were the only one willing to take the time, a lot of time, to make sure I passed. I'll never forget that."

"It was the right thing to do."

"Yeah, but most people, like me, don't always do the right thing." Cynthia paused, then continued. "You're a true person, someone who will go far. It's not just your looks, which I'd kill for, but the person within that gorgeous body that makes you special."

Joy blushed and waved Cynthia off. "Come on, Cyn, you're embarrassing me."

"No, I'm the one who should be embarrassed, embarrassed for being an asshole. But because of the example you set, I'm a better person. I envy your humility."

"Really, Cyn ... stop."

"Oh, don't worry, I'll always be spoiled and self-centered. I think it's genetic. My mother is, as is my grandmother, the queen of mean! I'm pretty certain she doesn't even like herself, much less me or anybody else. But from you, I've learned that being that way isn't what gets you respect ... in fact, it's the opposite."

Cynthia took a breath. "So, Joy, thanks for being my tutor, not just in calculus and Spanish, but in life."

Cynthia waved her arm in the air. "Remember how I mocked you that first year? I gave you that royal wave and flaunted my bracelet?"

"Yeah, I remember. It was pretty crappy on your part."

"That's an understatement. I would have punched anyone who did something like that to me, and if I had a gun ... well, I'd be doing life in some penitentiary."

Cynthia paused, then said, "Here, take this." She removed her Tiffany heart bracelet and pressed it into Joy's open hand.

"I want you to have it. I could have ordered a brand-new one for you, but I wanted you to have mine, the one I've worn for years. I think it means more to me that you have something of mine than something off a shelf from a fancy store."

As Joy held the bracelet in her hand, she knew it wasn't just a piece of jewelry. It was an apology, a heartfelt gesture of humility, and a bridge that connected their past to the present. She fastened it around her wrist, the tiny heart catching the light. Maybe it was symbolic of how far they'd come, from rivals to something deeper. Despite their differences in personality and circumstances, they had found common ground, built on respect, and perhaps, just perhaps, the beginning of a lifelong friendship.

Joy admired the bracelet. "Cyn, no, it's far too valuable."

"Not as valuable as your friendship. When you wear it, I want you to think that that snotty kid from Porter's realized that you were a far better person than she."

Joy was touched and smiled. When Joy finally spoke again, her voice was soft. "Cyn, I think you've always had a good heart. You didn't want anyone to know. Maybe afraid, or too guarded."

Cynthia laughed. "Yeah, or maybe I just didn't want to use it because it might get hurt.

CHAPTER 9

Bewitched

College was the next big challenge for Joy. Miss Porter's guidance counselor had helped her apply to a dozen or so schools, all in the top echelons of higher learning. And when she returned to Braga for the summer it was with a fistful of college acceptances. But it was Brown University in Providence, Rhode Island, that caught Joy's favor. The school was smaller than Stanford and Columbia, less structured than Harvard and Princeton, and "artier" than all the others. Joy intended to major in languages with a minor in fashion, and Brown had widely recognized departments for both.

Student excerpts printed in the college catalog answering the question, *What is the typical Brown student like?* greatly influenced Joy's choice.

"Brown students are liberal, environmentally conscious, politically aware, friendly, passionate, independent, quirky, laid-back, competent, fun-loving, supportive, and enthusiastic," wrote Josh.

Another comment from Stacey resonated with her: "Most students, especially girls, are fashionable, but those who prefer sweats fit in too. There are many wealthy students, and the socioeconomic gap is sometimes apparent, but those on scholarship or financial aid won't find it an issue."

Acceptance came with a full scholarship, which was particularly impressive given Brown's reputation as one of the most elite Ivy League schools. Known as the seventh-oldest institution of higher learning in the United States, Brown accepted only the cream of the crop and was famously parsimonious about handing out free rides. Joy's stellar academic record, extracurricular activities, and highly positive personal interview were just what Brown sought. Unquestionably, her extraordinary looks garnered favor from the predominantly male admission committee.

Joy loved Brown, and it was no surprise to anyone that she excelled. At the end of her first year, her roommate, Samantha McCoy, had some exciting news.

"Joy, you're never going to believe it!" Sam said, bursting into their dorm room.

"What, Sam?"

"It's Ned."

Ned was a seriously serious naval officer studying at the Naval War College (NWC) in nearby Newport.

"So, what about Ned? Is he being transferred somewhere?"

Sam paused, scratching her head. "Why, yes, but how did you know that?"

"I didn't, but it was a good guess, huh?"

"A good one, but that's not all. You see, Ned is hinting around about, well, getting serious."

"Serious? I'd say you're already serious. You date him exclusively, and you spend every weekend at the Shoreside Motel. By his nature, Ned is the most serious person alive. I don't think I've ever seen him smile. Maybe you'd better check to see if he has teeth, 'cause I've never seen them."

"Joy! Don't be ridiculous. Of course he has teeth. And he does smile, once in a while. But I agree, he's pretty serious. He told me he plans to become an admiral someday, and admirals are super-serious people."

Joy chuckled. "Yeah, he's certainly practicing at it."

"Come on, Joy, you're getting me off track. I think he's getting close to popping the question. I'm pretty sure he will after the NWC Cotillion."

"That's great! I'm so happy for you."

"Thanks, Joy. But I asked Ned to fix you up with one of his buddies so you can go to the cotillion and be there when he pops the question."

"Seriously, Sam? I don't think so."

"Please, Joy. I need you there. And besides, Ned says the party is really something special. All the officers in full-dress uniforms file in with their dates or wives on their arms. They parade past the commanding officer, a huge orchestra plays waltzes and 1940s music, and the couples dance around the ballroom. Just like Cinderella. After all the pomp and circumstance, they turn up the heat, and the band blares."

Joy didn't know much about the Naval War College. She instinctively didn't like the name *War College* but later learned about its historic campus in Newport, dating back to 1884. Service members from all branches attended, not just the Navy, to earn a Master of Arts degree. Many of these officers would go on to become generals, admirals, and even a president.

Since the War College was a graduate program, Joy figured that whoever Ned was setting her up with would be at least four or more years older and already a college graduate. But the opportunity sounded magical.

"So, you want me to go to this cotillion with some guy I've never met?"

"Yeah. Ned says he's nice. And cute too."

"Does he smile?"

"How should I know? Just come and stop being so negative. You love to dance, and who knows? You might meet Mr. Right."

"Or Captain Right..." Joy laughed.

The cotillion was scheduled for the last Saturday of the month, and Joy's father sent her a little extra allowance to buy a new dress. After shopping around, she found herself drawn back to one of her favorites, a quaint little thrift shop in downtown Newport called *Play It Again, Sam.* The irony of the name didn't go unnoticed.

Sam's, as the locals called it, was more boutique than thrift shop. Its windows were a treasure trove, featuring famous designers like St. John and baskets brimming with artfully arranged shoes, everything from Christian Dior to Gucci. The high-end clothing came from wealthy women who had either tired of their wardrobes or simply needed to make room in their closets. Some items still had their original sales tags, never worn; others were pristine classics that never went out of style. The shop was spotlessly clean, elegantly decorated, and perfumed with the unmistakable scent of old money and expensive fragrances. Even the clerks, many of them volunteers from St. Edmund's High Episcopal Church, were gracious, well-dressed, and polite.

Joy knew fashion and had shopped there before. She had a knack for spotting pieces with "good bones," beautifully made garments that had somehow fallen out of favor and landed on the close-out racks for mere pennies on the dollar. One of her greatest thrills was rescuing those mark-downs and transforming them with her own special touch, adding, subtracting, restyling, until she created something entirely original.

Her fellow students often admired her outfits and would ask, "Wherever did you get that? It's gorgeous!" And Joy would just smile inwardly. *If they only knew.*

"Can I help you, young lady?" an elderly woman asked as Joy entered the shop. "I'm Mrs. Littleton."

"Yes, please. I'm going to the NWC Cotillion and need something special to wear."

The woman looked Joy over from head to toe. "Wait, you look familiar." The clerk tried to recall but just couldn't place Joy. "God, you're gorgeous! Are you a model?"

Joy blushed and shook her head. This wasn't the first time she'd been asked that question, probably the hundredth.

"Well, dear, I'm sure we'll find you something, and it will be perfect."

Joy was a size two. Being so petite, the choices were limited as she sorted through the evening gown rack. The kind saleslady came over to help scroll through the rack to be sure.

"No, dear, there's nothing here for you. But I think I have something special in the back that just came in yesterday. It hasn't been priced or tagged yet, but I'm pretty sure it will suit you!" The clerk rushed to the back of the shop.

When she returned, she uttered breathlessly, "Here you go, dear. Isn't it exquisite?"

The clerk took the plastic off the gown and hung it on a hook. It was an excellent, hand-tailored copy of a Carolina Herrera design. Joy recognized the designer's name. The ultra-simple white silk gown, with its understated elegance, screeched class and glamour.

"It's stunning."

"Well, dear, try this beauty on. It doesn't have a size or label because it's custom-made. But if need be, you can always have it altered."

"I'm handy with needle and thread myself," Joy smiled.

"You know, dear, I met the woman who brought this in. She's a New York glitterati, who surreptitiously travels to Asia and hires seamstresses to copy famous designers. It gives her a kick to pull one off on her society friends. And the best part? She wears them once, then ditches them here. She wore this one only once. Not a spot on it; it looks brand new."

Joy's eyes lit up. "Oh my God, it's so elegant. May I try it on?"

"Of course, dear, that's why you're here. Now, go in there, and let's see."

When Joy walked out of the dressing room, the saleswoman gasped and dramatically whispered, "I'm bewitched."

Two other shoppers stopped and admired Joy as she twirled in front of the three-way mirror. "Look, Denise, she's gorgeous. I remember when you were that size!"

"Yes, Deanna. And I remember when you were that young."

Joy turned to the saleswoman and said, "I never thought I'd ever have anything so beautiful." Suddenly, concern set in. "But how much is it? I only have $224.00."

The saleswoman knew that amount would never cover the price, but the store manager hadn't officially priced the dress yet. Sometimes mistakes happened, she thought, and things got mispriced.

"Well, Dear, I'll check in the back and see what we can do."

In the back room, the clerk glanced through comparable gowns, all priced between $350 and $1,400. She knew this particular gown would likely fall on the high end of that range. Peeking out, she saw Joy admiring herself in the mirror. The dress fit her perfectly, and Joy looked magnificent. Suddenly, the clerk had an idea.

She wrote up a sales ticket for $1,249 but then "accidentally" smudged the first digit on the price tag. Feeling a pang of guilt for shorting the church, the volunteer saleswoman, who was well-off herself, decided she'd personally cover the difference between what Joy paid and the gown's true value. It felt like the right thing to do, and she knew her husband wouldn't mind; it was tax deductible.

The clerk emerged holding a price tag. "You are indeed lucky. The dress is priced at $249, but since you're going to a military ball, we can offer you a courtesy armed service discount of 15 percent. That brings it to $211. And don't worry about alterations; the dress fits you to a tee. Just a pair of heels, and you'll be the most beautiful woman at the ball."

Joy swirled around in the mirror again, thinking I couldn't possibly make this dress more perfect. "I won't touch a thread."

Joy couldn't believe her good fortune. "Oh my, yes, I'll take it."

"I'll wrap it up. And take a look at these shoes, they're perfect. Salvatore Ferragamo Try them; if you like, take them on approval. You can return them during my shift. I'm here Mondays, Wednesdays, and Saturdays."

"Thank you so much. You're unbelievable. I'll always remember your kindness, Mrs. Littleton."

Sam made the introduction. "Joy, please meet Kevin. Kevin Perry. He's Ned's best friend and comes from Columbus, Ohio."

"Hi, Kevin, I'm Joy."

Kevin couldn't believe his eyes. Knowing from experience that most blind dates require a sense of humor and a low bar for expectations, he was thrilled to see this stunning woman. She was breathtaking, dressed like a princess, and had confidence that radiated through the room. Dumbfounded, he stammered, "Nice, um, to meet you … um, Joy."

Joy wasn't disappointed either. Sam wasn't kidding when she said Kevin was cute. He was very cute, clean-cut with an impressive military bearing in his dress blues. She guessed he was about twenty-three or twenty-four, around six feet tall. His close-cropped haircut gave him a rugged look, but his eyes seemed warm and kind.

After the formal introductions and the obligatory parade of officers, the orchestra struck up the first song. Kevin turned to Joy and extended his hand. "May I have this dance?"

The song was Johnny Mathis's classic "Chances Are." A midshipman, backed by the full naval orchestra, crooned the iconic lyrics. As Kevin pulled Joy closer, she felt a wave of emotions she hadn't experienced in years. Silly as it seemed, she felt like Cinderella, and Kevin was her prince.

They danced to every slow song afterward, each step and each spin drawing them closer. As the night progressed, Kevin leaned in and whispered in her ear, "Will you see me again?"

Joy whispered back, "Of course."

The night ended with a surprise, though not the one Sam was expecting. Kevin and Joy slipped away to the terrace, eager to escape the noise of the ballroom and steal a quiet moment together.

The terrace overlooked Newport Harbor, its waters aglow with reflections from the city lights and the softly rocking boats anchored nearby. The moon hung low, casting a silvery glow that illuminated the scene like a romantic painting. A gentle breeze rustled the leaves, adding a soothing hum to the otherwise tranquil night.

Joy shivered slightly, the cool air seeping through her silk gown.

Kevin noticed immediately. "You're cold?"

"A bit, but I'm fine."

Without hesitation, Kevin removed his uniform jacket and draped it over her shoulders. "Better?"

Joy smiled, feeling the lingering warmth of the jacket and catching a faint, familiar scent. She couldn't place it at first, but then, in an instant, Travis came to mind. Yes, it was that same rugged, magnetic musk, a man's man.

The memory stirred something deep within her: a bitter-sweet ache as she recalled the void Travis had left in her heart. She wondered if anyone could ever take his place. For a brief moment, she allowed herself to feel the weight of that loss before shrugging it off with a practiced smile. "Yes, much better. Thank you, Kevin."

Kevin grinned, his boyish charm on full display. "So, Joy, tell me something interesting about yourself. What's your passion?"

Joy tilted her head thoughtfully. "Passion? Oh, I have so many ... art, music, design ... But I think my real passion is fashion. I'd love to be a designer someday."

Kevin nodded. "I don't know much about fashion, being in the military, Uncle Sam picks my clothes every day. But if you can design dresses that make women look as beautiful as you do tonight, you'll be a smashing success."

Joy laughed. "Oh, I didn't make this dress. I wish. But no, I can't take credit for it."

"Whoever made that dress should be grateful it ended up on you."

Joy blushed, her smile soft and genuine. "Thank you. And how about you? What's your passion?"

"Me?" Kevin thought for a moment. "I guess my passion is serving my country. My mom thinks I should go into politics someday."

"Politics? Why does she think that?"

"She says I have the face for it. But honestly, I think it's because I believe so strongly in this country and want to see it become even better. My mom is my biggest cheerleader."

"Well, she's not wrong," Joy said. "You do have the kind of face people would trust and admire and, depending, vote for you."

Kevin chuckled, slightly embarrassed. To shift the focus, he looked up at the sky. "Look at the stars."

Joy leaned back on Kevin's shoulder, her gaze following his. A sea of tiny pinpoints sparkled against the inky darkness, each one a silent witness to nights like this, nights filled with fleeting moments and memories waiting to be made.

"They're beautiful," she whispered. "So far away and yet so bright."

Kevin nodded. "I'm a pilot, you know. But even when I'm flying at 30,000 feet, the stars still seem so far away. It's humbling."

Joy laughed. "A pilot, huh? Like Tom Cruise in *Top Gun*?"

Kevin grinned. "Not nearly that glamorous. But it's exciting, I'll give you that."

They lingered there, talking about everything and nothing at all. For the first time since Travis, Joy felt something stir, a flicker of hope, a glimpse of possibility. She wasn't sure what it meant, but she was willing to find out.

Meanwhile, back inside, Ned was nervously preparing to propose to Sam. His buddies, who had indulged in a bit too much champagne, were eagerly watching from a distance, whispering and laughing as they anticipated the big moment.

Unfortunately, Ned wasn't handling the pressure well. He stumbled slightly as he pulled Sam into a corner.

"Sam," he slurred, "you're... you're my dream girl."

Sam, anxious and excited, nodded enthusiastically.

Ned fumbled in his pocket for the ring but came up empty. Panicking, he tried the other pocket and finally produced the solitaire diamond. As he dropped to one knee, he wobbled precariously.

"Will I ... will you ... marry me?" he stammered.

Before Sam could respond, Ned lurched forward, and the ring went flying through the air, landing thirty feet away under the bandstand.

His mates, just out of sight, erupted in laughter, their guffaws echoing through the ballroom.

Sam, mortified, hissed, "Ned! Everyone's staring at us! You're embarrassing me. Get up off the floor and find that ring!"

CHAPTER 10

❦

For God and Country

H ere's to you," Kevin said, lifting his glass.

Joy smiled and clinked her champagne-filled flute against his. It was their six-month anniversary as a couple, and Joy was in love. Her doubts and trepidations had been smoothed away by her renewed faith in the notion that "love conquers all." Although she knew she would never forget Travis, she came to understand that this is simply the way it is with first loves. She and Kevin became inseparable. When he could get away from school, he walked Joy to her classes on the Brown campus and waited patiently outside.

Joy's attention would drift as she sat in the classroom, peering out the window at her handsome warrior. As for Kevin, he too was smitten, but a tinge of worry began to creep into his mind. Joy, his wonderful distraction, might derail his focus on his military career. After class, the two would often drive off in his six-year-old Buick, a hand-me-down from his uncle, to their favorite spot, Nick's.

Nick's, just north of Providence, was tucked away in a somewhat secluded spot. Like almost everything else in Rhode Island, it had history. In the 1930s, Nick's had been a roadhouse owned by a member of the Patriarca crime family. Born with a club foot that earned him the nickname "Nick the Foot," the owner couldn't be an active mobster. Instead, during Prohibition, the family set him up in a remote roadhouse under the guise of a tourist camp. Nick was the first cousin of Ray Patriarca, an influential mob boss who controlled most of New England.

In its heyday, Nick's hosted a lively and eclectic clientele that partied into the early hours, consuming gallons of homemade hooch. The remote location ensured privacy from the vigilant eyes of police and federal agents looking for illegal alcohol consumption and, more notably, gang members and stills. Rumors and myths persist to this day that high-level Mafia chiefs met at Nick's to discuss "family" business. Upstairs, a labyrinth of rooms conveniently allowed them and their mistresses, called *cumari* occasional trysts. In the barroom, a hidden door led to the basement, where Nick and his minions produced highly illegal moonshine, supplying half of Providence.

After Prohibition ended and the Mafia's grip loosened, Nick's was seized by the government and sold off. It changed hands a couple of times, eventually becoming "New Nick's," a charming roadhouse B&B with tall columns and a second-story porch decorated with large window boxes filled with seasonal flowers. One suite was left intact, complete with bullet holes from a shootout between "wise guys." The original massive entry door, featuring a speakeasy-style peephole, now served as a nostalgic glamour piece.

The couple sipped from their half-full glasses.

"How was class?" Kevin asked.

"Class? Oh, great. It was great," Joy replied, though she hadn't focused on her Philosophy II lecture, preoccupied as she was with thoughts of amour. They had decided that on this, their anniversary, they would finally be together, Joy's first time.

Kevin and Joy arrived at Nick's just in time for an early dinner.

"Good evening, folks, welcome back," Anthony, the co-owner, greeted them. He stood in the small but attractive reception area that once served as a hat-check room. A crude sign hung over some cubbyholes behind the counter: *Leave Your Gun at the Door.* An old Italian flag adorned the wall. Rumor had it that Louie, the butcher, once hid in a secret space under the floor for three days with nothing but a bottle of Chianti and two pounds of salami.

"Will you be dining now," Anthony discreetly paused, "or perhaps later?"

Joy blushed and looked at Kevin, who answered for them: "For now, we'd like a table."

"Very well. And will you be requiring a room later? I have just one available, and Gianni will make it up for you ... if you would like."

Gianni, Anthony's younger and far more attractive partner in both business and life, walked into the room.

"Miss Joy, so good to see you. Beautiful as ever, even more beautiful since the last time I saw you."

Joy grinned. "Thank you, Gianni, and you look well too."

Gianni smiled broadly and struck a pose. What Gianni lacked in business acumen, he made up for with sizzling sex appeal. Kevin gleamed with anticipation as Gianni added, "Dinner first?"

Upstairs in their room together, Kevin gently steered Joy to the bed, where she sat nervously. He sat next to her and kissed her neck, his mouth traveling up to her ear. "No pressure, Joy. I want you to be certain."

He was such a gentleman, Joy thought. And this time, she was ready to step into that unknown. It was pre-dawn when Kevin dropped Joy back on campus. She quietly entered her room so as not to wake Sam. Slipping into bed, she replayed every moment of their evening. Joy had come to love Kevin deeply and was thrilled at the prospect of spending her life with him. Most importantly, she felt ready and able to give her heart entirely to someone again.

The days sailed by, with countless sweet moments the couple shared and treasured. Joy was in love, and Kevin was "perfect." Their standing Friday-night dates were even more special now. She was truly content.

But as perfect as it seemed, Kevin wrestled with conflicting emotions. He was unquestionably committed to Joy; after all, he felt deep and sincere love for her, and clearly, she loved him. She was the kind of woman any man would kill to spend the rest of his life with: kind, intelligent, loyal, loving, and, as a bonus, she was absolutely stunning, the most beautiful woman he'd ever seen. Their physical connection was ideal, every touch and glance resonated with passion and tenderness, forging a bond that transcended the physical and reached deep within their core ... not merely an attraction but a deep and lasting quenching of life's thirst for love with a pinch of erotica.

Yet there was something else. He could not quite pinpoint it, but nonetheless, it was a growing and increasingly intense feeling that gnawed at him. While he loved Joy, he was simultaneously bound to the military. He knew, deep within his soul, that his duty to his country and his fellow warriors could come between them. He worried that Joy might not understand this and that his overwhelming allegiance to duty might fracture or even destroy their relationship. Joy was the love of his life, yet he knew that someday he would face a heart-wrenching decision that would force him to choose between her and his career. And that day arrived sooner than he ever imagined.

—— ❧ ——

Kevin took a deep breath and approached Joy.

"Joy, I have something important to say," he began.

Joy's heart leaped. Was this *the* moment? Her mind raced with excitement.

Kevin's tone turned serious. He looked at her square in the eyes.

Joy braced herself, as wedding bells and white lace rushed through her mind, preparing to answer "Yes."

"You see, babe, there's a mission in the Gulf, and my program is training men for a vital operation. Yesterday, the word came down asking for volunteers to go. I felt I had to sign up."

Joy's expression changed from idyllic anticipation to consternation. Her mind raced, and she felt a slight tremble course through her body as if to predict something she couldn't quite grasp yet."

"What do you mean? Go? Go where?"

"I mean I'm going to be deployed. Week after next."

Joy's dreams of introducing Kevin to her parents, designing her wedding dress, and planning a simple church service at St. Lucia's in Braga vanished like the last remnants of winter frost under the heat of the late morning's sun. But what did he say? He had volunteered!

"But wait ... did you say volunteered?"

"Yes."

"So, they're not making you go?"

"No, but I'm the squad leader, and my men expect me to go with them. It's my duty, for God and country."

Joy felt devastated and betrayed. "God and country? What about Kevin and Joy?"

Kevin reached out, but Joy instinctively pulled away.

"You always knew how much the military means to me," Kevin said. "It's my life. I've trained for it, and I think I was born to serve. I've always made that clear. Can't you understand that?"

But Joy couldn't understand that at all. Not for a second. For the first time, she realized she would always come second to Kevin's calling. There had been little hints, here and there, but now, it was out there, on the table, clear as day.

Was it selfish to crave the kind of love her mother and father had, where each reigned supreme within the other? She had seen what true love looked like with them: every whispered promise, every tender caress, quietly affirming their shared understanding that their universe belonged to them alone. Kevin's choice, though born of noble sacrifice, was as dangerous as it was virtuous, a perilous defiance of fate that risked shattering the delicate balance between duty and desire.

On the day of Kevin's deployment, a note was slipped under Joy's door:

Dear Joy,

I don't know how to say this without breaking my own heart in the process.

I love you, more than I ever thought I could love anyone. But I also know that the man you deserve is someone who can always put you first, and I don't think I can be that man.

You've given me the happiest moments of my life, and part of me wants to throw everything away just to stay by your side. But that wouldn't be fair to you.

You once asked me if I would always choose duty over love. I didn't answer then because I didn't know how. Now I do. And it kills me to say that the answer is yes.

I know I may regret this for the rest of my life. I hope someday you can forgive me.

With all my heart,

Kevin

CHAPTER 11

A Side of Ice

Despite the undeniable hurt and disappointment from Kevin's abrupt departure, she suppressed her feelings and convinced herself that perhaps what happened was meant to be. As Kevin said, it was better to be honest with each other. She didn't regret losing her virginity to him, she knew in that moment, their love was genuine. She tried to reason that it was not meant to be. Gradually, her heart healed as she focused on life at school.

Joy relished Brown's academic life. She loved her classes and the experience of expanding her mind in so many disciplines. Although she focused on language studies, she savored the design and fine arts classes she took and excelled at them all.

Socially, Joy found Brown "interesting." She made friends quickly, both male and female. The boys in her fashion classes were more interested in what she was wearing than what was underneath it, and soon, the handful of male design students became "just friends." In addition to her major, Joy took core courses required for a degree. They were challenging, but nothing she couldn't handle with ease, maintaining excellent grades. In the core classes, the boys were quite different. They were either smitten with her and too shy to approach or bold and aggressive, looking to date her, hopefully having a shot at something more provocative. This wasn't a new scenario for Joy. It was déjà vu from her prep school experiences.

Carlos, a junior in her Economics I class, was her first real encounter with a "Brownie." He was a tall, thin, exotic Latin type with a crop of bushy black hair and came from a wealthy family in El Salvador. They met one night at Sharpe Refectory, the main dining hall the students affectionately referred to as The Ratty. Carlos had spotted her on the first day. She was the prettiest girl in class and probably in the school, and Carlos was determined to meet her. It was dinnertime on a Tuesday, and Joy walked into The Ratty. That's when Carlos made his move.

"Excuse me, aren't you in my econ class? Professor Claton?"

Joy looked at him for a moment. The class was large, held in an amphitheater with over ninety-seven students. "Well, maybe. I am in his 9:15 class."

"Yes, that's the one. I've seen you several times and just had to meet you. I hope you don't mind. I'm Carlos, Carlos Mendoza, from El Salvador."

Joy nodded. It wasn't uncommon for unknown men to come up to her and introduce themselves, something that had happened since her earliest years. "Nice to meet you, Carlos."

"How about you and me skip the 'mystery meat' at Ratty's and go out for a real meal? Like some great hamburgers at Nick's or a steak somewhere nicer?"

Nick's, she thought. *Oh God, I'd rather die than go back there.*

"No, I can't. I have a fine arts quiz tomorrow and need to get back and study."

Carlos was excited; this girl was stunning, and he had to figure out a way to spend some time with her. He already had her talking, and all he had to do was reel her in like a fish. She was chatting with him and didn't tell him to get lost. Then, he recalled a flyer in the student center and gave it a try. "Fine arts? Have you seen the Picasso exhibit in Newport? It's at one of those mansions. I saw a brochure on it."

"No, I haven't seen the exhibit, but I heard about it. My professor hopes to get a bus and bring our class to see it. But, so far, no luck. It's not in the budget, and he's trying to figure out if the kids want to chip in for the ride."

Carlos seized the opportunity. "Well, today may be your lucky day. It just so happens that I have the ride, a brand-new Corvette convertible that knows its way to Newport and back, round trip, free of charge. We can go anytime.

Joy looked over at this handsome young man. He was tall and well-groomed, wearing expensive loafers and tight jeans, and his physical appearance reminded her of the boys back home. She vaguely remembered seeing him around campus but decided to pass on his offer. "Thanks, but I'll wait and go with the professor. It will be more informative with him as our guide."

"Yes, I understand, and it makes perfect sense." Carlos's wheels were turning. He just had to take this gorgeous creature out. "Well, then, how about tomorrow night? Are you free? Brown has a movie in Manson Hall, and afterward, we can go for something, pizza maybe? It's a classic film, *On the Waterfront*. Come on. It will be fun."

A campus date was far more appealing than going off campus with someone she barely knew. Joy pondered: he was handsome, and it could be fun; seeing a classic film like *On the Waterfront* wasn't an everyday offering. Joy weighed the invitation and came to the conclusion: it was time to move on.

"All right, but we'll have to be home early; I have an 'eighter.'"

"It's a date! I'll meet you out front of Manson at seven. Don't be late."

"I'll be there."

The movie was great. Carlos was a perfect gentleman, and they had lots of fun. Joy, for no reason at all, thought she'd hold off telling him she was fluent in Spanish and would let it be a surprise later. Subsequent dates included a scenic drive in his red convertible to a deserted Newport beach for a picnic, followed by a few evenings enjoying movies at the newly opened super theater at the Providence Civic Center.

Carlos's generosity knew no bounds. He always took her to nice places and surprised her with thoughtful gifts, like a stuffed Bruno the Bear, the school mascot, wearing a pinafore embroidered with her initials, or a monogrammed school keychain. He sent two dozen red roses to her dorm on Valentine's Day. She felt truly wooed, and she loved every moment of it.

Carlos was enjoying the bragging rights of dating the prettiest girl on campus, maybe even in the state of Rhode Island. He loved having her on his arm or walking hand in hand around Providence. It was a tremendous status symbol to him, one that fed his male ego.

After four months, Carlos was getting restless. The more he catered to Joy, the more he wanted back and even felt entitled to. Each time they were together, he became more personal and aggressive. Joy was careful about setting limits, and Carlos reluctantly accepted her deflections, although he became increasingly frustrated. Latin culture demanded more than handholding and a goodnight make-out session.

When Carlos proposed going to an after-hours club frequented by the Latin community, Joy, a music lover, jumped at the chance to hear live music performed by talented locals. The couple arrived just after midnight. Carlos was a regular and the bouncers waved them through without even looking at their id.

"Joy, you are going to love this place. The music is wild, and the drinks are really great. They make a wicked frozen mojito with fresh mint and lime."

The couple made their way up to the bar, and Joy sat on a stool, taking in the vibes. A live Latin trio blared out some familiar tunes, and the flashing colored lights painted the tropical décor. It was an unusual place to have in Rhode Island, more something found in Miami or New York, where there were much larger Latino communities. She had to hand it to Carlos; he knew all the right places.

Over the months, Carlos gave Joy a peek into his background.

"You know," he explained, "I come from a wealthy family in El Salvador. I'm the only son of an only son of a wholesale food distributor, and our company pretty much has a monopoly on importing most dry goods to the island country."

Joy imagined her crazy friend Cynthia's words of wisdom if she had been privy to this conversation. "He'd be a good catch indeed. And oh yeah, what does he look like naked?"

However, as Carlos delved into the details of his situation, Joy's eyebrows furrowed with concern.

"You see, Joy, there are a few chosen families that control the commerce in my country," he explained.

Joy looked quizzically at Carlos. "Chosen? Chosen by whom?"

Now it was his turn to look puzzled. After a moment of thought, he said, "I really don't know. It's been that way my whole life and my father's too, and probably his father's. It just is."

"And how about the ones who are not 'chosen'?"

Carlos shrugged. "I don't know. I guess they work for us. The families, as they are sometimes called, employ most of the people. But being part of this elite club comes with a lot of responsibility and risk. Life isn't what you might think."

He continued, "We live under guarded conditions due to the perilous nature of the place. Kidnappings and extortion are almost like a national industry. I had an uncle who owned a bank who was kidnapped and kept underground for six months before a ransom was paid and he was rescued."

"Oh my God, Carlos, that's awful. Is he all right now?"

"Sort of. He has issues and needs a lot of coddling. They spend a good amount of time in Miami now, and he's better there, not as nervous."

Joy struggled to grasp the reality of Carlos's life. He told her they had around-the-clock armed security, walled homes, and bulletproof cars with escorts everywhere they went.

She remarked, "It's hard for me to imagine."

Carlos nodded. "But it's the price we pay for wealth in that environment."

While Carlos stood beside her, Joy looked at him in the dim light. He was handsome and charming, and in time maybe she could have even deeper feelings for him. But then, her concerns about the challenges that came with Carlos's background posed the question of whether such a life was worth having. However, for now, those worries were put on hold, and she focused on nothing more than her present life, and, of course, passing Friday's art history quiz.

As they waited for the bartender, a young Hispanic kid approached.

"Carlos, hey, amigo."

The short, dark kid, walked over and patted Carlos on the back. Joy was surprised that he would be a friend of Carlos since he looked more like a gang member than a college student. The backward baseball cap, multiple tattoos, low-hanging jeans with a leather nail belt, and silver chain looped from his pocket were quite different from Carlos's preppy Ralph Lauren look. Joy noticed the boy had very dilated eyes and suspected that this kid was on drugs.

Carlos didn't introduce Joy, and the two boys' conversation, in Spanish, which was in whispers and meant to be private, filled the air. Joy strained to hear, simultaneously translating as she listened:

"Juan, did you bring them?"

"I did. They are the best roofies around. Two will do the trick; just put them in her drink. They work in minutes, and you'll get the whole night out of her."

Juan looked over, licking his lips as he checked out Joy. "I can see why you couldn't wait to get these."

"Yeah. Give them to me."

"Not so fast."

"Okay, okay, how much?"

Juan looked at Joy again, made a crude gesture, and gave Carlos a steely-eyed stare. "The price is ..." he paused. "I get her after you."

"Are you crazy?"

"That's the deal, Carlos."

"You're insane! You can't be serious?"

"Deadly serious, my friend. And if you don't agree, I have a cousin who will make you regret it."

Carlos's inner panic was palpable. He couldn't believe his ears. What had he gotten into? He looked at Joy and then back at Juan.

He didn't want to proceed with this scheme, especially not allowing Juan to be involved. Carlos feared that if he backed out, he'd be knifed or worse by this unnamed cousin. Trapped and desperate for self-preservation, he reluctantly nodded in agreement.

Joy absorbed every word, translating the exchange in her mind with mounting horror. She couldn't believe what was being set up.

In that chilling moment, it became starkly evident: Carlos, disguised as a gentleman in Polo Black Label, was orchestrating a plan to drug her and abuse her. Worse yet, he was willing to allow Juan to partake in this despicable act. It was unthinkable. He lacked any sense of decency or honor and was a coward no less.

Joy was devastated. She had grown quite fond of Carlos and had envisioned a deeper, more meaningful relationship. Now, shock and fear churned within her as she fought off waves of panic-induced nausea. She needed to get out of there fast. *Stay calm*, she thought, *play it cool. THINK!*

"Carlos, those drinks look delicious. Could you order me a side of ice while I go to the ladies' room? I'll be right back. Don't start without me, I want a proper toast."

Joy, knees shaking, walked to the ladies' room, turning briefly to give Carlos a flirtatious wink while inwardly cringing.

When Joy was out of Carlos's sight, she bolted to the exit door, ran across the street, and flagged down a passing car.

"Help, I need your help."

"What's the matter?" asked the driver.

"A couple of guys are in there trying to drug my drink. I need to get out of here … now!"

Joy lucked out. The driver was a Brown student returning from a URI party. "Get in. I'm Luke, Luke Pitcher, and I know you."

"You do?"

"Yeah, I'm in your anthropology class. And everyone knows you because you are the prettiest girl at Brown."

The ride back to the campus was a silent one. Joy trembled and held back tears as long as she could, eventually breaking down.

"It's going to be all right. We're almost there."

When they arrived on campus, Joy had filled Luke in on sordid details. He was appalled, and before walking Joy back to her room, he told her he would check on her in the morning.

"Look, Joy, don't let this jerk worry you. Me and my friends will take care of you. I'm on the hockey team, and we'll take this guy apart if he so much as comes near you. Now get some sleep; I'll call you in the morning."

Joy's roommate, Sam, was also just getting in. As soon as she saw Joy, she knew there was trouble and was horrified to hear the story.

"He seemed like such a nice guy. Respectful and low-key. And it didn't hurt that he was rich and handsome. You two made such a nice couple."

Joy was too upset to talk any longer. "I need to get some sleep; I'm exhausted. All of this is surreal; I'm so traumatized."

As Joy waited for sleep, she prayed and thanked God, who delivered her from the unthinkable. She was so angry with herself. How could she have misjudged Carlos so much? She considered reporting the incident to school authorities but decided her word against his could get complicated. But she worried: Would Carlos and his thugs come after her?

CHAPTER 12

❦

More Than Gratitude

Recovering from Carlos's atrocious scheme was slow. Nightmares and signs of post-traumatic stress became less frequent as time moved forward. Fortunately, their economics class ended. Although she wasn't sure, she felt that Luke and some of his friends might have had "words" with Carlos, for he clearly went out of his way to avoid her.

Luke continued checking on Joy, worrying about her. It was late afternoon, after hockey practice, Luke had showered, dressed, and donned his favorite Patriots jacket, the one his dad had given him just before he left for Brown, and headed over to Joy's dorm. He softly knocked on her door.

"Can I come in?" he asked in a low, steady tone.

"Sure," Joy replied, her voice filled with surprise. "Luke, it's you, come in."

Luke, she thought, was a true hero. He was such a clean-cut young man who loved sports and played hockey like a pro. He had long blond hair, almost the color of hers, and people often thought they might even be related. Yes, he was a sweet guy, and despite his massive, hunky exterior, there was something unexpectedly gentle about him.

Luke stepped inside, his gaze steady and unyielding.

"Hey, how are you doing? I was just in the area on my way back from practice, heading to my room, and I thought I'd stop by to see you. Is that OK?"

Joy smiled. How sweet asking if it was OK. "Yeah, it's OK," she replied.

But was it really? Ever since Carlos, she wasn't sure if she could trust anyone; everything seemed so tainted. Yet with Luke, she felt different, secure and safe.

Luke pulled up a chair, squeezing his massive frame into the undersized seat as he sat across from Joy, who was at her desk with an open book. He knew that although time was a healing agent, her experience was still fresh and troublesome.

"So, how are you doing? Everything good?"

Joy smiled and turned to face Luke. His handsome face was a reassuring beacon of their friendship, and she began to open up.

"You know, Luke, for a long time after it all, I felt scared... like I was falling apart. Like the entire ordeal was my fault. But now, I know that wasn't true. Now, I feel like I've moved on, that tomorrow will be better, and the day after that even more so."

Luke listened and then softly offered his thoughts:

"I know nothing I, or anyone else, can say will erase Carlos. But I want you to know, I'm not going anywhere. I'll help you through this, however you need me."

Luke paused, took a deep breath, and spoke from the wisdom of having his own demons, ones he had never had the courage to face, much less the opportunity to share. "There's nothing I can do to fix what happened, but maybe I can be part of the process of helping you heal and move on, like you said."

Joy sighed. "It's funny, the human capacity to move on. How even the most horrendous things can, to some degree, be put aside. In retrospect, I was really lucky; lucky to know Spanish, lucky to be quick-minded, and lucky that out of the thousands of people I could have asked for help, it turned out to be you. Maybe there is a silver lining for everything."

Joy's eyes shimmered with fragile hope as she looked up. "Thank you, Luke. I know, you and your buddies are like guardian angels. I'm grateful. Thank you..."

Luke nodded, his voice a quiet vow. "We'll take it one day at a time."

"Yeah, one day at a time." Joy looked a bit closer at her hero and felt perhaps something more than gratitude.

For the first time in a long time, Joy had stirrings of emotions she hadn't dared to feel. Not just gratitude. Something deeper. Something warmer.

CHAPTER 13

The Truth Be Told

Later that month, Cynthia unexpectedly visited. Joy was amazed at how close they had become, who would have thought it? Cyn drove from Boston to Providence after a long, late-night phone call from Joy, who had shared her nightmare, a true and loyal friend.

A sleek yellow convertible pulled up in front of Joy's dorm and parked in one of the four handicapped spaces. It was Cynthia's third convertible in that many years, after various on-road mishaps. But Daddy always came through, and besides, yellow was a nicer color than the others.

She opened the door and slid out of the front seat, her skirt so short it might be mistaken for a wide belt.

"Hey, sweetheart," a voice rang out. "You're parked in a handicapped spot!"

"Really? Well, I am handicapped," Cynthia shot back.

The handsome, middle-aged security guard walked over. "You don't look handicapped to me."

"Well, if you don't think being rich, entitled, and insatiably hot isn't a handicap, you don't know jackshit."

The security guard shook his head in disgust, but his remark left Cynthia feeling shamed.

"All right, all right, 'Sheriff,' I'll move," she warned, "but you better watch out, or I'm going to come over there and show you just how handicapped I really am. And by the way, I love your pistol."

The reunion was thrilling: "Oh my God, Joy, you look fabulous. More gorgeous than ever!"

"Thanks, Cyn, and you look great too."

"Yeah, Liar. Honey, next to you, no one looks great ... you're the reason half the co-eds on campus are in therapy. It isn't fair, but what the heck. God hates me.

As usual, Cynthia was overstating. She looked about the same as she did when they graduated from Miss Porter's. Her hair was a bit longer and styled differently, but she looked great, still slim and put together, in the latest and most exclusive clothing ... this time, a rather low-cut Valentino blouse and a skirt that hardly qualified as one. Joy noticed that Cynthia's boobs looked more prominent, but then again, she probably had on one of those "push-up" bras she insisted on wearing or as she put it, "they're cock magnets,"

"If the headlights are on high beam, the guys can't miss them."

The old friends walked over to the campus coffee bar and settled in for one of their girl gab sessions.

Cynthia reached into a designer bag big enough to transport a dozen gold bars, pulled out a pack of Newports, and lit one up.

"You smoke?"

"Yeah, a habit I got from Jacques, some French dude I picked up in Saint-Tropez last summer. I met him on the topless beach. He was walking with some other guys. I took one look at him in that Speedo and thought he was smuggling grapefruits."

Joy cringed at the image.

Cynthia took a deep drag and continued: "Well, I had to have him, so I did. He smoked like a chimney, the French all do, and well, when in Rome, do as the Romans... or maybe I should say, in Saint-Tropez, do as Jacques does."

"You're too much, Cyn. So, what happened to Jacques?"

"Poor guy, I wore him out. When I was ready to leave France, he could barely stand up straight. You know what they say about the French... well, it isn't true. They peter out. But don't worry, I bought him a first-class ticket to Bali, and I'm sure he's recuperating on some beach."

"You're too much. Are you still in school?"

"Yeah, well, sort of. I'm doing my sophomore year for the second time, and the way it's playing out, possibly going for a third time. I'm at Fently, a co-ed school just outside of Boston. The place is filled with kids like me, seriously unserious about learning anything and just spending their parents' money. You'll love this. I changed my major three times. I started as a lit major, but when I found out how many books they make you read, I dropped it like... well, like Jacques. And then I matriculated." Cynthia paused and continued: "You're impressed that I knew that word, aren't you, Joy? As I was saying, I matriculated in ballet."

"Ballet? You can't dance. You have two left feet!"

"I know, but all these cute guys in tights were a big draw, and that didn't work out either."

"No? Because you couldn't dance?"

"No, because the guys weren't into me."

"Figures. Then what did you do?"

"I looked over the catalog, and the only major left I thought I could do was women's studies."

"Women studies? What's that like?"

"I don't know, and I don't think the school does either. We just sit around and berate men, how stupid most of them are and how they haven't got a clue about what women really want. And speaking of men ..."

Cynthia stopped abruptly. "OMG, I'm so sorry. I came here to see how you were doing, and here I am going on and on about me ... So, deary, how are you? Carlos, that asshole. It must have been awful."

"I'm doing well. It's becoming more of a distant memory now, and I have a couple of people who are very supportive, helping me move on."

"That's great, Joy. Any of them men?"

Joy's face told the story.

"There is someone, isn't there? Well, as you know, my philosophy is when life pitches you a strike, you don't collapse, you hold your head high and swing anyway, turning every strike into a lesson and a chance to come back stronger. So, who is he, and is he hot?"

"Well, I am sort of seeing this guy; his name is Luke."

"Luke, like Luke Perry? Tell me he is not as handsome as Luke Perry. Is he a 'ten'? If he is, I will kill you right here and now. Get me a knife! It's not fair that someone as gorgeous as you is dating someone as gorgeous as Luke 'Dylan McKay' Perry on *90210*. And to think I got stuck with Jacques ... God hates me."

"I thought you said Jacques was a looker?"

"Well, he was, but not a ten, maybe an eight and a half in all the right places."

"Oh, Cyn, you are such a drama queen. It's always about you, isn't it?"

"Of course. Who else is there? If I don't look after myself, no one will. I'm pretty sure my parents tried to sue the doctor after he delivered me. I was such a difficult child, and it only got worse. But, come on, tell me about your Luke. Is he good in the sack?"

"God, cut it out. You are always holding a pity party for yourself, and it's none of your business whom I sleep with."

"Go on, tell me more about LUKE!"

"He's a junior and goalie on the Brown hockey team."

Cynthia lit another cigarette and bounced up and down in her seat: "Hockey team? A goalie. I love it. Goalies are the best; they spend the whole game with their legs spread apart. So, when?"

"When, what?"

"When am I going to meet this goalie? You know, if he's too gorgeous, I may steal him away. Not that I'd even have a shot at it the way I look next to you."

Cynthia got to meet Luke a couple of nights later. Afterward, she sulked for an hour, tormented by the idea that anyone that cute, that tall, and so "Luke Perryish" wasn't with her. When she left to go back to Boston, Cynthia leaned her elbow on the rolled-down window of her convertible and reminded Joy, "Don't forget, send Luke to Boston if you get tired of him. I'll show him how to really handle a puck. Ciao!"

Times with Luke were sweet and fun. He always came up with neat things like playing Frisbee on the deserted beaches or visiting the Newport mansions, which was especially interesting given that he was studying architecture and Joy, design. A stop at the local hot dog joint was as much fun as any gourmet dinner. Joy loved so much about Luke: he was handsome, athletic, and, like she, interested in many of the same things.

Luke, too, was relishing life with Joy. He found a profound sense of contentment being with her. Unlike many of her contemporaries, usually selfish and contriving, Joy was different. Her astounding good looks and lack of conceit humbled him. He felt such a strong connection, a mutual admiration, maybe even a kind of love. But he was young, inexperienced, and confused about matters of the heart.

Luke was delighted when Joy agreed to attend the big game. The Brown Bears had an ongoing rivalry with the Yale Bulldogs. Both teams were Division I and fiercely competitive for the Ivy League championship. It was a home game for Brown.

"Joy, I'm so glad you are coming. It will be my good luck charm. If we win, we go on to play Harvard, and if we win that game, we're the Division Champs. It would be the first time for Brown in decades."

"I'll be rooting for you! You can be sure of that."

The game was a blowout. Brown stomped Yale 3-0, and the fans went wild. After the game, Luke showered up and joined Joy and his friends at the local beer garden. The festive mood was contagious, and Joy was excited to see Luke happy with his teammates. Around midnight, the party broke up. Luke walked Joy back to her dorm, and they reminisced about the night's excitement.

"You know, Luke, I never liked hockey very much. I went to a few games at the boy's school near Miss Porter's but until now didn't take much interest in the sport."

"Oh, and now you do?"

"Well, yeah. Maybe more interest in a particular goalie than the game."

Luke blushed.

When they arrived at the dorm, Joy leaned into Luke and gave him an affectionate kiss on the cheek. "You know, you are my hero. You practically saved my life that night, and now you are Brown's MVP."

Luke blushed again. "Thanks, Joy. You are the most beautiful girl I've ever seen. And the nicest too. If I were to choose a partner, it would be you."

Now Joy blushed. She waited for Luke to declare himself. But he stopped short of that. She reasoned that he was either too shy, intimidated, or maybe both. Their time together was precious, and he was the ultimate gentleman, always treating her with respect. She chalked that up to his upbringing, being from Montana and reared by parents who stressed solid values.

The couple sat on the steps in front of Joy's dorm and held hands. She looked into Luke's eyes and sensed he wanted to say something but was having difficulty articulating it. Rather than push him, she simply laid her head on his shoulder and patiently waited. A chilly breeze picked up, so Joy nestled closer to Luke, savoring the warmth of his masculine body. She felt so safe and content.

It took a while, but Luke finally spoke: "Joy, I think we are pretty good friends, maybe more than friends."

Joy snuggled closer and waited to hear the words she'd been longing for. Luke was her knight in shining armor, she loved his shy, unassuming nature and how unaware he was of his own desirability. She adored everything about him, his kindness, intelligence, athleticism, sensitivity, and, of course, his handsomeness.

Luke continued in a low, uncertain voice, "But I think friends are all it could ever be with us."

Joy's heart leaped; was there someone else? Did Luke have another love interest, maybe back home? That would explain a lot, she thought. She pulled away and desperately asked, "There is someone else, isn't there?"

"No, no, no one else. I swear, I'd never do that to you."

"Then what?"

Luke hesitated and collected his thoughts, shifting his substantial frame as he sat on the step. "You know, Joy; you are the best woman I've ever known. You are so intelligent and kind and sweet ... and so much more. If I brought you home to Montana, my mom would love you. I could just hear her saying, 'You'll make beautiful children together.' And my dad, well, he'd be thrilled to know you. You're the type of girl every father wants for his son."

Joy listened intently. Where was this going?

"In Montana, other than hockey, I didn't have much of a life. I wanted to go to college and needed a scholarship, so I had to earn it by playing hockey and studying... really studying hard. But that was a good thing, the scholarship and leaving Montana, because in Montana, there isn't room for me."

"Room for you? The last time I looked, Montana is an enormous state."

"Yeah, it is. It's filled with good, God-fearing people, like my parents, who have wholesome ideals and devotion to the things that count."

Joy, now totally lost, asked, "Luke, what are you even talking about?" She wondered if he wanted to be a priest or something.

Luke took a deep breath. He had to make a decision he'd long avoided in fear of hurting Joy. But this decision was now a declaration.

"Joy, I am telling you that we can never be. As much as I want it, and I even prayed for it, it just can't be. From way back, I always knew that marriage and children were not in the cards for me."

Joy, clearly confused and frustrated, asked again, "What are you saying, Luke?"

Luke hung his handsome blond head down, and tears welled in his piercing hazel-green eyes. Joy sensed a deep, bone-wrenching tremble in his large frame. He looked up and forced a brave smile. "Joy, I won't cheat you out of the life you deserve." Luke took a deep breath. "How can I be right for you if I'm not right for myself?"

Joy was puzzled. "Luke, I don't understand. You're talking crazy."

Luke squeezed Joy's hand and spoke words he'd never had before. "Don't make me say it … it hurts too much. I can't even admit it to myself. I've never acted on this, and maybe never will, I'm too frightened, but it haunts me, day and night. I could never subject you to living with a liar, a denier, a fraud, maybe even what some might call a degenerate." Luke paused and wiped a renegade tear from his eye.

"Joy, I'm a lot of things, but one thing I'm not is dishonest, and I know I'm not the man you deserve; in fact, I'm not the man any woman would want."

Joy held her breath and shuddered as an epiphany clutched her, unraveling the fragile hope she had held for them. It vanished like a flash of lightning, leaving only the stark truth behind. She saw it now, he wasn't pushing her away out of cruelty but out of kindness, respect, and a deep concern for what she deserved. His heart, she realized, could never truly be hers, not because she wasn't enough, but because his path lay elsewhere. Despite his genuine affection, his inner turmoil only added to his confusion and torment. He knew she deserved honesty, not deception.

That night in bed in her dorm room, Joy recalled the quiet distance in Luke's arms when they embraced. His touch, though gentle, lacked the passion she so desperately craved. Suddenly, everything that had confused her before became painfully clear, his avoidance of certain conversations, his reluctance to offer even a hint of commitment. The conflict in his eyes made sense. He was fighting demons he might never conquer. At that moment, she realized the depth of their unsolvable dilemma and knew his struggle was not hers to fix. Despite her heartbreak, she understood she must let him go with dignity and compassion, honoring his truth even as it shattered her own.

Tears welled up in her eyes, and she cried for Luke, the truth be told, he was a noble soul locked in an unwinnable argument between his heart and his nature. But she also wept for herself, for the fruitless unconditional love she had given him, only to find he couldn't give her what she most longed for: someone to love and to be loved in return. Her tears couldn't wash away the sting of heartbreak or the despair of losing in love once more.

"Is this to be my fate?" she whispered, recalling the words of the Roma gypsy woman who had warned her long ago. The memory sent a shudder through her. Was she cursed after all?

CHAPTER 14

Hypersexuelle, Ma Petite Cherie *

(Oversexed, my little darling)

Summer Abroad

The years at Brown flew by, feeling like just a couple of months. Spending summers in Braga allowed Joy to be close to many other European countries. She traveled as a no-frills student visiting the historical highlights: Rome, London, Prague, Milan, and Paris.

It was in Paris that Joy made the final decision that fashion, not languages, would be her career.

Strolling down the historic boulevards of Paris, Joy absorbed every whisper from the ancient buildings and charming nooks and corners that the city so abundantly provides, like little treasures collected over the years. She knew that Paris was filled not only with history but also with innovation, and she felt a deep pull to be part of it. She embraced the vibrant energy of the elegant cafés, stylish boutiques, and timeless ateliers, uniquely Parisian, defying time yet thoroughly modern.

Joy marveled at the small, out-of-the-way shops near Montmartre, where she discovered vintage fabrics and intricate sketches that beckoned with possibilities, just waiting for a designer to seize them and transform them into wearable art. Her eyes gleamed with anticipation at the thought that she, too, would be part of this living art. She walked through the winding streets with her ever-present companion, her notebook, making sketches and taking notes. Ideas danced off her pencil as she filled page after page: a design for an elegant cape, an outrageously chic chapeau, and a breathtaking ball gown, all destined to be crafted in workrooms filled with talented cutters. Without a doubt, Joy felt that Paris was not merely a destination; it was a muse calling her to a life of fashion and art. She was ready to embark on the journey, fully aware of the determination and grit it would demand, yet still haunted by one lingering question: how?

The daily routine was simple: wake early, grab a café at Madam Noel's, and set out exploring. Often, she would read about trade events and gain entry.

It wasn't that difficult getting in, given her good looks, her mastery of French, and her natural congeniality.

She would simply show up, and people would assume she was a well-known model. Security would often wave her past, focused on her extraordinary good looks, which were to them credentials enough.

But it wasn't modeling that interested Joy; it was design. Every spare moment, she worked hard drawing sketches using her God-given talent for creating beautiful fashions, hoping to someday be able to produce and market them. Volumes of sketches filled her modest room, some pinned to the walls, others piled high on her vanity table.

While attending a runway show at a hidden gem and somewhat under-recognized design house, Joy crossed paths with Monsieur Pierre Longchamp, the charismatic maestro of Maison de Paris. The elderly gent was a fashion visionary well into his seventies, and yet as vital and creative as designers half his age. Joy decided to take the chance and meet the maestro.

"Excuse me, Monsieur Longchamp," Joy began hesitantly, her eyes wide with admiration as she approached the distinguished gentleman. "Your show, your vision, is unlike anything I've ever seen."

Longchamp, initially puzzled as to who this young woman might be, smiled warmly. "Ah, mademoiselle, fashion is not merely about frocks and accessories, it's about passion and art. It's about transforming something as esoteric as fibers or hides into creations that are not only functional but beautiful. It's about breathing life into the ordinary, preserving time-tested traditions, and creating new ones. For me, it's about life itself ... without passion, there is no life. Do you understand, *ma chérie*?"

Joy listened intently as she scribbled notes in her ever-present notebook. "Yes, Monsieur, I understand."

Longchamp continued, his voice gentle yet earnest, "Trends and fleeting beauty are not what matter, it is the art of creating through cloth and color."

Leaning in, Joy replied, "I feel as if every piece here speaks a language, one that is understood differently by each who views it. How do you capture such timeless emotion?"

He pondered her question and then replied thoughtfully, "Time, my dear, it is time. What truly matters is the passion that fuels creation, passion that grows with time. Like life, each creation carries the secrets of the past and the promise of the future. And, like life, it must be both bold and tender. *Comprenez vous*?"

"I've always believed that true style comes from deep within," Joy confessed softly yet determinedly. "Your work has awakened something inside me, an urge to express my own dreams."

Longchamp nodded. "That, mademoiselle, is the very essence of art. Do not fear to be bold; let your creativity speak for itself and let your spirit transcend all else. If you do this, you will be among the great. But if you allow yourself to fall into the trap of monotony and greed, you may end up what some might call a 'department store hack.' No, no, *ma chérie,* never allow that to happen."

Joy smiled and quickly wrote his words down.

"What is this you're writing?" Monsieur Longchamp demanded. "Are you a reporter?"

"Oh, no, Monsieur, I am a student of design," Joy answered.

Abruptly, Longchamp reached out and took the notebook from Joy's hands. "Let me see this."

Carefully, he flipped through the worn pages, pausing now and then. "Are these all your own thoughts?"

"Oui, Monsieur. They're all mine."

"Well, they are excellent, beyond excellent. You have promise. And in case I haven't said it before, you are very, very beautiful. Even an old man like me cannot ignore that."

Joy blushed. "*Merci,* Monsieur. *Merci.*"

"So, you fancy being a designer? Well, come by tomorrow, and we shall see what we shall see. Tomorrow at nine, *oui?*"

"*Oui, oui,* of course, I'll be there. And thank you, Monsieur, your words give me hope and the courage to follow my dreams. I am beyond grateful."

Monsieur Longchamp was enthralled by Joy's elegance, charm, and undeniable "*C'est allure.*" He could not resist the magnetic pull of her presence and befriended her. Joy kept that early-morning meeting at Maison de Paris. And it was then that maestro offered Joy the golden ticket to enter the world of fashion ... an exclusive summer internship in his cutting-edge atelier.

He explained, "My child, you do understand; you will work long and hard hours, in the third-floor salon, with very little pay but tremendous exposure to the industry."

Joy willingly nodded. "*Oui,* Maestro"

"It's settled. You start Monday. I see you then. Seven a.m. sharp."

"Attention, Attention!" bellowed Messier Longchamp. "This *c'est magnifique* creature is here to study the trade, and you all are here to help her learn. She is to do, how do you say, everything from the bottom up."

The half dozen or so craftspeople in the shop looked around.

Lorraine, the senior cutter turned to Bernise, an assistant. "Who is this little chickadee? Maybe Messier's lover? *Pas possible,* she is too young, and Messier could hardly walk, much less *levez-le.*" She made a gesture for a limp penis.

"I do not know," admitted Bernise. "How could I?"

Monsieur clapped his hands. "Voila! So, get to work."

Joy looked around the room, filled with skepticism and distrust. She knew it wasn't going to be easy to win over these seasoned workers, but she was determined, too.

Day after day Joy showed up early prepared to do whatever was asked of her, be it sweeping the floors, untangling thread, or steaming wrinkles from completed outfits. Every morning and afternoon, Joy cheerfully delivered the cafés to Lorraine and the others, and then did the wash-up. In between her mundane duties, she intently watched and learned.

Although Maison de Paris was not as well-recognized as other design houses, it produced some of the finest garments in the industry. Often, the giants and well-known houses would commission Maison de Paris to produce clothing and then private label their designs for sale in their own well-known and prestigious salons.

The staff soon warmed up to Joy. Her engaging and kind manner gained their respect. She was a hard worker and clearly exuded enthusiasm and talent. Eventually, the cutters allowed her to assist them, and she mastered the skill handily.

Lorraine explained, "You see, *ma cherie*, you must know how a garment is constructed to be a good designer. It's like when you build a *maison*. You don't just draw a pretty picture; you must start at the foundation and understand how it all goes together... *oui, you comprendre?*"

Joy nodded. For years, she had puttered around with sewing, fixing or changing a few things here and there on an outfit or accessories. But Madam Lorraine was right, technical skills were essential and learning them was necessary for true mastery. And this was her chance.

As the summer passed, Joy's mastery of French and enchanting looks secured a spot in everyone's heart, especially Francois, Messier Longchamp's middle-aged married son and heir apparent. For most of the summer, Joy navigated herself out of tight corners or dark closets as Francois pursued her.

Francois would demand: "Mademoiselle Joy, please, go into the stock room and find me bolt 129, the Italian silk, it's blue, sapphire blue." No sooner had Joy arrived in the closet, than Francois would be behind her, closing the door.

"Look, for it, Mademoiselle. It's usually underneath the shelf with all the greens on the bottom."

Joy gracefully bent down to look and was greeted by a pair of very aggressive hands belonging to Francois.

"Please, Francois, I don't like when you try and touch me. You should be touching your wife."

"*Ma femme, cette sorcière.* No, no, no. She is a hag. I desire only you. You must know, we French men have a wife to clean, wash, and raise children for us, not to touch, like I want to touch you, Mademoiselle."

"Monsieur Francois, that is not true. Your wife, I've met her, and she's very nice. I don't think she'd be happy with you fooling around like this."

"Oh, *ma petite cherie,* she would not care. She thinks I'm, what you call it … ah, *hypersexuelle.* Poor thing. She is so wrong. I'm not oversexed, I'm just under-touched. *Pauvre de moi.* No, no, not oversexed, I'm just right sexed … and, of course, French men, well, they need women, lots of them, and often! You know, like a tom cat …."

It took a bit of time, but eventually, Joy figured out how to handle Francois. He was like so many other men that Joy had dealt with for most of her life, and she had come to accept it as part of the curse of being beautiful.

The summer was ending, as was Joy's internship, when the maestro summoned Joy to his small office overlooking Roux Marie Antoinette. His desk sat in front of a large Palladium window that framed the vibrant French street three stories below. Racks of dresses, in various stages of completion, hung helter-skelter around the room, and the oversized leather lounge chair where monsieur often napped sat quietly in the corner.

"Mademoiselle Joy." He began. "You have done well here at Maison de Paris. My workers all love and respect you, and I hope you feel the same."

"*Oui,* Monsieur, of course I do, well, most of them anyway."

"Oh, *oui,* of course. Francois. He is a naughty boy but harmless. He acts that way because he thinks it makes him young. But like a cat trying to catch a large mouse, he wouldn't know what to do with it if he caught it."

Joy thought, *Naughty boy, my foot, more like a dirty old man, and I'm not so sure about Francois not knowing what to do if he had the opportunity.* But one thing for certain, he would never get that chance with her.

Monsieur Longchamp continued, "I have seen your sketches, and they are impressive, and how do you say ... *Innovante.*"

"Innovative? *Merci,* Messier. *Merci.*"

"So, as a reward for your work, I will allow you to produce one of your designs. My staff will assist, but the work must be your own. And you must do the *travail de grognement* ... the grunt work ... on your own time."

Joy was thrilled. "Oh, Messier, thank you. It will be a privilege to have this opportunity, and I will make something divine, and you, all of you, will be proud. I promise."

"So," Messier Longchamp continued. "Mademoiselle Joy, you must begin. Your remaining time here is short. *Bonne chance, Mon cher.* We shall see what we shall see...."

CHAPTER 15

✧

A Focus on Life

Joy returned to campus after her summer internship to complete her senior year. She had transformed into a woman in every sense, no longer the naïve kid who started at Brown just four short years ago. Along her journey, she acquired a few battle scars as evidence of her experiences, some more painful than others. But now, she exuded sophistication and confidence. Her time in Paris was well spent, not only learning her trade but also becoming a woman.

Diligently, Joy completed her core courses early on, leaving senior year to pursue some upper-level specialty subjects that she felt would serve her well. Advanced chemistry was an unlikely course for a fashion designer. Still, Joy felt that the developing science of new synthetic fabrics was the future, and knowing chemistry was the first step in understanding the potential. A course in business management was another excellent choice. Being a designer was a natural talent for her but knowing how to run a business was not. Instinctively, she was preparing for the future.

Another interest was photography, and it was serendipitous when Joy saw a notice on the bulletin board in the Fine Arts building and decided to apply.

Attention Fine Art Majors

Brown is proud and honored to announce that Giuseppe Di Legno, CPP, renowned artist and fashion photographer, has accepted a post as Artist-in-Residence for a full term.

Mr. Di Legno has an impressive Curriculum Vitae, including winning first place for three consecutive years in the International Fashion Photography Competition (IFPC) held in Milan, Italy. Di Legno has also been published extensively in prestigious venues, including The New York Times, Vogue, Glamour, and Italy's Grazia and Io Donna. His peers have recognized him in industry publications like Capture, Shutter, and Black+White magazine. Di Legno's work has been shown in galleries worldwide. He is celebrated with permanent exhibits at the Fashion Museum of Paris and the New York School of Design library, among others.

Brown will host Mr. Di Legno in an eight-week photography symposium, open to a limited number of Juniors and Seniors via lottery, matriculating in the Fine Arts program. To enter the lottery, contact Repelda Krasnaborski, Dean of Fine Arts (Borski@brownfaculity.edu).

Luck was in Joy's corner when she received the email notifying her that she was one of the fourteen students randomly chosen for Di Legno's symposium. Learning that the school would provide a professional quality loaner camera was exciting. "Meetings," as they were called, were held three times a week at ten p.m., which Joy thought odd. The first meeting was on a cold Monday evening in November.

"Good evening, ladies and gentlemen," began Di Legno.

"My name is Giuseppe Di Legno. But I go as 'D.'" He paused, put his hands in his jean pockets, and strutted around the room, counting his charges.

In his unmistakable continentalism, he continued: "I see we are all here, all fourteen of you. And fourteen of you are really lucky, because, as you will come to find out D. is no ordinary person. No, he's *come nessuno che tu abbia mai conosciuto. ...* That means like nobody you ever known. And why, you ask?"

D. walked to the back of the room, forcing the students to turn toward him. "Because he will make you do things you never thought possible. He will teach you things, but more than that, he will show you things, not just photography, but life.

"I know, to some, the hour may seem late, but to D., the day has just begun. You see, I live nocturnally, my energy comes to a boil at night. So, we shall begin. But first, a few frames of reference, a bit of philosophy, and, of course, the ground rules."

Joy listened intently as she studied Di Legno. He couldn't be more than forty-two or -three, perhaps forty-five at most. Yet he appeared much younger than his years. Unlike most professors in button-down shirts, loafers, khaki chinos, and the occasional well-worn blazer, Di Legno dressed more like an avant-garde artist. Joy thought, perhaps even a rock star ... an Italian version of Mick Jagger.

He wore his thick black hair pulled back into a stubby man bun, and he was bone-thin yet muscular. A Gucci messenger bag with the iconic green and red strap hung over his shoulder, just as European men often wore. His slim-fit cotton shirt, barely reaching his belt and left mostly unbuttoned, revealed a smooth, lean, nearly hairless torso that most women would find irresistibly sexy. Skin-tight, hip-hugging, low-rise designer jeans, Versace, she recognized, clung to his frame, and a full crop of bushy pubic hair provocatively peeked out just below his navel whenever he dramatically flung his arms about. Above that pelvic area, she caught a glimpse of a tattoo.

D., like many Italians Joy knew, animatedly waved his arms as he talked. Straining to get a better look, Joy finally saw the tattoo, a downward-pointing Cupid's arrow entwined with the words *Qui è dove troverai amore* ... Here is where you find love. Joy thought to herself, *Boy, you can't make this up. He must be hot, really hot, but not my type.*

D. continued, "Most people think that being a photographer is nothing more than a person aiming a camera and pressing the shutter, no, no. How wrong they are. These people are not photographers; they are, *come si dice?*" He squinted, "How do you call it?.... Snappers, worse, camera bugs.

"You know, like this." D. waved an imaginary camera around the room in exaggerated gestures, once again exposing his provocative tattoo. Joy couldn't help but smile and thought, *Oh my God if only Cyn could see this...a real Italian stallion!*

The class listened intently as this charismatic master went on.

"You see, *miei amici*, being a true photographer comes with a responsibility and requires focus, a focus on life. That responsibility is to pierce the surface and expose the soul of the subject, be it a beautiful person, an ancient building, a scene of nature, an elegant gown or a pile of *merda. Si*, it is the responsibility of the artist behind the camera to make the world see; the beauty, the ugliness, the filth, the joy, the horror and the complexity of his subject. In other words, *la verità*, the *truth*!"

D. strutted around the room, commanding attention as he addressed the class with a theatrical flourish. "But I find that doing this is a God-given gift, not a skill learned, like, *come si dice?* How do you say? Riding a bike or making wine. Sure, there are technical skills and equipment to learn, but anyone can do that. It is the gift given only by God that makes one great. And God has blessed me with such a gift. I have known this, always."

He paused, his every move deliberate, heightening the tension in the room. His intensity drew every gaze, and he stepped closer to the front row. The room fell silent as he leaned in, his face mere inches from one of the boys who now appeared wide-eyed and terrified. In a near-whisper, his voice carried a mix of gravity and reverence, almost as though he were praying, D., hissed, "So, we will find out if God has given any of you this gift ... I pray He has."

The words hung in the air, charged with an almost electric energy. The boy blinked, frozen under D.'s piercing gaze, while the rest of the room remained enthralled, waiting to see what might happen next.

D. paused and walked around the room, stopping at each of the students, putting his face next to theirs, and asking, "Do you have the gift? And you? And you? Well, we will soon find out."

But when he reached Joy, D.'s eyes suddenly found hers, locking on with an intensity that sent a shiver down her spine. Their gazes met, and he offered her an almost sensuous glare before reaching out, and gently touching her chin, tilting it slightly upward. "*Mio bel fiorello* ... my beautiful little flower," he said softly, his voice laced with intrigue. "Perhaps you are yet another gift from God, for D.?"

Suddenly, it was back to business. "I know you are here because you want to be a famous fashion photographer like me." D. modestly bowed his head reverently. "And with my help, maybe you will become one too." He shrugged, "Unlikely, but maybe." The eager students looked around the room, wondering if they were among the chosen.

D. walked up to the whiteboard with purpose and began writing. Turning to the class, he explained, "I have divided this course into two parts. Part *una,* one awakens your spirit, allowing you to find your soul and unleash the 'gift' you might have. Part *due,*" he held up two fingers, "is the easy part; learning the mechanics of being a photographer, the technical skills that you all came here to master."

He paused for emphasis, scanning the room with a knowing smile, then continued, "And in this journey, we will have some fun. We will learn a lot and do so much together. Like I said, we'll learn the process, how to use the equipment, visit some fashion houses, attend a few exhibitions, maybe a fashion show in New York, and even do an actual photo shoot."

The room was electric with anticipation, as a sea of heads nodded and smiled. D., despite all his eccentricities and blatant egocentrism, hit a home run with these wannabe photographers.

"I will take a picture of each of you, so you experience the way a true artist takes photos.

"But before you can do that, you must witness and understand real life through the camera's lens. So, I have prepared an assignment for each of you, and it goes like this.

"In this box are fourteen pieces of paper upon which I have written a subject. It could be an object, a person, or a building. Each of you will draw from this box and select a topic that will be yours exclusively. *Capisci?"*

The students eagerly nodded in unison.

"*Bene,* now let's get started."

When it was her turn, Joy reached into the box, drew her pick, and read it, " You are to find an old woman, as old as you can. Then, you are to spend time with that person and learn who she is. Her dreams, her fears, her philosophy, and her love. Once you have done that, you will photograph her in black and white."

D. looked at the clock, which read 11:45 p.m. He jumped up on a chair and waved enthusiastically:

"We are done for tonight. You have three weeks to complete your assignment. Carry it like a torch, out of mediocrity, toward greatness. Until we meet again next Tuesday night."

CHAPTER 16

─────── ❧ ───────

Whispers, Wrinkles, and Wisdom

Joy left the classroom with an unmistakable buzz. D. was not just a character, she mused; he was an inspiration, possibly a revolutionary, and maybe even a genius. The alluring Italian had left an indelible mark on her, and she couldn't deny her excitement. Having admired his work in magazines like *Vogue*, she was now filled with artistic envy. The opportunity to study under such a rare talent was beyond extraordinary, and she was determined not to waste a single moment of this once in a life time opportunity. And ... besides all that, he was undeniably entertaining with an abundance of charm and sexuality!

Finding an older woman at Brown University, where the average age was probably twenty, maybe fifty-five if you counted faculty and administration, wasn't going to be easy. But Joy was a resourceful person and figured it out quickly. Just on the outskirts of Providence, Joy found a lovely retirement home. The complex looked like a series of connected New England cottages strung together, each painted in the rich blues and Nantucket reds of homes up North. Crips black shutters surrounded the windows, and charming attic dormers popped through the roof seemingly waving at the passersby. A central building with a welcoming, navy canvas awning bore bold white letters: Brightstar. Joy briskly entered and asked to speak to the administrator, who eventually joined her in the cheerful parlor.

As she waited, she looked around. There was a fireplace and lots of books and magazines in every nook and corner. Oversized comfortable faux leather furniture was liberally placed around the "great room," and the large-screen TV blared at an ear-piercing level. Small groups of elderly people, some seated and quietly chatting, while others seemed to be elsewhere, unaware of their surroundings. Joy was sure that she had found the right place. Most everyone was in the sunset of their lives.

"Good afternoon, I'm Mrs. Linden, the managing director of Brightstar; how may I assist you? Do you have a relative interested in joining "our little family?""

"How do you do? I'm Joy Nordstrom. I'm a senior at Brown." Joy presented her student ID.

"How do you do, Joy? Please sit down over here, and we can talk." The director led Joy to an out-of-the-way corner. She could not help but notice how very attractive Joy was, thinking: *this girl could be in the movies or a cover girl.*

"Thank you." Joy sat and continued: "I'm working on a very special project. The project involves meeting, interviewing, and photographing a particular person, an older woman, one willing to share their thoughts and insights and has earned the right to be listened to and respected."

"I see; go on."

Joy explained the assignment in detail: a famous artist/photographer was mentoring the project, and everything was on the up and up.

"So, Mrs. Linden, do you think one of the women here at Brightstar would want to share their story? My assignment requires me to interview and photograph the subject."

Mrs. Linden smiled warmly. "We welcome visitors of all ages, especially the young. It's a thrill for our residents to have young people visit. Many have no one left at all, no family, no friends, much less young folks.

"As for the photos, well, that would be up to each resident. Some are a little camera shy; others, well, say the word 'cheese' and they're all smiles."

"Oh, Mrs. Linden, I would never take a photo of someone without their agreement," Joy said earnestly. "Everyone is entitled to their privacy. My assignment is to take a very special kind of photograph, one that captures the heart and soul of the subject, not just a casual headshot. I hope we can find just the right woman... and that she'll be willing to help me."

"Hmmm." Mrs. Linden paused, considering the proposition. "A woman, you say?"

"Yes," Joy said. "My assignment requires that I choose a woman, an elderly woman."

"And what would become of this photograph?"

Joy had rehearsed answers to many possible questions, but she hadn't anticipated that one. Truth be told, she really didn't know. "Well, all of the students in the class have this assignment, some are shooting buildings, others nature, and so on. I assume Mr. Di Legno will pick the best ones and return the photos to the student photographers. The subjects would remain completely anonymous, of course, and they could have as many copies as they would like."

"Interesting. Very interesting, young lady." Mrs. Linden smiled thoughtfully. "Let me think about it. If appropriate, I'll discuss it with a few residents, and we'll have to get management's approval as well. And naturally, the subject would need to agree and approve everything, too."

"Naturally," Joy nodded.

Later that afternoon, Mrs. Linden called Joy with exciting news.

"Three women at Brightstar volunteered to be considered," she said. "And based on several factors, I would recommend Beatrice Gerkin. She's eighty-nine years old, a former psychologist, and a retired assistant professor at the University of Rhode Island. I think you will love Miss Gerkin. She's so bright and alert, and she jumped at the opportunity to participate. Would you like to meet her?"

"Yes, of course!" Joy said eagerly. "Can I come by after dinner tonight?"

When Joy arrived, she was led into a cozy sitting room where Beatrice Gerkin was waiting, poised in one of the faux-leather wingback chairs. Mrs. Linden made the introductions.

"Joy, I'd like you to meet Miss. Gerkin, Beatrice Gerkin. Bea, this is Joy Nordstrom, the Brown student I told you about."

Joy stepped forward. "How do you do, Miss Gerkin? It's a pleasure to meet you. Thank you for allowing me to have this interview."

"Oh, dear, you are welcome," Beatrice said warmly. "I had no idea you'd be so beautiful... so breathtakingly beautiful!"

Joy blushed. "Oh, Miss Gerkin, thank you. That's very kind of you. But this is all about you, not me."

Joy had done her homework and prepared a list of questions she wanted to ask Beatrice, some mundane, others probing and philosophical. She hoped the exchange would give her a window into

Beatrice's personality, something she could later capture on film. What followed, however, came as a complete awakening for Joy.

—— ❧ ——

Joy returned to Brightstar a few days later for the formal interview. Outside, it was snowing lightly, turning the grounds into something out of a Christmas village, tiny buildings dusted with white, like a model train scene under a tree. Inside, the scent of evergreens filled the air, and a fresh Christmas tree stood proudly in the oversized bay window. The warmth of the place lifted Joy's spirits as she checked in at the desk.

"Good afternoon," said the receptionist, a nicely dressed woman in her sixties. "May I assist you?"

"I'm Joy Nordstrom. I'm here to see Miss Gerkin."

"Of course. Mrs. Linden told me you'd be coming. She set aside the card room for your meeting. Third door on the left." She pointed. "I'll go fetch Miss Gerkin. Please, make yourself at home."

Soon, Bea entered, walking slowly but with dignity. The interview stretched over three intense hours, a marathon of questions, stories, cups of tea, and revelations that left both women utterly drained.

Miss Beatrice Gerkin, eighty-nine years young, sat poised in a smartly tailored jacket and matching skirt. Her thin frame radiated elegance. Around her neck hung a hand-crafted necklace of semi-precious stones, which she absentmindedly fingered from time to time, a gesture that seemed to mirror the thoughtful, deliberate rhythm of their conversation. Her demeanor was composed yet commanding, her spirit sharp, and her mental acuity remarkable, every bit as quick as someone half her age. Years as a counselor had made Bea a natural at reading people, a skill she wielded effortlessly.

From the outset, Bea had made it clear that this wouldn't be a one-sided exercise.

Joy, notebook and tape recorder in tow, began cautiously, easing into the interview with simple questions about Bea's upbringing, education, and early life.

She remembered D.'s late-night lectures, emphasizing that great portraits were born from understanding the subject deeply, not just surface facts.

"Get into their minds, their hearts, their psyches," D. had said, quoting photographers like Diane Arbus and Roger Ballen. "Strip them bare, figuratively, and then, and only then, will you capture a picture worth taking. A glimpse into their true being, one no costume or façade can disguise."

As the hours passed, Joy scribbled notes and adjusted the recorder, while Bea answered with a mixture of candor and humor, often absentmindedly fingering the beads of her necklace.

When the session ended, Bea leaned back in her chair, smiling.

"My dear," she said, her voice soft but deliberate, "you've been most conscientious, and I'm flattered you'd take such an interest in an old lady like me. But perhaps ... perhaps you could indulge me as well?"

Joy tilted her head, curiosity piqued. "Of course. What are you thinking about?"

Bea studied her for a moment, her expression unreadable. Her face, lined with the dignified etchings of time, carried a depth few ever achieved. Her bright eyes shone with wisdom, gained through firsthand experience.

Finally, Bea smiled and touched the necklace again.

"Let's wait. Let's get to know each other better first. Once we trust one another ... then I'll tell you more of my story of love lost, of life."

Joy nodded. She smiled in acceptance, thinking, *Who knows? Whatever Bea had in mind might just be worth the wait.*

Later that evening, back in her dorm room, Joy reviewed her notes and listened to the recordings. She loved Beatrice, her insights, her strength, the confidence in her voice. Her years as a lecturer were evident.

But of all the questions Joy asked, one answer would be forever imprinted in her memory:

"So, Bea," Joy had asked, "have you ever lost love?"

The recording captured Bea setting down her cup of strong mint tea and taking a deep breath.

"Love," Bea said, "oh my dear, what an impossible question. Let me start with a true story that happened a long, long time ago."

She sipped her tea and continued.

"When you're young, true love is an illusion, something you've heard about, something you hope might come your way, and something that defies definition. Of course, I'm not talking about the love we have for our parents, that's different. Nor puppy love ... no, I mean the kind of love that comes but once. The kind you don't know until you know it. And the kind you don't realize you had until it's gone."

Joy paused the tape, rewound, and played that part again: *"the kind you don't know until you know it..."*

Beatrice's voice continued: "When I was a little younger than you are now, I fell in love, unexpectedly, accidentally. "During the war, I volunteered at a hospital while pursuing my undergraduate degree in psychology. The patients were victims of serious war injuries, scarred, disabled, dismembered. Many suffered from what we now know as PTSD, though it wasn't recognized back then. It was painful to see, and even more painful to live with.

"There was a young lieutenant, Bobby, from New York. A burn victim, with over 70 percent of his body affected. Oddly enough, his face and hands were untouched, and he was, well, handsome. Dashing, as the girls would say."

Beatrice's voice softened.

"We spent hours talking, reading. Friendship became admiration. Admiration became love. But Bobby was deeply scarred inside and out. He couldn't accept love. Under his clothes, his body was a patchwork of keloids. His shame was unbearable.

"I tried to tell him, what I loved wasn't his body, but his mind, his spirit. But he couldn't believe me. 'I'm repulsive,' he said. 'Your love blinds you to the truth.'"

Bea took another breath on the tape.

"He left me," she said. "Left me with a note. I carry it with me even now. Would you like to hear it?"

On the recording, Joy's voice hesitated. "I ... I don't know if I should. That seems so personal."

Beatrice insisted. "Let me read it to you."

There was a rustle of paper, and then Bea's voice again, cracked slightly with emotion:

"My darling Bea,

I am writing this farewell note. It will be brief and to the point, like our love affair.

I face a choice: stay, yield to the desire to be with you forever ... or spare you the pain and inevitable regret.

I love you too much to stay. I pray you understand and forgive me.

Whenever you look at the stars, know the brightest one will be mine, looking down and loving you for eternity.

Bobby."

Tears welled in Joy's eyes as she listened.

"So," Joy asked gently, "did you ever see him again?"

"Once," Beatrice said. "At his funeral."

Bobby ended his life a year later. A nurse, who knew Bea from the hospital, brought her the necklace. Bobby handmade it just before he died.

On the tape, Beatrice's voice dropped to a whisper: *"I wear it … because it's all I have left of him. And because, maybe, it reminds me to keep going, even when it feels impossible."*

The following afternoon, Joy returned to Brightstar for the photo shoot. She set up by the fountain near the chapel entrance. Through the lens of her Leica, she focused on Beatrice's face, deeply lined, rich with memory, a map of a life lived fully.

She snapped the final frame with tears in her eyes, understanding at last what Mr. Di Legno meant: *You must see the soul before you can photograph a picture that matters.*

When Joy turned in Beatrice's photograph, Mr. Di Legno took one look and gasped, *"Oh mio Dio, è fantastico!"*

Oh my God, it's brilliant.

"You have captured it."

CHAPTER 17

The Masterpiece

The mail brought an unexpected surprise for Joy: a formal invitation. Monsieur Longchamp was retiring, and Maison de Paris was planning a gala in his honor.

Joy knew she couldn't possibly attend. It wasn't just the cost; it was the time away from school, upcoming finals and soon-to-be due term papers. Accepting was out of the question. Still, even though she wouldn't be at the party, she wanted to do something special for the old man. He had given her a remarkable opportunity to learn the trade. Despite the unwanted attention from his lecherous son, François, the experience had been invaluable.

She racked her brain. *What do you give a seventy-year-old man?*

As she puttered around her closet, the answer came to her. Sudden, simple, and perfect. It wouldn't cost more than a couple of dollars, but it would mean something. She'd need a little help, and she knew exactly who to ask: Mr. Di Legno.

"Good morning, D."

Joy still felt a little awkward calling a teacher that, but he had made it abundantly clear it was what he preferred.

"*Buongiorno, caro,*" he replied warmly. "And seeing your sweet, beautiful face makes it a wonderful morning. *Sì,* wonderful." D. gave her an approving once-over.

"I was wondering if you'd help me," Joy began. "I want to do something special for a man who helped shape my future in fashion."

"And who is this man you speak of, *caro?*"

"His name is Monsieur Pierre Longchamp."

D.'s eyes lit up. "*Aspetta, aspetta,* wait, wait, I know this name. He's not from here, right?"

"Right. He's French. Lives in Paris. He owns Maison de Paris."

"Ah, of course, Monsieur Longchamp!" D. snapped his fingers. "He has a son, yes? His name is... wait... it will come to me... ahh, François! Yes, that's it, François. He's ... how do you say? An asshole, yes?"

Joy nodded but chose not to comment.

"Monsieur Longchamp gave me a break years ago when I was just a novice freelance photographer, struggling to make a name for myself. He let me shoot his spring line. His designs were fine, not groundbreaking, but my photos made them look twice as good," D. said with a modest shrug. "So, what's this all about?"

"I interned at Maison de Paris. At the end of my stay, Monsieur Longchamp let me create one of my own designs. His staff helped, but the design and most of the work were mine. I finished the last stitch the day before I left France. He never saw it completed."

"I see," D. nodded. "Go on."

"As a retirement gift, I'd love to send him a beautiful photo, taken by you, maestro, of me wearing the gown. I think it would mean a lot to him. He was very fond of me. He often had me model for clients, and it helped move merchandise."

"Of course it helped," D. said. "Anything on that perfect body with that perfect face will sell."

Joy blushed. "D., I bet you say that to every woman."

D. smiled, offering no confirmation either way.

"So," he asked, "where is this masterpiece?"

"I have it carefully packed in my room. It's the most precious thing I own."

"*Sì, naturalmente.* Naturally, you'd feel that way. Now let me be sure I understand. You want me to photograph you in your original creation to send to Monsieur Longchamp?"

"Yes, please. It would mean the world to me. Will you?"

D. rubbed his hands together, studying her from head to toe. "Maybe ... if."

Joy gave him a puzzled look. "If what?"

"If you'll be my girlfriend and run away with me to the mountains of Italy. We'll make good wine, love every day, and you'll sit for me while I take the most breathtaking photos of your divine beauty. The world deserves to see you as only I can capture you."

Joy blinked, stunned. "You're joking, right?"

"Maybe," D. replied with a grin.

"D., I like you, but I could never be your girlfriend. Not now, not tomorrow, not ever. You're my teacher, nearly twice my age, and even though I find you charming, and yes, even sexy, it just wouldn't be right."

"*Caro,* I am your teacher. I will teach you the ways of *amore.* Your body is that of a goddess, and I am here to worship it." He paused. "Wait. Did you say you find me sexy?"

"Very. I find many men sexy. That doesn't mean I want to run off to the hills with them."

D. stroked his chin. "But still, you do find me sexy, *sì*?"

"Yes. I already told you that."

"And running away with me is ... how do you say ... out of the question?"

"YES. Completely out of the question!"

"*Caro,* are you sure? I promise a lifetime of excitement and passion."

Joy rolled her eyes. She'd heard lines before, François Longchamp had a whole book of them, but D. took the cake. This hot-blooded Italian had all his blood flowing away from his brain, and it was definitely affecting his judgment.

"Let's face it, D. You'd be like that until the next so-called 'goddess' came along. It's your nature."

"Mamma mia! You know D. better than D. knows D. So, you win, *caro*. I'll help you. But one matter remains. Non-negotiable."

Joy narrowed her eyes. "What is it?"

"You must agree to sit for me. Not in the gown, but in a studio session. Let me capture your radiance, your majesty, your uncanny beauty, for my portfolio. In return, I'll photograph you in your gown for Monsieur Longchamp."

Joy considered it. "Maybe. But I have a condition too. If you shoot me, it'll be in a public studio, and no funny business."

"Funny business?" he repeated. "*Che cosa significa,* funny business?"

"It means a legitimate photo shoot. Nothing exotic. Nothing explicit. And you know exactly what that means."

"*Mi arrendo. Tu vinci.* I surrender. You win. You'll have your picture, and I'll have mine."

D. booked a studio near campus. He hired assistants, invited the class, and even arranged for a dresser to help Joy with the gown.

When Joy stepped out of the dressing room in her original creation, the room gasped. She looked stunning, almost ethereal.

Joy's creation was a gown sculpted to accentuate her perfect silhouette. It was encrusted with tiny shimmering crystals that caught the light with every movement, each one hand-sewn by Joy during late nights and stolen weekends, creating a mesmerizing effect. The neckline, a fashionable strapless, framed her beautifully, drawing attention to her long, regal neck.

The skirt flowed like liquid silk, cascading to the floor in translucent layers that rippled with each step. A dramatic slit along one side revealed a glimpse of her leg, a modern, bold twist on classic elegance.

The color was a breathtaking blend of moonlit silver with undertones of pearl, shifting subtly in the light. The back of the gown was just as striking, plunging almost to her waist.

Joy paired the dress with a simple string of cultured pearls, a gift from her namesake grandmother, Julianna. The final touch was the train, which floated behind her as she walked, adding an otherworldly quality to her presence. She didn't just wear the gown, she became it.

D. moved around the studio like a ballet dancer. He adjusted Joy's head, then changed his mind and adjusted it again. He nudged her shoulders and hips this way and that, altered the lights several times, and made countless tiny refinements. More than an hour passed before he clicked the shutter.

When he finally did, he took only four shots.

"We are done. It is going to be *magnifica*," he declared. The room erupted in applause.

Joy looked confused. "But D., you only took four shots. Is that it?"

"My angel," D. said with a smile. "To be honest, I took three too many. The first was the money shot. The others are insurance in case the light was off."

As the session wrapped, D. approached her and whispered in her ear. "You didn't change your mind, did you?"

"About what?"

"About the mountains in Italy and making babies?"

"No," Joy said with a sly wink. "Never."

Joy kept her promise. After sending the print to Monsieur Longchamp, she sat for D.

To her surprise, he kept his promise too and behaved like a consummate professional.

The sitting was instructive. Joy got to observe the master at work, how he set the lights, how he positioned her body, how he fine-tuned every detail until he saw what he was looking for.

In the end, he took fewer than twenty photographs. He destroyed all but one, the single image that spoke to everyone who saw it.

D. had created a masterpiece. Joy was his photographic Mona Lisa.

And little did she know what that picture would come to mean.

CHAPTER 18

———— ❦ ————

Pomp and Circumstance

Friday morning broke over the Brown campus like most mornings in late May. The sun shone through high, overhead clouds, tossed about like fluffy white pillows on a blue coverlet. Joy had been up late the night before, but she dared not sleep in on this particular morning. It was graduation weekend. The time not only she, but her parents, had waited years to see arrive.

As consciousness crept in, she opened her eyes and looked around the room, one she would soon leave behind, likely forever. She thought of her parents, comfortably settled in a charming B&B within walking distance of campus. They had arrived a day earlier, and their excitement was impossible to hide. Being in the United States, on American soil, to witness Joy receive her degree was, for them, a dream made real.

Joy lay there just a few moments longer, savoring it all; Graduation, the moment she had worked so hard for, the moment her parents had sacrificed so much to make possible, and the moment that would forever mark the end of one chapter and the uncertain, exhilarating start of the next.

Her phone rang, ending the warm glow of her memories.

"Hello,"

"Joy, are you up? "

It was Cynthia.

"Of course I'm up." Joy fibbed. Joy had to beg, borrow, and practically steal to get a third ticket to the festivities. Brown was as tight as a pensioner on a fixed income regarding graduation tickets. But the event would be short something if Cynthia weren't there. They had become like sisters from another mother, despite being completely opposite on almost every level. It was the contrast that made it all work; a serious contender towards achievement, and a ne'er-do-well rich kid who thought morals were optional.

"So," Cynthia, continued. "I'm here. Arrived a little while ago, but I almost was going to miss it."

"Why?"

"Well, you see, I flew in, and the driver, a total mega-hottie, picked me up at the airport. And, well ... you know me, always one to reciprocate, so I picked him up too. He had a gig driving to New Jersey and kind of invited me to ride along. But then good sense kicked in, and I had him take me to the hotel instead. I gave him a really great tip, if you catch my drift, which, by the way, was a hell of a lot better than the back seat of an Impala. After that, I sent him on his way. And now... I'm here for you."

Joy rolled her eyes and thought, "And that's why I love this crazy person."

Brown's graduation was a weekend affair, beginning Friday night at nine with the beloved Campus Dance, a tradition open to graduates, families, alumni, and faculty, held on the College Green. The Brown Orchestra blared out a lively mix of traditional and pop music as attendees danced under hundreds and hundreds of whimsical paper lanterns, their soft glow lighting up the night and creating an atmosphere laced with romance and memories.

The foursome, Joy, her parents, and Cynthia, grabbed a little table near the bandstand, and Joy's father asked her to dance. It was a slow dance, and Jonathan held his daughter close, knowing deep down that he had done his job, the job every father dreams of doing: raising a child who finishes her education and steps boldly into the world.

He and his wife were thrilled with Joy, who had graduated from Brown with high honors and numerous awards. But what filled Jonathan with the greatest pride wasn't the accolades. It was seeing the transformation of his little girl into a young woman, confident, wise, and ready to make her own way in the world, armed with everything she needed and more.

As the dance ended, Jonathan leaned in and gently kissed Joy's beautiful hair, whispering, "Sweetheart, you are my pride and joy. Mama and I are incredibly blessed." Tears welled up in his eyes as he finished his very special thought. "The world is out there, honey. Go out and make it yours, and always remember, no matter how far you travel or what you're doing, you will always be in our hearts."

When father and daughter returned to the table, they found a small crowd gathered. Seven or eight young men had surrounded it, all seemingly vying to get closer to the main attraction: Cynthia. And as usual, she had dressed for the part, nothing short of eye-popping.

But when Joy rejoined the group, the young "gents" suddenly shifted their attention. The contrast between the two young women was striking, one like a flame to moths, the other a portrait of timeless grace. The evening wound down after one o'clock, and Joy decided to turn in early. Graduation was just hours away, and she wanted to be fully rested for the day she had worked so long and hard to reach. Cynthia, on the other hand, rushed off with a couple of what she laughingly called "leftovers."

Joy stirred early, around seven. It was her day, and she wasn't going to miss a second of it. The long black graduation gown hung freshly pressed on the back of her door, as if to say, I'm ready. And the cap, square shape, like a bricklayer's mortarboard, hence the name, sat waiting to adorn Joy's beautiful hair.

She remembered the dress she would wear, the one she and her mother, Carmella, had picked out together. It was the perfect outfit, this time brand-new and from a nice department store in Providence.

The fitting room

Carmella had held up the dress to Joy with a grin. "I think this one fits you, the color is perfect, and I love the style," she said.

Joy slipped it on and twirled in front of the mirror, grinning back. Cocking her head left, then right, as if weighing a different perspective, she delivered her verdict with the conviction of a Supreme Court justice, "I love it too, Mama, but you know me ... I'll have to tweak it just a little."

Carmella sighed. "Of course you do. Add that little bit of Joy magic.

Joy had laughed, smoothing the fabric thoughtfully, envisioning what it needed.

"It's almost perfect. Maybe just something simple, like a little appliqué at the shoulders."

"That sounds perfect, and then off the rack becomes a Joy original," Carmella said, teasing but proud.

As the clerk packaged the dress into a fancy garment bag, imprinted with the store's name and logo, Carmella leaned in and whispered like it was a great secret.

"You're going to be the most beautiful girl on that stage. Not because of the dress, but because you're you."

Joy blinked back happy tears.

"Thanks, Mama. For everything."

The dress was blue, with simple but elegant lines. True to her plan, Joy added her special touch later, a sweet appliqué on each shoulder in a slightly lighter blue. Her enhancement was perfect. It made the dress hers, and made the day feel even more like a celebration of all they had built together.

The graduation ceremony was as traditional as Brown itself. Century-long customs, familiar music and the moment that every senior and their beaming parents waited a lifetime to hear:

"To Juliana Joy Nordstrom: By the authority vested in me by the Corporation of Brown University, I confer upon you the degree of Bachelor of Arts, summa cum laude, with all the rights and privileges thereto pertaining."

Joy shook hands and walked across the flower-bedecked stage set on the majestic Brown Green, and every head in the audience turned to watch this stunning young woman take her place in Brown's history. And little did they know, how could they, that Joy was destined to make history of her own.

——— ❦ ———

CHAPTER 19

Wash Her Mouth Out ...

After graduation, Joy interviewed for a couple of positions in New York at some "off-the-rack" design manufacturers, but they didn't hire her, claiming she was "overqualified." She considered returning to Paris and applying for a job at Maison de Paris. But Messier Longchamp's retirement meant that Francois would be in charge. And working under Francois would literally mean "under Francois." And she knew the only raise she'd ever get from him wouldn't be in francs.

When Cynthia tracked her down and called, Joy was staying with June, a fellow graduate, at her parents' home in Short Hills, New Jersey.

"Joy, it's me, Cyn. I hear you are sequestered in a place called Short Hills ... Where the hell is that? Are you a prisoner?"

"Sequestered? Of course not, Cyn. I'm staying with June Albright, a girl from Brown."

"A girl from Brown? I would have thought you'd be cohabitating with Luke Perry. You never did tell me what happened to that hottie."

Joy paused. "It's a story for another day, Cyn."

"He dropped you? What am I saying? No one in their right mind would drop gorgeous perfect Joy." So you dropped him … tell me what happened."

"As I said, it's a story for another day."

Cynthia knew not to push further. "I told you I'd take him when you finished with him. You know how I love goalies."

"I don't think that's a good idea." Joy changed the subject. "So, are you still at Fently?"

"Yes, such a prestigious institution. You know, Joy, you ended up an Ivy Leager, and I ended up with poison ivy. Fently hands out crayons with their textbooks. There's an AP course there called 'showing up.'"

Joy laughed into the phone. "Oh, Cyn, you are too much. So, are you up in Boston or not?"

"Not! You see, the dean of women, some has-been washwoman, and I had a parting of ways. She had some weird notion that students are required to attend classes. So, when I extended my spring break for a few weeks, she read me the riot act and threw my butt out. I told her I was on a learning vacation in Zermatt, but she didn't buy the act. By the way, you just have to go there … Zermatt. The skiing is unbelievable, and the guides are hot despite the subzero weather. I met Hans, and he showed me a lot of tricks, not just on the slopes but off too. It's all about cervelats over there … trust me."

"Cervelats? What's that?"

"It's the national sausage of Switzerland. I couldn't get enough of it."

"Oh God, Cyn …" Joy groaned into the phone.

"Seriously, what are you doing in that place ... Short Hills? Do they really have short hills there?"

"I'm looking for a job in New York, and it's commutable by train. June's family offered to put me up until I find something."

"Hey, Joy, I just got a brainstorm. My father owns a couple of companies in New York City. I'll get him to give you a job. Better idea, I'll get him to give both of us a job. I'm school-less now and need to do something. What do you say? We can get a place together. It would be a blast. We'd be 'beauty and the bitch.'"

Joy couldn't stop laughing. "You know Cyn, you always make me feel happy. You're so funny. But honestly, I couldn't just take a job someone's father created for me. No, I'd have to have a job that contributes and one that would be worthy of a salary."

"There you go again. That 'goodie two shoes' ethic. Why can't you be like me and most of the other girls out there? Just take whatever, smile, and say thank you. Then go shopping."

Cyn stopped talking for a moment to think. "Look, I'll ask my dad to set up some interviews for real jobs, and you will have to convince whoever interviews you that you are qualified. I'll make my dad swear not to influence anybody."

It was a fair plan, and Joy agreed. She felt confident that she would be able to be a valuable employee wherever she worked.

The interviews went well. One of Cynthia's father's companies imported and marketed cosmetics. Not high-end ones like Chanel, Estee Lauder, or Elizabeth Arden, but the kind found in drug and down-scale department stores. The kind offering buy one get two free. Cynthia also was hired, and at her request, part-time. Joy was to be a junior executive assistant to the senior vice president of Fashion and Marketing, and Cynthia worked in the marketing department developing brand names and promotional ideas. Marketing Vice President Manny Rose ran the division. He was in his late fifties and had a good marketing eye and a keener one for the ladies.

Cynthia's father insisted that they live in a safe and decent place. New York wasn't a city where you could live just anywhere. It was Cynthia who found the perfect apartment.

"Here we are. You are going to love it, Joy. I put a deposit down, and they are holding it pending your approval."

Joy stood in front of the old brownstone building and read the address on the faded awning. *100 Christopher Street.* "I like the sound of the address."

"Yeah, me too."

"Come on in; the agent is meeting us. You'll love it... two bedrooms, one big and one smaller, and there's a tub in the bathroom. It doesn't come furnished, but that won't be a problem. My mother has stuff in storage from all our old houses, and she'd be glad to get rid of some of it."

A week later, a moving van pulled up in front of 100 Christopher Street. The sign on the truck read "City Haul," and two muscle-bound men jumped out and prepared to unload. Cynthia was missing, nowhere to be found, so Joy managed the move herself. It was already decided that Joy would get the smaller room and that Cynthia, who insisted on paying two-thirds of the rent, would get the larger one. As the last lamp was unloaded from the van, Cynthia arrived at the second-floor walk-up.

"Where were you, Cyn? I was worried."

"Worry, never." Cynthia looked at the taller mover, now covered with perspiration, and blew a low whistle. "If I knew this guy was here, I wouldn't have been so late. I love them sweaty. Did they put the bed together yet?"

—— ❧ ——

Joy took the junior position at the cosmetic firm on 48th Street seriously, even though the firm was called "Monkey Business." The company, a British enterprise, was acquired by Cynthia's father three years earlier, who saved it from bankruptcy.

The firm was "cheeky," as the president, a Brit, liked to say. The firm's mission statement attested to that: "Smell good, look good, and most of all, be naughty!"

It didn't take a week before Vice President Manny and Cynthia hooked up. He loved her free spirit and thought she was rather clever, witty, and particularly risqué, dressing on the slutty side.

Manny assigned Cynthia to the lab to develop a new line of "hip" lipsticks. Monkey Business planned to introduce them at the fall market for Christmas. Cynthia's only instructions were that the firm's target was the teenage girls' market. She spent weeks in the lab and got to know the cosmetic chemists intimately, especially Carl, a former Olympic swimmer from Germany. Often after work, Cynthia invited him to the apartment and prepared her favorite dish: cervelats.

At a regular weekly morning meeting, Manny invited Cynthia to present what the team had developed for the coming Christmas market.

"Folks, this is Cynthia. She's new here, and I handed her a tough assignment. Let's see how she did. Remember, she's a newbie ... so be kind and listen carefully."

Cynthia was no stranger to being in the limelight; she savored it. That morning it took her an extra hour to choose what to wear for the meeting. She asked herself, "What does one wear to a meeting at a company called Monkey Business?" Ultimately, she decided on a hot pink miniskirt, paired with a white low-cut sheer top over a rhinestone studded super-sizer black push-up bra. That outfit, she felt, was worthy of Monkey Business.

"Thanks, Manny, and good morning, guys. I'm Cynthia; most people call me Cyn; that's spelled CYN, not SIN."

Cynthia pulled a presentation box of lipsticks closer to her and opened it. "Here we go, folks, buckle up!" She pulled the first tube out and held it high for all to see. "I call this one: Plant One On, Fuchsia.

"The next one is a pretty pearlescence tone, which I called Tasty but Not Salty."

Cynthia continued to go through the tubes, one after another: "This is 'Can't Kiss Me Off,' a dark burgundy, like wine. *Kisses as sweet as wine ...*" melodiously rolled off her lips for all to hear.

The presentation continued. "And here is a light rose hue, My Lips on Yours; followed by Orange You Lucky Tangerine, and for the more adventuresome, Lickity-dickity, a creamy moisturizing cherry red."

Cynthia paused and took a giant slug of her double espresso café latte.

As she unrolled the next tube, she explained: "This one here is my personal favorite: Naked Pink. It comes in a flesh-colored tube wrapped in latex sheath." Cynthia continued to unroll the latex wrapper, imprinted with the company name, Monkey Business, and liberally applied the creamy substance to her plump lips, followed by a thorough smoothing with her tongue.

All eyes were on Cynthia's face, except for Manny's, whose gaze was fixed on Cynthia's glitter-trimmed push-up bra.

"Oh, yeah. I forgot the glosses." Cynthia picked up the first gloss tube: "This is Stiffer Upper Lip, a gloss for all occasions. It comes in four tantalizing flavors."

Cynthia opened the first tube, applied the gloss to her lips, and generously licked them: "Sperm-mint. Oh my God, what a rush!"

"Next," she said, "is Gag-a-licious, nothing more to say about that one, followed by Pucker Up, like sucking on a lemon, and lastly, Mouthful, featuring a savory, exotic, sweet and sour tang, with a pinch of salt. Divine!"

Cynthia laughed. "That one should come with a warning! Ha, ha."

She put the last tube down on the table. "Thank you for your attention."

A couple of attendees looked around the room at each other and smiled, but Manny grinned like a Cheshire cat in heat. At one end of the table was Mildred, a chubby woman pushing sixty and a twenty-year veteran marketeer on loan to Monkey Business from the parent company. She was sipping coffee when she heard the flavor names for the glosses, causing her to spurt out a mouthful, spraying the conference table.

"Oh my God, this child is … is … pornographic. Somebody wash her mouth out with soap. No one will accept this blatant in your face … what can I say… slut talk!"

Manny glared at her. "Mildred, get with it; welcome to the 1990s! You're not back at your old company, which catered to preppy Catholic schoolgirls. Kids put the Barbie dolls away a long time ago and they are out there and a lot savvier than you think. This kind of in-your-face marketing is what young people relate to, and young girls are our market."

Manny addressed Cynthia, "Well done, Cynthia, well done. After the meeting, see me in my office. I have a surprise for you."

Cynthia smiled broadly. "Surprise? Oh, I love surprises...what is it?"

CHAPTER 20

❦

Life on Christopher Street

Cyn was rarely at their place on Christopher. If it was not one new love interest or another, she was always off on weekend trips to fabulous places. Joy, on the other hand, preferred to stay home, endlessly working on her sketches and designs.

Joy had come to love their building, the super and his wife, a couple with an adorable baby on the third floor, the gay couple on the fifth floor who threw the best Halloween and Christmas parties, and a nice guy with a dog in the basement apartment.

She was returning from the market one weekend when she spotted her neighbor's dog, Noush, walking down the street alone. She immediately recognized the dog because of her distinctive collar and beautiful, shiny coat. Joy put her groceries on the stoop and called out for the dog, "Hey, Noush, how are you doing, sweetie? Come see me; I have a treat."

Joy reached into her grocery bag and removed a piece of cheese. Noush recognized Joy, and her calming voice convinced her to come close enough for Joy to grab her harness.

"Thatta girl. Good girl. Where's your daddy?"

Joy pulled Noush into the hall and down the half-flight of stairs leading to Davis's apartment. She knocked and called out: "Hello? Hello, it's Joy. Are you there?"

Davis's voice came from inside, immediately recognizing both Joy's voice and familiar perfume. They had met before, but just in passing. "Joy, is that you?"

"Yes, and I have Noush here. How did she get out?"

He opened the door, and Noush rushed in.

"I don't know. I was working on a piece and not paying much attention to her. I must have left the back door open when I took out the trash."

"Really? Well, it's a good thing that I came along just when I did. You should be more careful ... someone could get into your apartment too!"

"Oh, yeah, I hear there are bands of thieves looking for unpublished music." They both laughed.

Davis bent down and hugged Noush. "Bad dog, Noush. You are in trouble."

Noush knew she was, tucking her tail and scurrying into her bed just beneath the old baby grand piano. Joy would later learn that this piano was special, at least to Davis. It had belonged to his music teacher, who dearly loved Davis. She left it to him when she passed away, and it was Davis's prized possession.

Joy could see how attached Davis and Noush were and vowed that someday she would have a furry companion, one who would give her unconditional love, a rare commodity in humans. But it was a matter of practicality for her. Finding someone she trusted to watch a dog while she worked would be a problem, and she knew she could never leave any dog she had in a kennel. For now, dog parenthood was out of the question.

"Would you like to come in, Joy?"

Joy hadn't been invited in before this and thought declining would be unneighborly. "Sure, I'd love to. I hope I'm not interrupting anything."

"Nope. Not at all."

Joy thought Davis to be maybe two or three years older. He was tall and nice-looking, not like the pretty metrosexual guys she met in New York or the ultra-pampered wealthy men with their two-hundred-dollar haircuts and clear painted manicured nails, the cling-ons, as Cynthia would say. No, Davis was masculine and strong, someone you'd want to be with in an emergency. That day, he wore an old USMC t-shirt that exposed his broad shoulders. There were some vague signs of bruising, more like faded scars, that peered out. His face was handsome and showed worldliness and character.

"How about some coffee? Or maybe something else?"

"Coffee sounds great."

"You know Joy, there's a lot you learn in the Marines," he said, his voice carrying the sound of authority. "Discipline, resilience, and that instant coffee should be banned in every corner of the earth."

Joy looked around the modest apartment. It was almost sterile but neat and orderly. Everything had its place, it seemed, a no-frills bachelor pad.

"I know the place is probably not much, but I like it that way. Less to fuss over. I'm not too good about keeping house. Mrs. Campanella comes in and helps me."

"I love her and Mr. Campanella."

"She's a saint. She fusses over everyone in the building."

"When my roommate and I moved in, she brought us biscotti to die for. And Mr. Campanella is constantly washing the front stoop or taking out the trash."

"Yes, Tony. Well, Mrs. C.'s like a second mother to me, better. She doesn't ask questions or nag. And what a cook! She's always bringing me something. Sometimes I think she cooks extra just to have something for me. I don't know what I'd do without her."

Davis came over with two cups of coffee. "Cream or sugar?"

"No, black is fine." Joy sipped the coffee. "This is divine. Much better than instant," she joked.

Joy enjoyed the conversation. She learned that Davis was a former Marine, a musician, and a songwriter. For a while, he had a budding career, but that was years ago, before the Marines. Joy realized that, obviously, things didn't work out career-wise, but she didn't push for more than that.

"Now I write music for advertising jingles and do voice-over commercials. It's something I can do right from here, which gives me a lot of time to take care of Noush, and there's no commuting. I hate the subway!"

"Me too. I'd rather walk. The subway is always so jammed, and you never know who's just around the corner.

"I'd rather walk too," Joy said. "The subway's a nightmare, half the time it feels like someone's trying to talk to me, or worse, brush up against me. I've even been followed once or twice. I switched to the bus, but really, I'd rather walk."

Joy looked at her watch. "Oh, it's late; I have to run. Let's do this again. I had a good time."

"Me too, Joy, and thanks for saving Noush. She would be in a shelter if it weren't for you, and I couldn't live without her." Davis reached out and petted Noush. "Say goodbye to your new friend."

Noush actually walked over to Joy and gave her hand a big lick.

"Well, bye for now. I'll let myself out."

As she left, Joy thought, *There is something intriguing about this guy, Davis.* He was clearly intelligent, well-educated, and super easy to be around. She wondered what his back story was. She paused, smiled, and once again rationally confirmed, *He's cute but not my type. I hope he finds someone someday. He deserves it.*

CHAPTER 21

❦

Laden with Lasagna and Secrets

Davis soon became Joy's coffee buddy when she was around. When he discovered she was from Portugal, he made special trips to a market a few blocks away that carried a dark roast similar to what she had at home. There was still a little air of mystery about Davis, though, as if he held some of himself back. But, Joy had discovered that *The New York Post's* Page Six had nothing on Mrs. Campanella as a source of information and gossip.

The older woman lived on the first floor with her husband, Tony, a robust, retired MTA transit worker. Mrs. Campanella had taken a particular liking to Davis, treating him like an extended family member. Being an old-school Italian, she often cooked far more than she and Tony could eat, and Davis was the grateful beneficiary of her culinary overabundance. Her specialty was lasagna, which she delivered to him at least once a week, much to his delight, and his waistline's dismay. It forced Davis to double his workout efforts to balance out the indulgence.

Occasionally, when his laundry piled up, Mrs. Campanella would do a few loads for him, and every now and then, she would sneak into his apartment and do some spring cleaning, a fact Davis rarely noticed.

"Men are lousy housekeepers, and Davis gets the Pulitzer Prize for that," she often told Tony.

On one such day, Joy had arrived home to find Davis's dry cleaning hanging in the foyer. She noticed his apartment door slightly ajar and knocked.

"Hello? Davis, are you there?" she called out.

When no one responded, she peeked inside and found Mrs. Campanella vigorously polishing Davis's old piano.

"Heavens, dear, you startled me," Mrs. Campanella had exclaimed.

"I'm so sorry, Mrs. Campanella. I found Davis's dry cleaning in the foyer, and I didn't want anything to happen to it. When I saw the door ajar, I thought ..."

"How thoughtful of you, dear. Come in," Mrs. Campanella interrupted, waving her inside.

"Where is Davis?" Joy asked, stepping into the apartment.

"He and Noush are at the gym, he goes three or four times a week. That body speaks for itself. If I weren't so old, Mr. Campanella would have something to worry about," she said with a wink. "Poor Davis, he's so gorgeous and doesn't even know it. But that's what makes him even more endearing."

Joy smiled, recalling the times she'd seen Davis working out in the small backyard behind the brownstone. His large frame would move effortlessly through dozens of jumping jacks and push-ups, sweating profusely as his loyal dog eagerly waited to join him in a playful tumble on the grass. Even Cyn had noticed his physique, but she was determined to land an "obscenely rich husband", which took Davis out of the running.

"What should I do with this?" Joy asked, holding up the dry cleaning.

"Well, I'm covered in polish, so why don't you hang it in his closet? It's in the bedroom, just past the bathroom, on the left."

"Sure."

Joy made her way to Davis's bedroom. The space was stark, no pictures, no decorations. "Maybe he's a minimalist," she mused as she hung up the dry cleaning. Through the clear plastic, she noticed the distinct detailing of a military uniform, dress blues.

When Joy returned to the living room, Mrs. Campanella was hard at work mopping the entry area.

"I'll bet those dress blues look great on Davis. How long was he in the service?"

"I really don't know how long, but I do know, he's a hero."

Mrs. Campanella sat down on the armrest of a well-worn sofa, clearly ready to share more. "Davis doesn't brag, but I found something while dusting the other day, by accident, of course."

"Of course," Joy said, stifling a laugh.

"Well, our Mr. Davis Hatfield is quite the man of mystery. I came across something that you might find interesting," she said, lowering her voice, as if to reveal something classified.

Mrs. Campanella pulled open the top drawer of Davis's desk and retrieved an official-looking leatherette folder embossed with the Marine Corps logo. Inside was a citation from the Department of the Navy. She pointed to a section in the middle.

"Look at this part," she urged.

Joy read quietly:

For extraordinary heroism while serving as Platoon Commander, Captain Davis Hamilton Hatfield demonstrated exceptional courage and selflessness during a critical engagement in Afghanistan. Under heavy enemy fire, Captain Hatfield led a daring rescue mission, saving the lives of his team while sustaining significant injuries. His actions upheld the highest traditions of the Marine Corps and reflected great credit upon himself and the United States Department of the Navy.

Therefore, with the authority of the President of the United States and full Congressional approval, the honor of the Navy Cross is presented with the highest honors.

Joy looked up, stunned. "He ... he's a hero."

Mrs. Campanella nodded proudly. "And not just any hero. He was awarded the Navy Cross." She retrieved a leatherette presentation case from the same drawer. "See? This. That's one step below the Medal of Honor. Mr. Campanella looked it up. Can you imagine?"

Joy tried to reconcile the quiet, unassuming coffee buddy she knew with the decorated hero described in the citation.

"That's Davis for you, quiet and private," Mrs. Campanella said. "But now you know, dear. There's more to him than meets the eye."

Joy's thoughts swirled as she handed the folder back.

"Have you ever heard him sing?" Mrs. Campanella asked, snapping Joy out of her thoughts.

"Not really, maybe a few notes here and there," Joy replied.

"Well, let me tell you, he has the voice of an angel. I just don't understand why he didn't pursue it professionally."

"It?" Joy asked, raising an eyebrow.

"Singing! He's better than almost any of the big names. He went to that fancy music school in Connecticut, what's it called? The Hartt School."

"I've heard of it," Joy said. "It's prestigious."

"Well, one day, I came across a CD. Naughty me, I borrowed it and brought it upstairs for Mr. Campanella to play."

Joy laughed. "You mean you stole it, Mrs. C."

"Borrowed," the older woman corrected, feigning innocence. "Anyway, the CD cover had Davis's picture on it, oh, how handsome he looked! I just couldn't resist. Shame on me, right?"

"Shame on you," Joy said with a playful grin.

"Mr. Campanella was furious when he found out. But when we listened, even he had to admit, Davis is incredible. His voice, his piano playing, everything. One song after another, each one more beautiful than the last."

"Does he ever play for you?" Joy asked.

"No, never. But sometimes, when I pass by his door, I stop and listen. I even dragged Mr. Campanella down once, but you know him, he doesn't have the patience for anything that's not online poker or food. Me? I could listen for hours. I'd even pay for the privilege, and I'll bet others would, too."

Mrs. Campanella paused, looking around as though someone might overhear, then leaned closer and whispered, "Do you know what I saw?"

"No idea, but I have a feeling you're about to tell me."

"Well, one day, I saw a Navy car parked in front of the building. Naturally, I was curious."

"Naturally," Joy said, stifling a chuckle.

"So, I walked up to it. Inside was this sweet young woman in uniform. She rolled down the window and asked if she could help me. I thanked her for her service and, of course, asked what she was doing here."

Joy folded her arms, intrigued.

"The young woman explained that she was part of a detail that assists at military funerals. She told me her teammate was inside, getting Davis."

"Funerals?" Joy asked, suddenly concerned. "Was Davis okay?"

"Oh, yes, perfectly fine. She explained it all. Davis and Noush are part of a special unit that performs at military funerals across the tri-state area. And not just funerals, sometimes they attend birthday celebrations for old World War II and Korean War veterans."

"That's why he keeps his dress blues so immaculate," Mrs. Campanella added. "Jake at the cleaners presses them for him every week, for free, no less. Jake only became a citizen five years ago, and I think it's his way of giving back. Patriotic, don't you think?"

"Very nice of him," Joy said.

"You know," Mrs. Campanella continued, lowering her voice again, "if Davis had a woman around, she'd press his uniform for him. It's a shame so few women iron these days."

Joy smiled. "Maybe, but it's not exactly a popular skill anymore."

"Well," the older woman huffed. "I'm not sure about this, but I think he might have a girlfriend. Maybe a fiancée."

Joy's interest piqued. "Why do you think that?"

"Well, I found a ring box in his drawer, purely by accident, of course. It had a lovely ring inside. Nothing flashy, but nice. I just don't know what to think about it. Maybe he's going to give it to someone, or maybe it's from the past. Maybe some ungrateful witch returned it to him. Pardon me, but I get very maternal when it comes to Davis."

Joy laughed. "All I know is that if he has someone in his life, it's his business. I hope he does, though. He deserves someone wonderful."

Mrs. Campanella sighed. "You are absolutely right." But curiosity was killing Mrs. Campanella...did he or didn't he?

CHAPTER 22

≈

Firestorm

Joy's time at Monkey Business was a learning experience. It was two years after she took the job when life changed in ways no one could have imagined. It all began quite fortuitously when the Arts and Leisure editor at *The New York Times* reviewed Giuseppe Di Legno's latest exhibition at New York's Fashion Institute. That article lit the match that set Joy's world ablaze .

Over the last couple of years, Di Legno's status as a celebrated photographer had skyrocketed, and his work was published everywhere. The 'net, now essential to everyone's lives, overflowed with his photographs, and every A-list celebrity wanted a photo taken by D. But D. was a smart marketer, he limited the photo commissions he would accept, making his work even more sought after. And he had landed an agent, Bernie Rubin, who was always scheming to make him an even bigger star in the photography universe.

At the institute's exhibit, *The New York Times* editor noticed Di Legno's two photographs of Joy: the one in the Parisian evening gown taken for Messier Longchamp (as a gift to him), and the other, a breathtaking portrait from Brown. The editor, along with hundreds of the exhibit attendees, was mesmerized by the face that stared back. It literally gave him goosebumps. The editor begged D. to allow him to run an article for the Sunday Arts section and print the pictures.

Naturally, D. agreed immediately, knowing that this exposure would further enhance his already flourishing career. The feature story appeared the very next Sunday. The article included only one picture, Joy's portrait from Brown, because the editor felt that anything more would detract from its impact. The headline boasted: "The Most Beautiful Woman in the World."

"...rarely does one come across a living being who is the true manifestation of sheer beauty and innocence."

The editor continued:

"...Giuseppe Di Legno is a maestro with a lens, but the real wonder of this piece is not the artist who shot the picture, no disrespect to his talent, but the subject herself."

The article rambled on for several paragraphs and ended with:

"Only once before has the title, 'The Most Beautiful Woman in the World' been bestowed upon anyone. That honor belonged to the legendary Gina Lollobrigida, an international movie star now retired in Italy after starring in a movie of the same title. But history has repeated itself, and Di Legno has impeccably captured what only God could create: an utterly perfect and seemingly flawless human being. We should all be humbled when we feast our eyes on this creature ... indisputably the most beautiful woman in the world. But who is this mysterious goddess?"

D. sat in his dimly lit studio, the faint scent of developer chemicals lingering in the air, as he scanned *The New York Times* review. A tornado of feelings raced through his mind, from jealousy to anger. How could that twit of an editor shift the focus onto Joy instead of celebrating his overwhelming, God-given talent? The photo had taken on a life of its own, and there was nothing he could do about it. D. realized that although he had received some kudos from the editor, the whole world would now be talking about Joy, not him. His Italian ego couldn't stand it. "*Sono stato fregato* . . . I've been screwed."

Yet deep in his heart, he knew one thing was true: Joy truly was the most beautiful woman in the world. And with that realization came an undeniable truth, he would have to content himself with being the maestro who immortalized her beauty for posterity.

He tossed the paper onto his desk, his fingers drumming against the edge. The phone buzzed incessantly, messages from agents, magazines, and clients begging to know who this woman was. Everyone wanted a piece of her, the very woman he had framed, lit, and captured. And now she was the story, not the work, not the art!

The firestorm of interest that followed was relentless. National news networks picked up the story and flashed Joy's picture everywhere. Part of the hype was that this face belonged to an unknown, not a celebrity or femme fatale, but an utterly enigmatic figure from an unheralded place. Talk shows and commentators all asked, "Who is this woman? Where is she?"

D. was inundated with questions from everyone, yet he wisely kept Joy's identity a secret. He reasoned that the longer the mystery persisted, the more ravenous the public would become, keeping him center stage. Even Joy's coworkers, most of whom didn't read *The New York Times,* remained oblivious to the article. And those who did weren't entirely certain it was her, given the nature of the photograph and its out-of-context presentation.

It seemed most unlikely that "the Most Beautiful Woman in the World" could be found working at Monkey Business.

At work, Joy began to wear her hair in a ponytail and sported unnecessary horn-rimmed glasses; she felt that toning down her appearance was a clever way to hide in plain sight. She didn't wear makeup, and the one time a co-worker said, "You kind of look like that photograph," Joy laughed so uproariously that it wasn't brought up again.

Each passing day, the public's curiosity grew more insatiable. Late-night shows even hired detectives to track down "TMBWIW," all hoping to scoop their TV competitors with an exclusive.

It was Bernie Rubin, D.'s agent, a.k.a. D.'s babysitter, who ultimately leaked Joy's identity, defying D.'s explicit instructions to keep it secret. Bernie acted covertly while D. was away from his combination studio living loft, shooting a fashion gig. Getting into the studio was never a problem for Bernie, who always kept a backup key; after all, D. frequently lost his own. Too often, a frantic midnight call from D. would request someone to unlock his place, usually while he was engaged with some young thing in the elevator.

Once inside the loft, Bernie snooped around for anything that might reveal the name he sought. It was a massive space with industrial columns and exposed air ducts. D. was living well these days, Bernie noted. There was no proper bedroom, just an area enclosed by sheer drapes that desperately needed cleaning. The rumpled black sheets were less than inviting, yet the living space boasted extraordinary mid-century Italian furniture, like something out of a museum. The stained black floors were partly covered by large animal-skin area rugs, mostly zebra. Hung over a large marble block coffee table was an enormous crystal chandelier that belonged in a cathedral rather than a loft. A sleek stainless-steel kitchen with a black marble center island was tucked into a corner. All around the loft, red enamel easels showcased some of D.'s best work. As Bernie wandered the space, he mused: "It's different, but it all works, and it certainly fits this eccentric artist."

An out-of-place thrift shop desk sat by the floor-to-ceiling window. Bernie opened a couple of its drawers and found an address book. "Bingo!" He thought, *this could be it.* Most of the entries were in Italian, but he knew that D. had taken the celebrated photographs while lecturing at Brown University. Scanning the pages, he found only two names with Rhode Island addresses: George McLautan and Joy Nordstrom. George wasn't who he was looking for. But could this Joy Nordstrom be the one?

CHAPTER 23

"Leave It to Bernie"

Bernie waited until the following day to make the call. He crossed his fingers as he dialed the number.

"Hello, is this Joy Nordstrom?"

"Yes, who is this?"

"My name is Bernie Rubin, and I'm calling because you're going to need me very soon."

Joy tightened her grip on the phone. "I don't understand. Why would I need you? And by the way, who are you anyway?"

She braced herself. Probably just another weirdo. She'd had more than her share of strange men trying every trick in the book.

"I'm D.'s agent," Bernie said.

That caught her attention. "D.'s agent? Oh."

"Yes, his exclusive agent. And soon to be your angel. I'm the guy who's gonna make you a *macher* in this business. Look, cupcake, let Uncle Bernie get to the point. I'm a star-maker, the best. Like Houdini with a contract. I take nobodies, polish 'em till they shine like diamonds in Tiffany's window, and turn them into legends."

Joy blinked. *Cupcake? Uncle Bernie?* Was this guy serious?

Bernie steamrolled on. "And you, sweetheart, you've got the goods. All you need is me, a little glitter, and poof, you're a household name. Trust me, cupcake, with my *chutzpah* and your face, we're gonna make magic. I'm telling you, I'll be your Houdini, and you're gonna be big. *Really* big."

Joy hesitated. Was he crazy, or just crazy enough to know what he was talking about?

Bernie didn't miss a beat. "I'm sure you're aware of what's going on. It's everywhere."

Joy's heart skipped. *He means the Times photo.*

"Exactly," Bernie said, as if reading her mind. "We need to meet. You need someone who knows how to handle what's coming. Uncle Bernie here? I'm your man. Experienced, connected, and yes, even likable. I'm your fairy godfather, sweetheart, standing here with my magic wand, just waiting to make you famous. And rich. Ask D., he'll tell you. The guy worships me."

Bernie was, in fact, likable, a small man with frameless glasses who looked like everyone's father or grandfather. Despite his nondescript appearance, his quiet power and extensive network were undeniable. Over the years, he had represented dozens of celebrities, mainly in the arts and fashion industries, and had developed connections par excellence. Everyone from former Miss Americas to world-famous artists like Andy Warhol and Di Legno were among his clients. Bernie had even represented the Pope on a book deal proposed by the Vatican for U.S. publication. Unquestionably, the whole world took Bernie's calls, and practically no one ever turned down a Bernie deal.

"An agent? Why would I need an agent?"

"Well, sweetheart, what do you do now?"

Joy told him about her current job at Monkey Business and shared her true ambition, to design haute couture.

"Cupcake, all that's possible. But before you serve dinner, you've got to cook the meal, set the table, and make sure you don't burn the house down. Sometimes, there is a long on-ramp before you hit the highway. And once you're cruising, you can pick the exit that suits you best."

Bernie explained what that might look like. "And this is why, my dear, you need Bernie, you have no idea what's about to happen to you.

Joy wrestled with the idea of needing an agent. After all, just because an editor made some ridiculous remarks about a silly photograph didn't seem to warrant more than an "oh hum" or, better yet, "who cares?"

But Bernie presented a compelling argument, a vivid picture. Was this really the direction her life was taking? Could this foolish little man, who spoke in riddles, actually know what he was talking about or was he just another lech trying to manipulate her into something she neither understood nor desired?

He spoke of her becoming a high-paid model, appearing on magazine covers and runways with endless press coverage. Joy thought, *How unreal. Fashion design was my dream, not strutting down runways in other designers' creations.* And yet, perhaps this serendipitous article was an unforeseen path to the next step, perhaps an alternative way to move forward. After all, modeling and high fashion were intertwined.

Bernie was persistent, his charm as polished as his Gucci loafers. "Joy, my little cupcake, listen to your Bernie," he said, his voice smooth as honey. "What you have here is lightning in a bottle, a Dom Perignon of talent. With the right guidance, and the right strategy, you won't just be remembered as 'that face'; you'll evolve into a brand. And once you have that, you'll own the world. Every Sara, Silvia, and Sadie will be lined up to pay top dollar for brands you promote. Trust your Bernie ... I can do this, and so can you, Cupcake."

Joy, deep in thought, contemplated, was this opportunity really knocking on her door, or was Bernie simply another eccentric trying to con her? But his credentials spoke for themselves. He was D.'s agent, and D. was no fool, he had obtained celebrity status and international recognition. If Bernie was being truthful, then he was the real deal.

After convincing Joy that time was of the essence, she agreed to meet Bernie the very next day at her apartment.

Bernie arrived five minutes early, laden with a bag of bagels and a cream cheese salmon spread. After some preliminary niceties, he leaned forward, elbows resting on the table's edge, his expression earnest yet tinged with excitement.

"Joy, listen to me. You're standing on the brink of something extraordinary. You're not just the 'most beautiful woman in the world,' you're a phenomenon. But trust me, without the right guidance, you'll be a flash in the pan, yesterday's news. And worse, a squandered opportunity for greatness. Trust me, Bernie knows, he's been to this rodeo more times than you can imagine. Once you get on that bull, the ride is life-changing. Ask D., when I met him, he was just a couple of shutter clicks better than Alan Funt from *Candid Camera*, more 'Cousin Vito's wedding' than prize-winning magazine covers. But then Uncle Bernie worked his magic, and *voilà*, now he's a globe-trotting, big-bucks maestro of the lens. That's right, Uncle Bernie did it. From snapshots to stardom, from a slice and a Coke to a prime table at Cipriani's. Applause, please. Thank you very much ... Uncle Bernie." He paused as Joy absorbed his words. It was a once-in-a-lifetime chance that needed to be navigated with skill and experience.

Softening his tone, Bernie continued, "Look, Cupcake, I'm not here to sell you a pipe dream. This is about your destiny, your long-term future, a chance to fulfill your dreams, whatever they may be. You've just won the career lottery, and you need the right person to help you maximize your potential, to guide you through a world full of crooks, leeches, and opportunists. You need Uncle Bernie, a guardian angel who will open doors and truly care for you."

He slid his business card across the table. "Sweetheart, I know your mind is racing and you're at sixes and sevens, but what have you got to lose? A job at some *mashugana* place called Monkey Business selling cheap perfume? Think it over. I'll call you tonight."

Joy nodded and cautiously picked up the card as if it were a forbidden fruit, like the apple Eve once offered Adam. Was this really happening? Was she about to entrust her future to this unusual and eccentric man? *Perhaps,* she thought, *maybe this was something.*

Bernie got up from the table, looked around, and said, "Nice place, for now, but Uncle Bernie knows you're an uptown girl, and he's going to make sure you live in style." He slid the chair back under the table, smiled, and turned to leave. Pausing, he pointed to an everything bagel peeking out of an open bag. "Mind if I take that with me?"

That night, Joy signed on with Bernie, making him her exclusive agent, an honor, as Bernie put it, which incidentally came with a 10 percent cut of everything.

A master at his craft, Bernie got down to business immediately. He enrolled Joy in a crash course at Barbizon, New York's top modeling school. Selling Joy on the idea wasn't as easy as he had expected.

"But Bernie, I don't get it. Why on earth would I want to go to a modeling school? I'm a Brown grad, and I'm not even a model, nor do I want to be one."

"Sweetie, listen to Uncle Bernie," he said with a dismissive wave of his hand. "I know you don't want to be a model, but fate has delivered you this incredible opportunity, like getting two pickles with a Carnegie Deli sandwich when you're only entitled to one. Do you return the extra pickle? Of course not. You savor it, thinking, 'My lucky day!'"

Joy smiled as she connected with Bernie's analogy.

"Look, my little dumpling," Bernie continued, "you must seize this chance. Sure, you went to Brown, but Barbizon will polish you into the diamond you are. You'll learn to walk with poise."

Joy shrugged, unconvinced. "I walk perfectly well, and at Brown, being an Ivy League student already polished me quite a bit."

"Ivy Leaguer … pfft. I know plenty of them, half are educated nothings, the rest so busy admiring themselves they forget how to be civil. Cupcake, you must trust Uncle Bernie. When you become a famous model, you'll be rich beyond your wildest dreams, and then, "

"Then what?" she asked, folding her arms.

"Then you can be whatever you want! You can put your famous name on your own design firm and create all the gorgeous schmattes you desire. And the rich and famous will line up to buy everything you touch. And little ol' Bernie will be right there to help you."

The thought of funding her own design house was overwhelmingly appealing, hanging in the air like catnip. "Well, you may be right about that."

"Of course I am, *Bubbale*," he said with a sly grin. "You'll see. But like Eliza Doolittle, we must keep my little butterfly under wraps until she's ready to emerge from her cocoon."

A non-disclosure agreement with the school and private, one-on-one lessons were arranged to ensure that Joy's identity remained a secret until the perfect moment. Shrewdly, Bernie negotiated a full scholarship for Joy, leveraging *The New York Times's* anointment of her as "The Most Beautiful Woman in the World." He convinced Barbizon's director that having Joy as an alumna would bring unparalleled prestige. "Every aspiring model wannabe will be banging at your door," he declared, "but we must not make this public until after her reveal."

At first, the modeling course seemed frivolous to Joy, but, as with everything in her life, she took it seriously and excelled. Barbizon's seasoned professionals taught her how to walk and sit with poise, how to strut on a runway and strike the perfect pose. Masterful cosmetologists trained her in makeup application and the best treatments for her hair and skin, while dietary experts set her on a customized exercise regimen and stressed the importance of a balanced, healthy diet.

Barbizon's team all agreed that Joy's natural beauty was nearly impossible to improve upon. By the end of her training, they were convinced she had maximized her potential, cementing her reputation as "The Most Beautiful Woman in the World."

Joy completed the crash course with flying colors, and Bernie decided she was ready for the "unveiling." Until then, the public had seen only one picture of Joy, *The New York Times* photograph that had sparked the media frenzy.

Bernie masterminded an elaborate rollout. He planned to present "The Most Beautiful Woman in the World" at a national press conference in the Waldorf Astoria's prestigious press room. Behind the scenes, he had already lined up deals with three major late-night talk shows, knowing this exposure would make Joy Nordstrom a household name. And to appease D., there were plenty of publicity opportunities for him as well.

Joy's appearance on *The Tonight Show* exceeded even Bernie's lofty expectations. She walked onto the stage in a stunning pale blue silk dress, sent by one of the fashion houses vying for her endorsement and carefully selected by Bernie. The dress's simplicity highlighted her natural beauty, while the delicate Tiffany-gold cross she wore around her neck subliminally signaled innocence and purity, a touch Bernie had insisted upon.

Bernie worked his magic. Knowing how much it would mean to Joy, he arranged for her parents to attend the broadcast. Two first-class tickets and a suite at the Plaza came with the invitation. Cost was no object, it was an investment, one Bernie expected would be paid back in ten percent increments.

Carmella and Jonathan had front-row seats in the studio audience. As the lights dimmed and the red light above the cameras flickered on, Carmella looked over and saw her beloved husband beaming with pride. She reached over and squeezed his hand, her heart pounding in disbelief; their Joy, their baby girl, on national television!

The guest host, Jack Handy, welcomed Joy with a broad smile. "Ladies and gentlemen, please give a warm welcome to the one and only, Joy Nordstrom, the most beautiful woman in the world!"

Thunderous applause greeted her as she gracefully took her seat. Poised yet genuine, she smiled as the cameras zoomed in, capturing every angle of her radiance.

Handy leaned in, his voice tinged with curiosity. "So, Miss Nordstrom, how does it feel to be the most beautiful woman in the world?"

Joy paused, her expression thoughtful, as the audience hung on her every word. "Well, Mr. Handy," she began, her voice steady yet warm, "I feel that every woman should feel beautiful in her own way, inside and out. Beauty isn't just what you see in a photograph; it's how you carry yourself, how you treat others, and how you see the world."

The crowd erupted in applause. Her genuine charm, freshness, and delightful personality captivated everyone. It wasn't merely her looks; it was her authenticity that drew people in.

By the time the show ended, Joy had won over not only the studio audience but millions watching at home. The show's ratings hit a record that night. Her appearance sparked a flurry of headlines the next day, each praising her grace, wit, and elegance.

Within a week, Bernie's phone wouldn't stop ringing. More than six major clients wanted to sign Joy as their "fashion face," and Bernie couldn't wait to share the news.

"Joy, Bernie here. How are you, my little darling?"

"I'm well, Bernie. And you?" Joy replied.

"Perfect; thank you for asking. I'm better than perfect, and you will not believe what's happened."

"Happened? What do you mean?"

"Well, to start with, they're fighting over you like cats and dogs."

"What? Who's fighting over who, and for what?" Joy asked, exasperated.

"You, my precious, you! They all want you, Dior, Louis Vuitton, Chanel...and more."

Bernie explained that these major brands were eager to have Joy represent them. His voice brimmed with excitement. "Joy, sweetie, you will be the next big thing. Bernie will make sure of it. Buckle up and get ready, after all, you are 'The Most Beautiful Woman in the World.' And," he paused dramatically, "I'm your Bernie!"

Joy began to respond, but Bernie hung up before she could get a word in. "What the heck?" she muttered, shaking her head.

Bernie, as promised, worked his magic. He told Joy to leave her job at Monkey Business, a directive she reluctantly followed. It wasn't long before he signed her to the "big three": Estée Lauder, Chanel, and Ralph Lauren. Bernie's clever strategy positioned Joy for different aspects of each brand, Estée Lauder for fragrances, Chanel for haute couture, and Ralph Lauren for their "All-American Preppy" line.

Joy's new life was exhilarating but daunting. She traveled extensively, spending less and less time in her cherished little apartment on Christopher Street.

Their days at Monkey Business were over now that Joy had left her job, and Cynthia was flying around the world chasing who knew what. Like a gnat, Cynthia was always out and about. She would spend weeks away from their Christopher Street apartment, only to pop in for a few days, just enough time to pack up for another adventure.

Then came something big. Really, really big.

It was one of those late nights. Joy had just been visiting with Davis and Mrs. Campanello and had hiked up the two flights of stairs to her place. She was shutting off the bathroom light after removing her makeup when the apartment door suddenly flung open.

At first, it startled Joy, and she was near panic. Then she realized it was Cynthia. Her friend stood there, out of breath and practically glowing.

"Joy! Joy! It's me!"

"I can see that. What's the matter? You look ... weird."

"No, not weird, excited, thrilled, panicked, out of my mind with excitement."

"All right, spill it, Cyn."

Cynthia pushed Joy away from the bathroom door and barreled in. "I'll tell you everything, but wait, I need to pee first." The door slammed shut.

The toilet flushed, and Cynthia emerged, breathless and bouncing on her toes.

"Okay, okay, you better sit down. Brace yourself. This isn't my usual *'you won't believe this' story*, it's bigger."

Joy walked over to the fridge, poured herself a glass of white Bordeaux, and plopped onto the sofa. "Oh God. What is it now? You found yourself a billionaire who rescues puppies?"

Cynthia laughed. "No, but that does sound pretty good. My news is even better. *I'M GETTING MARRIED!*"

Joy choked on her mouthful of Bordeaux.

"Married?! To whom?! I can't even imagine that. You're the quintessential non-committal dater, the girl who can't even commit to a magazine subscription. The girl who thinks men are like razor blades: use them, toss them when they get dull, and move on to the next one."

Cynthia danced around the room with her arms wide open, nearly delirious with excitement.

"Oh, that was before! I've changed. I've met the man of my dreams, a prince. I mean a *real* prince. One who actually has a country, Liechtenstein or something like that." Cynthia giggled. "Gosh, I guess I'm going to have to learn how to spell it."

She kept going, bubbling over: "And he has a family castle, with crests and stuff like that. He showed me pictures, no shit, Joy, he's the real deal. And for fun? He's a Grand Prix racer."

Joy's mouth dropped open. "You're kidding."

"Nope. Prince Charming, *my* Prince Charming, with a body like a New York Jets linebacker and the package ..."

Joy held up her hand. "Enough, Cyn. Way more than I need to know."

Cynthia poured herself a second glass of wine and mused, "Maybe I'll even get to sit on a throne someday, wear a tiara, wave at peasants, the whole thing."

Joy burst out laughing. "Does Liechtenstein even *have* peasants? It's a pretty wealthy country."

Cynthia grimaced. "Well, if they don't, I'll have some imported."

Laughing, Cynthia grabbed Joy's hands, pulling her up from the couch and twirling her around the room.

"Joy, can you imagine? Me, attending coronations, hosting royalty, naming bridges after myself. I'll have to act royal, but you know, not *too* royal."

Joy smiled. "Well, I hope you'll still stay in touch with us little people."

Cynthia winked. "Oh, don't worry." invoking the Royal We, "We will."

"We?" Joy tossed a pillow at the over-the-moon, soon-to-be princess.

Cynthia was packed and, before Joy knew it, gone. The apartment was now entirely hers when she could get there, for her travel schedule was filled with business trips and appearances. Her visits grew infrequent. She could afford a much better place, but Christopher Street still felt like home and when she did return, it was her refuge. She loved curling up in her pajamas on the old sofa from Cynthia's mother's summer house, reading a good book. Though she could easily redecorate, she felt attached to the space, it grounded her in a life that still felt authentically her own.

Bernie, however, had other ideas. He pressured her to move uptown to a luxury apartment on Fifth Avenue between 68th and 69th Streets, the poshest of New York neighborhoods.

"Lamb chop, you're going to love it," Bernie gushed. "It's a duplex, the kind you see in movies, on the sixteenth floor, with a terrace. I can see you now, walking down that spiral staircase like Loretta Young in a flowing gown."

Joy shook her head, amused and said firmly. "Stop, Bernie. I know you mean well, but I'm not going anywhere. I love Christopher Street. Even though Mrs. Campanella and Davis aren't movie stars or famous, I want them around me."

Bernie sighed dramatically, throwing up his hands. "All right, all right. I'll get the deposit back. You can stay in this ... this hovel."

Joy shot him a look. "It's not a hovel. It's my home, and I intend to stay here as long as I'm in New York."

Bernie, ever the pragmatist, let it go, for now.

One of the things Joy loved most about living on Christopher Street was the community. Her elderly neighbor, the effervescent Mrs. Campanella, doted on her like a surrogate grandmother, and then there was Davis. Joy enjoyed spending time with him, mainly because he was oblivious to her newfound fame, and that was exactly why she valued his company. Davis didn't read fashion magazines and avoided pop culture entirely. His world revolved around music, playing it, composing it, with the occasional voiceover gig to pay the bills.

Joy found his uncomplicated existence refreshing. With Davis, she didn't have to be "Joy Nordstrom, The Most Beautiful Woman in the World." She could simply be herself. They often "vegged out" together listening to his music, eating takeout, or enjoying meals cooked by Mrs. Campanella.

She remembered the last time Mrs. Campanella had barged in, pot in hand, with her usual flair.

"Hello, young people!" she exclaimed, her voice as warm as her smile. She bustled into Davis's apartment, carrying a huge pot of homemade turkey barley soup. "Look what Mama's made, plenty for both of you!"

Joy and Davis, amused, broke out with broad smiles.

"Thank you, Mrs. Campanella," Joy said sincerely. "You're the best."

"And here's some homemade garlic bread, smothered with fresh butter and herbs," Mrs. Campanella added, placing a basket on the table. Then her expression grew serious. "You look too skinny for my liking. Are you eating enough?"

"Of course I'm eating," Joy laughed. "And tonight, I'm going to splurge, I'm not foolish enough to miss out on that bread. It smells heavenly!"

"Shoot," Davis teased. "I was hoping you'd skip it so there'd be more for me."

"There's enough for everyone," Mrs. Campanella replied, patting him on the shoulder. "And if not, I've got another loaf back at my place. So, *mangiare,* kids, I've got to get back to Mr. Campanella, who really should be skipping the bread. *Arrivederci!*" She headed for the door, then paused. "I'll be back for my pot tomorrow. And maybe, just maybe, I'll bring a batch of biscotti."

Joy cherished these moments, especially those rainy nights when she and Davis would sit around talking about everything and nothing, their conversations flowing effortlessly. Their relationship was simple and platonic, like that of a brother and sister, and Joy appreciated that Davis was perfectly content with it staying that way. As she often said, Davis was a nice guy, kind and fun, loyal and considerate always there for each other but squarely in the "friend zone." She took comfort in knowing she could be herself around him, no pretense, no constant performance. And gratefully, unlike Cyn, Davis never asked to borrow her shoes or use her perfume ... and for sure, absolutely no drama.

It was clear: Joy was here to stay at 100 Christopher Street.

CHAPTER 24

And Then There Was Jamie

When the sleek Rolls Royce pulled up in front of the East 64th Street townhouse, Claude, the driver, instinctively shut down the engine and settled into his familiar routine. It was another late-night chauffeuring his employer, the enigmatic and undeniably magnetic James Harper-Smyth known simply as Jamie to his inner circle.

Jamie wasn't just an international investment banker; he was a playboy with a pedigree that demanded attention. His lineage sparkled with historical significance. His great-great-grandfather, Allister Harper-Smyth, the Fifth Earl of Westford, was a member of Parliament and one of the wealthiest men in the United Kingdom. His holdings included vast estates in Wales, the Cotswolds, and a massive crescent townhouse in Kensington, along with countless other properties scattered across Britain.

Jamie liked to joke that bad behavior ran in the family, and he wasn't entirely wrong. Through a maze of tangled marriage lines no one could exactly pinpoint (nor cared to), the Harper-Smyths were loosely linked to the illustrious Spencer-Churchill family. One of their most colorful and public figures was Jennie Jerome Churchill, a legend in her own time.

Jamie first heard about "Cousin Jennie" from the sherry-soaked aunts who ruled holiday dinners with half-true, half-invented stories. They sniffed at her as a "gold digger" who had married up, but the tales of scandal and audacity fascinated young Jamie.

As he grew older, he devoured everything he could about Jennie Churchill and came to see himself in her reflection ,rebellious, entitled, and determined to chart his own course. His true inspiration came from this infamous ancestor, the indomitable Lady Jennie Jerome Spencer Churchill.

Times were different now, more accepting, more liberal, which, to Jamie, meant he could reinvent Jennie's spirit in a way that suited him just fine.

Lady Jennie was the stuff of legend. Born in Brooklyn, New York, she defied Victorian convention at every turn. Scandalizing both British and American society, she married Lord Randolph Churchill and became a fixture in the highest echelons of power and privilege. Although factually not confirmed, rumor had it that she bore a tattoo of a coiled snake, a bold symbol that whispered of her daring nature.

Lady Jennie's charisma was unparalleled. Even decades after her death, whispers of her allure still lingered in the gilded drawing rooms of New York and London. She captivated everyone she met, including the Prince of Wales, later King Edward VII, who entertained her regularly.

Consuelo Vanderbilt Balsan, herself a titan of New York's Gilded Age, wrote of Jennie in her memoir *The Glitter and the Gold*:

"She was still, in middle age, the mistress of many hearts, and the Prince of Wales (later Edward VII) was known to delight in her company. Her grey eyes sparkled with the joy of living and when, as was often the case, her an,ecdotes were risqué, it was with her eyes as well as her words that one could read the implications. She was an accomplished pianist, an intelligent and well-informed reader, and an enthusiastic advocate of any novelty."

The stories of her wit, and her unapologetic zest for life were enthralling to Jamie, and it was as if her spirit had passed itself into his DNA, making him a man of charm, intrigue, and ambition, a modern echo of her legacy.

His uninhibited cousin's philosophy resonated within Jamie. Her moral margins exceeded the acceptable norms of the times, and her philosophy was more like an "I dare you" list.

And when he faced choices that could define or destroy his career, he would imagine what Cousin Jennie would do: put aside what others might say, follow your gut, and then just do it. Lady Jennie's example had taught him many things, and the more he read and learned of her, the more he admired and respected who she was and how she lived her life. He never really knew her, she died well before his time, but he felt the connection, the vibes, and most of all the convictions she had that life was one's own to live and be damned the chorus of naysayers. That, coupled with his own personal success and wealth, meant Jamie felt entitled.

Jamie always took command of a room, a deal, a woman, whatever he wanted. Wealth, heritage, and charm were his weapons, and he wielded them without remorse. In his mind, the world didn't just offer opportunity; it owed him its rewards.

The Rolls waited in front of the impressive double-wide townhouse covering over sixty feet of street frontage. A stately dual limestone staircase flanked the entrance, providing a grand entry for the 1898 classic mansion. It was one of Jamie's family residences, and by most standards, it was one of the most exclusive in the city.

Claude was no stranger to the late-night chauffeuring of Mr. Harper-Smyth's latest girlfriends. His boss had become fixated on the idea that he had to have only the most attractive women. Jamie was in his prime, just turning forty-five, and proud that he still had the looks and body of a thirty-year-old soccer star. But his appearance and vigor didn't come easily; two hours every morning in the gym with a personal trainer, a full-time nutritionist on staff, and oh yes, not one but two skilled functional longevity doctors, one specializing in virility and the other with a private room at Jamie's disposal at an exclusive Zurich clinic called Für Immer Jung ("For Ever Young") catering to the rich and famous obsessed with their looks.

Tonight's paramour was a tall willowy brunette named Monica, all of nineteen and a half years old. She was a Romanian, here with her father, a low-level diplomat. Monica was almost six feet tall and more with her Jimmy Choo stiletto heels, and Jamie liked to think of her as "delicious."

It was around dawn when Monica rolled over in the California king bed. She was covered with perspiration, not just hers but his. Her body ached and felt as if she had been split in two. She gazed upward to see the ornate ceiling mural. It was something out of a museum and reminiscent of something one would see in a great medieval hall. She wondered where it came from. The scene depicted a group of goddess-like women lying naked in a circle around a puddle of milk spilling out of a nearby vessel lying on its side. A perfusion of flowers and birds filled the background and a huge white stallion peered down from a hillside.

Noise from the bathroom caught her attention, and she peered through the opened door to see Jamie in the massive glass-enclosed shower. Steamy water poured down in all directions onto his fit form. Monica jumped up from the bed and dashed towards the main attraction.

"How's the water? May I join you?"

"Of course, nothing like a chaser after a big night."

Monica had no idea what that meant. English being her second language, off-the-cuff, tongue-in-cheek remarks often escaped her. But what did not escape Monica was that Jamie was ready for round three, and she was a willing-sparring mate. Quickly she opened the door and slid in.

Jamie wasted no time, pulling Monica close beneath the steaming water. He pressed her against the marble wall, his touch practiced and relentless, hands like a trained potter who molded clay into the perfect form. To her, it felt like surrendering to something primal, irresistible. By the time it ended, she had yielded for the third time that night.

"Oh my God, Jamie." Monica whimpered. "I can't get enough of you; I'm addicted."

Two hours later, she was back in her low-cut, stunning beaded dress from the night before. It exaggerated her decisively enhanced breasts. Monica descended the limestone steps, pausing to wave.

"Bye-bye, sweetie," she bellowed in a somewhat intoxicated Romanian accent. "Call me; remember *you* promised, Jamesy. I love the bracelet. Night, night." She looked up at the brightening sky. "Good morning," she giggled.

Monica entered the rear of the Ghost, rolled down the window, and once again wildly waved her wrist bedecked with the Louis Vuitton bangle that James had given her for being such a good girl.

"Thanks for the trip to the moon; I loved every minute, of it. You are the best ... the biggest and the best ... and oh so naughty."

Claude rolled his eyes. He had heard all this before. If he had a dollar for every bangle bracelet Jamie Churchill had given out, he probably could retire. He wondered if his boss bought them by the dozen.

As the Rolls pulled away from the curb, Jamie stood at the top of the imposing staircase, wearing only his boxers. Turning to face the grand double front doors, he appeared relieved to see Monica leave. To him, their nights together sometimes felt less like passionate encounters and more like intense workout sessions, full of muscle flexing, sweating, grunts, groans, and a sprint to a climactic finish.

Mentally, Jamie chalked the night up as just another conquest, a notch in his belt like so many others. Being young, super-rich, and handsome was a given for him, and having any woman he wanted was considered an entitlement, a deserving reward for just being Jamie. He got almost anything he wanted. And when he didn't, watch out because he would be quite willing to do anything to have his way. He knew no limits and boundaries were for the little people.

Maybe next weekend I'll try a blonde, he thought, as he scratched his crotch and closed the door. *Yeah, a blonde and maybe one with real boobs.*

The mansion's door slammed as if to signal Jamie's inner thought: NEXT.

CHAPTER 25

Close Call

J oy arrived early for the Fashion Week Grand Runway show at Lincoln Center. She went directly to her dressing room, one reserved just for her, given her supermodel status. It was more like a salon than a dressing room. A full-blown make-up area was next to a comfortable seating area and a chaise lounge. A professional cosmetician was waiting to make her up. She sat in the salon chair facing the trifold mirror as a lovely staffer applied ever-so-light makeup to her flawless face.

"Excuse me, Miss, but you barely need a thing. You are naturally so beautiful.

"Thank you." Joy paused. "Your name is?"

"Sunshine, Miss."

"Well, thank you, Sunshine."

"I'll just put a smidgin of powder here and there to prevent glare from the lights. Besides that, you'll be all set with just a nip of lipstick. Do you have a preference?"

Joy smiled and remembered the "Naked Pink" stick she had always carried in her purse. She loved that shade because it was barely detectable and gave the impression of nothing, as well as because Cynthia had named it. Despite her endorsements for all the fancy brands, she secretly only used Naked Pink. "Yes, in my bag, I have a tube over there. I want to use that color."

She surveyed the sizeable room filled with flowers sent by admirers. A huge bouquet of pink peonies, her favorites, caught her eye.

She grabbed the card:

To the World's Most Beautiful Woman, Like an angel, you'll soar down that runway, making memories, breaking hearts, and turning heads. Go knock 'em dead, Bubbale!

Love,

Your Uncle Bernie

Joy smiled and clutched the card closely. "Oh, Bernie," she whispered. "He can be so sweet."

Bernie was sweet, at least as sweet as any agent could be. He came to love Joy like a daughter. It had only been a few years now since he took Joy on and skillfully navigated her into fame and celebrity. With his direction, Joy became one of the fashion industry's highest-paid and most sought-after models. All the major and most prestigious labels sought her to represent their brand. Louis Vuitton, Gucci, and Dior paid dearly to have Joy Nordstrom don their goods, walk down a runway, or appear in an advertisement. Of course, Bernie would love Joy; she had made him rich. Ten percent of every paid appearance, every ad, every testimonial, every everything made Bernie very comfortable. He guarded her like the crown jewels or maybe more crudely said, "the goose who laid the golden eggs."

Joy saw a dozen or more other flower arrangements as she walked from her dressing table. She picked the cards off each, put them together in a deck and read the top one.

To My American Beauty, Love Ali.

Joy closed her eyes and thought, *Ali.* He was a dashing middle-aged Arab who was part of one of those royal families over there. She wasn't exactly sure which country; she met so many people from around the world. Ali had been pursuing her ever since they met at an event held by The Fédération Française de la Couture, the gold standard in the fashion industry, in Paris the prior spring. She thought back to the night they met.

Hotel de Crillon, Paris

"Joy, I want you to meet a really good friend of mine, Prince Mohammed bin Salmān bin 'Ali, but everyone calls him Ali."

"Nice to meet you, Ali; I'm Joy Nordstrom, and Frederica ... thank you for introducing us."

Frederica nodded. She was a skilled "cling-on,"... that is, someone who surrounded themselves with celebrities and benefited by peddling them off as "dear friends." Her European family, among the wealthy in Milan, enhanced her access, giving her countless opportunities to mingle among the rich and famous. Unknown to most, including Joy, Frederica was handsomely rewarded for arranging introductions. And this one, to the prince, would pay off big time. Frederica was skilled in making these introductions seem haphazard and uncontrived. It was a natural talent for her and one that kept her in fine clothing, Hermes, Birkin bags and champagne.

"Joy Nordstrom, indeed, you are ... I dare say there aren't too many breathing men in the world who don't know who you are. 'The World's Most Beautiful Woman.'"

Joy blushing at the sound of that now-irritating title she virtually detested, blinked with an embarrassed smile.

Ali continued his schmoozing and downright flirting. "And I might add, the title befits you. I can certainly see why the world would fancy you. You are awesome."

Joy detected a decidedly British accent coming from the prince. Probably educated at one of England's famous boarding schools. He dressed in a modern Italian tailored suit, probably Brioni, and sported a monogrammed Gucci pocket square in red silk. Prada shoes, and a belt completed the designer look. *Not bad looking for a fifty-something.* Joy thought. *But definitely not my type.*

"My brother introduced Ali to me," Frederica explained. "They were Etonians and later studied at Oxford, been friends for years."

"I see." Joy now put it together. An Arab prince who was educated in England was now traveling worldwide on some yacht or private plane looking to party. A playboy! He probably never worked a day in his life. She got the picture, an all-too-familiar one.

Ali, clearly smitten by Joy's looks, stared. His eyes assessed her, imagining how she might be as a lover or even one of his wives if she converted to Islam. He thought she'd be the perfect number five.

Ali turned to Frederica. "Let's go up to my suite. I have some chums coming in for drinks, and I'd love to have you join me."

Frederica urged, "What do you say, Joy? I can have Sidney meet us up there as soon as he finishes up with some calls.

Sidney was Sidney Luchini, Frederica's oldest brother, a massively successful businessman, and Ali's long-time mate.

"Oh, I'd love to come, but I'm just not up to it right now. I have much to do before the show and am still fighting off jet lag. I need some sleep."

"Nonsense, of course, you'll come," insisted Ali. "And the last thing you need is beauty sleep; it would be redundant."

Frederica said, "Oh, please come; it will be such fun." She knew a handsome trinket was in the cards for her if she got Joy to join the prince.

Joy looked at Ali and then at Frederica, "I'm sorry, Frederica, but I must decline. Maybe next time."

Deflated and incensed, Ali backed off and let it go. He wasn't used to being denied whatever he wanted and had to suppress a rising rage. But he played it cool: "For sure, next time. I'm going to hold you to it. Right then, are you staying here at the Crillon?"

"Yes, for the next five days, until the show is over and back to New York, home sweet home."

"You live in New York; how clever. I have a little place in the city, in Sutton. Where are you?"

"The West Village."

"Oh, the Village, such a quaint place. I have friends on Horatio; I think 190. Whereabouts are you?"

"Christopher Street, right across from the Restaurant Le Blanc. Do you know it?"

"Yes, of course, best foie gras in the city. I would love to take you there sometime."

Joy waved off the invitation: "Yes, that would be nice, but I don't eat foie gras any longer. I'm not happy about how it is obtained, inhumane if you know what I mean."

"Really, I suppose, but I've never concerned myself about such matters."

"Now, I must excuse myself; I need some serious sleep. Au revoir, dear Frederica, good night, Ali."

"Au revoir, Joy. *En attendant de nous revoir.* "

"Yes, until we meet again."

As Joy rode the lift to the third floor, she thought about how insistent and crafty the prince was. It had taken a mere five minutes before he learned where she lived, and her compassion for animals! To top it off, he even asked her out. Very smooth, indeed. Joy had to admit that he was very, very sexy. The tall, dark, handsome type with a hypnotic stare and seductive British accent. She smiled and thought, *he probably looks as good in his underwear as he did in that $4,500 suit.* And then she scolded herself for yielding to such promiscuous thinking. *Shame on me,* she chuckled softly.

The next morning a respectful tap on Joy›s door awakened her.

"Room service," the staffer whispered.

Through the door, Joy replied, "Oh, I didn't order anything. It must be a mistake."

"No madam, you are Ms. Nordstrom, are you not *si vous plait?*"

"Yes, I am, but as I said, I ordered nothing."

"Oui, madame. It is not an order. It is delivery."

Joy slipped on her long Pucci robe and opened the door. "A delivery?"

"*Merci,* Madame."

As the staffer walked into the room, Joy suspiciously questioned him: "A delivery, from whom?"

"*Je ne sais pas.*"

"Very well, come in."

The staffer turned back into the hall, pulled in a trolley filled with boxes, and topped off with a vase containing four dozen white roses. "Voila!"

Joy immediately thought of Bernie and how he was always so thoughtful. "Thank you, Monsieur, and here is something for your troubles."

"*Merci,* Mademoiselle. Have a wonderful day."

There was a small handwritten note attached to the flowers. It was on what appeared to be a business card. "To Joy, from your friend, Ali."

Joy turned the card over. Printed in gold leaf was some coat of arms and Arabic writing. Below it in a flamboyant scroll, written in English: "To the most beautiful woman in the world. Until we meet again. Ali"

Although curious about the boxes and a bit flattered, Joy decided to return everything. She rang the bell captain and asked for a bellman to come up advising him that she would be returning the gifts. Within minutes the phone rang; it was the concierge.

"Madame, is there a problem? Do you not like the flowers? You prefer orchids? Maybe something else?"

"No, no. I do not want to accept anything. It has nothing to do with the flowers or the gifts."

"Please, madame, I cannot take this back. The prince made that very clear if I do, I will be fired. You must accept them, or he will be most unpleasant to the staff and me."

"Fired? How can he do that?"

"Madame, you don't understand, the prince's father owns the hotel, and the prince can do whatever he wants. Last week he had a poor beautician fired because he didn't like the haircut she gave him. You have no idea. *S'il vous plaît, S'il vous plaît!* You don't understand."

"That is outrageous. He will punish you and the staff if I turn these gifts down. Is that what you are saying?"

"*Oui, Oui,* he will. Please, Madame."

Joy was now clearly caught between doing the right thing for herself or doing the right thing for the poor concierge. "Very well, but I will give these things to the poor."

"I cannot help you with that, madame, *s'il vous plait.*"

"I see. Then I will drop them off at the church for them to dispose of them. And please, no more 'deliveries.' Do you understand?"

"I will do my best, Madame, I am at his disposal."

Joy's recollection of that incident continued as she sat at her dressing table, waiting to begin the show. She thought about how that meeting was the beginning of so much more. There were endless phone calls from Ali insisting that he send his father's Gulfstream to New York and take her to his villa in Sardinia. She did not accept the oh-so-many invitations to his Sutton Place penthouse.

At one point Joy searched the internet and learned that Ali was the father of twelve and had four wives. But in his world, that didn't matter. She was human and, yes, flattered by his attention but knew instinctively that any relationship with him was totally out of the question, despite Federica's urging and Ali's drop-dead sex appeal. .

But Ali was not one to give up. He was possessed with the thought of having the most beautiful woman in the world to be his, and his alone, one way or another.

A loud knock snapped Joy back to reality.

"Twenty minutes!" called the stage manager as he stuck his head into her dressing room. "Twenty minutes, Miss Nordstrom."

Joy adjusted her lipstick in the brightly lit makeup mirror, her hand absentmindedly shuffling a deck of gift cards from the dozen flower arrangements filling the room. When she stopped, her gaze landed on one card that slipped to the top. Its elegant script caught her eye:

"I want to meet you, and I will soon!"

It was signed with nothing more than a flamboyant "J."

"Hmm... 'J.'?" she murmured aloud. "Who's that?" She rolled her eyes at the audacity. "And what nerve to assume I'd want to meet him." Then she paused.

Scanning the flowers, she tried to recall which bouquet the card had come with. Was it the pink orchids overflowing from a golden basket? Or the five-dozen yellow and white roses?

At precisely nine o'clock, the pulsating thrum of techno music signaled the show's start. Her dresser, Maria, returned just in time to give the rack of outfits a final check.

"Good luck, Miss Joy. You look beautiful, as always."

"Thanks, Maria. I couldn't do this without you."

Maria smiled. "No problem, ma'am. These clothes are exquisite, but without you, they're just expensive rags."

Joy chuckled. "Oh God, Maria. I'd hate to hear what the Chanel team would say if they heard that."

"They'd have to agree ... unless they're fools like the snakes who follow you around."

"Maria! Cynical as ever," Joy teased, though she felt an unease creep in. Maybe Maria wasn't wrong.

After the show, Joy returned to her dressing room, removed her makeup, and changed into something comfortable. The thought of her quiet Greenwich Village apartment made her sigh with relief. Tonight, she longed to disappear into her sanctuary, away from cameras, catwalks, and the constant gaze of strangers.

The phone in her dressing room rang as she was leaving, but she let it go. She was too tired for small talk or more meaningless pleasantries. Instead, she headed to the rear entrance, where Bernie had arranged for a car to pick her up.

The sleek, oversized black SUV was waiting. Its imposing size made her chuckle; it was large enough to fit a small group, but that was Bernie, always preferring dramatic to practical.

"Good evening, ma'am," said the driver as he opened the door. "I'm George, your driver tonight."

"Good evening, George. Thank you for coming," she replied warmly, sliding into the spacious back seat.

"There's champagne if you'd like, or water, ma'am?"

"No, thank you. I'm fine."

The SUV rolled smoothly through the quiet streets of Manhattan. Joy leaned her head back, letting the city lights blur into streaks as they whirled by. Like an animated light show, the glowing colors merged into a kaleidoscope of neon and incandescent radiance.

George, ever-vigilant, couldn't shake an uneasy feeling. As a driver trained in evasive techniques, he was attuned to subtle details, and tonight, something felt off. A dark blue Lincoln had been trailing them, too far back to be overt, but its presence was consistent. He thought, *Nothing to see here, just being jittery, that happens when you're driving celebrities, over cautiousness,* he mused. *Comes with the territory.*

Glancing at Joy in the rearview mirror, he saw her eyes were closed. After hesitating, he spoke. "Ma'am, may I ask you something?"

Her eyes fluttered open. "Of course," she said, polite but weary.

"I have a teenage daughter, Dawn. She's your biggest fan. She tapes your pictures all over her walls and drives her mother crazy. Would you mind ... could I get your autograph for her?"

Joy smiled, warmed by his earnestness. "I'd be happy to." She pulled out a card from her bag. "Do you have a pen?"

George handed one over, and she quickly signed, "To Dawn, with love, Joy Nordstrom."

"Thank you, ma'am. Dawn will die when she sees this."

Joy smiled, remembering her younger days when she admired celebrities from afar, convinced she'd never meet anyone famous. She reached into her oversized Prada bag and pulled out a small, elegant hand-held mirror engraved with her initials, a gift from one of her many sponsors.

"Here," she said warmly, handing it to George. "Please give this to your daughter. Her name was Dawn, right?"

George's eyes widened in astonishment as he carefully took the mirror. "Oh my God, Miss Joy, thank you! She's going to treasure this forever. You've made her day, no, her whole year!

When they reached her brownstone, George got out to open her door. He paused, his eyes narrowing at the blue Lincoln parked down the block. The hairs on the back of his neck stood up. *Maybe I was too quick to dismiss this....*

"Good night, ma'am. Let me walk you to the door?"

"No, thank you, George. I'll be fine. Now get home to your beautiful family."

Joy got out of the SUV before George could move, waved him off and, dashed off to the steps of her building. As she fished for her keys, they slipped from her hand, clattering onto the stoop. She bent to retrieve them when a shadow loomed behind her.

"Hello, Miss Nordstrom," a low voice purred.

Before she could turn, a hand clamped down on her arm, the aroma of frankincense and rosewater invading her senses. Her heart skipped a beat, she knew that scent, but from where?

Suddenly, a growl pierced the air. Noush bolted from the building, teeth bared, fur bristling. Davis followed close behind.

"What is it Noush? Who's there!" Davis yelled

The man hesitated for a moment too long, and Noush lunged, snapping at his legs. With a curse in a foreign tongue, the attacker released Joy and bolted into the night.

Davis, hearing Joy's voice, rushed to her side. "Are you okay?"

Joy nodded, her voice shaky. "I think so."

As Davis escorted her inside, she couldn't shake the memory of the card she'd read earlier that night: *I want to meet you, and I will soon.*

Was this connected? And why did the scent of her attacker feel so hauntingly familiar?

That night, as she lay in bed, her mind spun. It had been a close call; thank God for Davis and Noush. For the first time, she felt her title as "The Most Beautiful Woman in the World" wasn't just a burden, it was dangerous.

CHAPTER 26

Drumroll, Please

Bernie was even more excited than he usually was when he called his favorite client. "Joy, it's your guardian angel."

"Are you calling from heaven?"

"No, but I have exciting news. You won't believe how lucky you are to have Bernie working so hard for his little bundle of Joy.

"Bernie, skip the self-edifying. You don't have to sell yourself every time we talk. Everyone knows, especially you, how great you are."

"Darling Joy, don't be so complimentary, but once you hear what I have to say, you'll be lighting candles at ol' Bernie's shrine. Now, listen to this, my little cupcake. Bernie has cut the deal of all deals. Your star will skyrocket, so sit tight and listen."

Joy pulled up a kitchen stool and sipped her afternoon tea. "I'm all ears."

Bernie began. "Last month, I got a call from a senior guy at Ogilvy & Mather International, but I haven't mentioned it until now. You probably never heard of them, but they are the Rolls-Royce of advertising and public relations agencies. If Moses were around, he'd use them to sell the Ten Commandments."

Joy moaned. "Everyone in New York knows who they are."

"Yes, and clients like IBM and Merrill Lynch; celebrities like Paul Newman and the Beatles, not to mention a long list of Middle Eastern monarchies and Hollywood legends all work with them. De Beers has engaged O&M.... You know De Beers, don't you?"

"Of course, diamond merchants."

"Right. So, now the incredible part. They have been asked to co-sponsor a world-class auction with Sotheby's for ... listen up ... 'The World's Most Beautiful Jewelry.' Now, get your camera out, sweetie, because here comes the money shot."

Joy rolled her eyes. *Here he goes again, speaking in some kind of code, like it's a language of its own.*

"Bernie, speak English."

"Well, a one-of-a-kind piece called *L'incomparable* diamond."

Joy knew French and that *L'incomparable* translated into eminent beyond comparison.

Bernie continued: "It didn't take rocket science for the suits at Ogilvy & Mather International to make the connection: The most beautiful jewels in the world and a necklace dubbed 'eminent beyond comparison' to think of you."

"Bernie, I'm lost. I don't get the connection at all. Why me?"

"You dear sweet innocent cherub ... modest to the core. The big boys at O&M are staging an auction in New York and want an international blockbuster. You know, to get mega publicity to stir up interest as one of the main attractions, they want you to model the premiere piece: L'incomparable diamond necklace and a couple of other bangles.

"Now, buckle up for this part." Bernie paused to catch his breath. "After Bernie got through with them, they agreed to pay you 1.5 million dollars for three days' work! That's $36,000 an hour! That's a lot of chicken salad, if you know what I mean."

Joy put her mug down and inhaled. "Bernie, are they crazy?"

"No, not crazy, smart. Having the most beautiful woman in the world model their stuff makes all the sense in the world. The rub-off is a natural."

"Rub-off? What do you mean?"

"Rub-off … You know, prestige by association. The most beautiful woman with the most beautiful jewels … Get it, sweetie?"

"But Bernie, 1.5 million is a tremendous amount of money."

"Chicken feed, my dear. The necklace alone is worth a cool fifty million plus, maybe more, and Sotheby's commission on that and all the other pieces will be staggering. So, 1.5 million for your endorsement is chump change. Less, 10 percent, for Bernie, of course."

Another deep breath and Bernie went on. "Now, here's the best part."

"There's more?"

"Drumroll, please," Bernie said, grinning. "Get ready to gen-uflect, sweetheart, because this saint just landed you the Sistine Chapel of deals, front row pew, next to the Pope. I negotiated something that will make your dreams come true.

Joy thought, *More Bernie drama. He missed his calling; he should have been a soap star or a carnival barker.*

Bernie sounded another drumroll on the other end of the phone, something he relished doing whenever he announced one of his incredible accomplishments.

"Old Bernie said he would only agree to the deal with just one condition. And that was if they would allow you to design and wear only your fashions, not just you, but all the models. And they would finance the manufacturing of the garments up to half a million dollars."

Joy gasped. "Are you serious, Bernie?"

"I swear on my *bubbe*."

"Who? Your *bubbe*?"

"My darling grandmother, may she rest in peace. She'd be proud of her little *yingaleh*. And speaking of resting in peace, Coco Chanel will roll over in her grave when people see your designs with that jewelry. And wait for this ..." Bernie sounded another drumroll. "You, Joy Nordstrom, get to keep all the outfits for your inventory."

Joy was a little lost in his "Bernieisms" but overwhelmed with his message: "But how did they know I can even design such creations?"

"I showed them the picture. You know, the one D. took of you in the gown you made in Paris. They loved it and were all in.

"So, get cracking, baby. We have eleven months to pull this off. Ciao." Bernie hung up.

Joy sat at the counter for a while, trying to absorb it all. Was she dreaming? she thought. No, she wasn't. But it all seemed so unreal. Bernie pulled off the deal of a lifetime. Now, what?

CHAPTER 27

———— 🍎 ————

Come Fly with Me

Ladies and Gentlemen, we are beginning our descent into JFK International Airport. The local time is 12:40 p.m. Crew, please prepare for landing.

Jamie Harper-Smyth deplaned the British Airways 747 a few minutes later. He was bummed out having to fly commercial, since he was accustomed to using his own aircraft. But his plane was not capable of transatlantic flights. His trip was a mixed bag. He had to attend to some "matters" back home, and he felt he was performing a delicate balancing act between his life in the UK and his other life in the United States. Still, the thrill of the experience was invigorating, and as far as he was concerned, he was going to have it all.

Although it was a long flight, he arrived refreshed, having a first-class ticket. He had lots of room to stretch his six-foot-four frame in the comfortable, British Airways lay-flat seat.

An army of flight attendants buzzed around him like caffeinated bees in a five-star hive, fluffing his pillows, refilling his glass, and practically fanning him with palm fronds. But Jamie hardly noticed, as entitlement was so deeply ingrained in his psyche that he simply thought, *Do I deserve anything less?*

Just after a sumptuous dinner had been served onboard, the purser, a striking redhead in her early twenties, approached Jamie with a polished British accent. "Sir, when you're ready, I'd be delighted to turn down your bed."

Her model-like beauty and the tailored uniform that fit her perfectly in all the right places immediately caught Jamie's attention. He had noticed her during boarding but hadn't had the chance for more than a passing glance. Now, up close, she was impossible to ignore.

"You'll turn down my bed, huh?" Jamie said with a wink. "Could it be for two? And your name is ... ?"

She glanced at her clipboard and read his name off the manifest. "Mr. Harper-Smyth, my name is Ronda, and as you can see, all our beds are singles." She struck a playful pose, hand on hip, and winked back.

Jamie couldn't help but admire her, a tall, sensuous figure with fiery red hair. Irreverent as always, he wondered cheekily, *Do the drapes match the rug?*

"Pity," Jamie quipped. "But I'd be willing to squeeze."

Ronda paused before giving the pat answer memorized in flight training. She was unflappable and well-practiced in handling attention. She let a sly smile play on her lips. "Tempting, sir," she replied, "but I'm working this flight. Plenty of passengers need me ... not just you."

With that, she turned and walked away, leaving Jamie grinning like a schoolboy caught in a harmless flirtation, calling after her, "Another time, then?"

Ronda smiled and waved as she moved away.

When the huge aircraft had landed on runway six and taxied into position next to gangway 12 in the international terminal, the flight crew lined up at the exit hatch and mouthed the obligatory "Bye-bye." And "Thank you for flying British Air."

Jamie flung his carry-on bag over his shoulder and approached Ronda, who was at the head of the lineup. "Nice meeting you. I'd love to show you around New York." He slipped his business card into the breast pocket of her uniform, winked, and deplaned.

He cleared customs in a flash, and since he only had a small carry-on bag, there was no need to claim luggage. As he entered the arrival hall, he spotted Claude.

"Welcome home, sir." He grabbed Jamie's carry-on.

A loud PA announcement blared as Jamie and Claude walked toward the exit: "Mr. Harper-Smyth, Mr. James Harper-Smyth please go to the nearest terminal phone and dial 890.

"They're paging you, Sir."

"Yes, I hear it. What do I do?"

Claude looked around and saw a yellow phone and a sign over it: Terminal Phone."

"Over there, sir."

"Hello, this is Mr. Harper-Smyth . What is it,"

"One moment, please." The efficient airport operator advised. A second or two passed, and she continued: "Go ahead; your party is on the line.'

"Hello, who is this?"

"Mr. Harper-Smyth, this is Ronda, the purser on your flight. It seems you forgot something on the plane."

Jamie was confident he had checked thoroughly and collected everything, so he was puzzled. "What?"

"Me."

Jamie couldn't help but smile. He gave the stunning redhead his address and arranged a rendezvous for the next evening. She mentioned she had a three-day layover, and he joked to himself that she might literally be getting one. As he walked out of the airport, he muttered with a grin, "I guess I'll finally find out if the drapes match the rug."

Claude, the driver, looked confused. "Excuse me, sir? What did you say? Something about drapes?"

"No, Claude. Nothing at all."

CHAPTER 28

Diamonds, Dresses, and Destiny

The months rushed by in a whirlwind of inspiration and anxiety. Joy was consumed with bringing her vision to life. Being a perfectionist, she struggled with getting everything just right. She would have sleepless nights hovering over her sketches and mood boards. And when it came to choosing a name for the fashion house, it was also a struggle. She wanted just the right one, one that said it all and yet wasn't officious, pretentious, or egocentric.

The name came to her in a flash over a cup of tea sometime after two a.m. on a Tuesday morning: "World Couture." This name encapsulated her experiences in New York, Milan, and Paris, embodying the idea that her creations would transcend borders and possess a timeless, universal appeal.

But where to begin this "magical journey," as she called it? Confidence in her designs wasn't the problem, Joy knew she had an eye for beauty and the skill to imagine it. The challenge was the business itself, a world she barely understood, with its labyrinth of supply chains, production schedules, personnel choices, margins, and market demands. And time? There was never enough.

Bernie, ever eager to help, offered his connections in the "rag trade." His Eighth Avenue friends, garment district gurus entrenched in the world of mass-marketing, and off-the-rack fashion, were a far cry from the elite realm of haute couture Joy envisioned. Their advice, while practical and reliable for standard department store lines, felt like trying to sculpt a masterpiece with a hammer and nails.

Joy stood at a crossroads. Would she stick to the safe, predictable path Bernie's well-worn network offered, or would she dive headfirst into the unknown world of high fashion, risking everything to forge her destiny? The stakes couldn't have been higher, but for Joy, the only way forward was up.

Instinctively, Joy reached out to Monsieur Longchamp. She knew he retired but sought his advice anyway. In a late-night call to Francois, she learned that the old master had left Paris.

"Francois? It's Mademoiselle Joy, Joy Nordstrom."

"*Oui, oui*, Joy, my *cherie*. You called to tell me that you are returning to Paris and will be my lover. *Oui?*

"No, Francois, not at all."

"So, why do you call? To break my heart?"

Joy made light of the question and quickly moved on. "I'm calling to speak with your father. I know he retired, but how can I reach him? Is he well?"

"*Bon ami*, you prefer my father to me? He's old, and how do you say: 'past his prime.' But, my *cherie*, Francois is not.... No, no, no, hardly...he will make you crazy with his passion, we will drink wine and make love, day and night, *oui?*

206

Joy knew that Francois was a self-proclaimed "sex maniac" and shrugged it off. "Francois, I would like to reach him. Can you please help? I need his advice."

Francois finally decided to let it go and act like someone who wasn't chronically in heat. "My papa is not here. When he retired, he moved. And *oui,* he is well, thank you for asking. The old man is fit as a bull and will live to a hundred like his father."

"I see. I'm pleased to hear he is in good health. Where did he move?"

"The poor old soul grew tired of the dreary Paris winters; he was always cold, wrapped up in an overcoat and sitting by a fire. So, he packed up and moved to warmer climates. And the old fool convinced Giselle, my senior cutter, to go with him for 'company.' He took a place by the sea. In Naples."

Joy's scowled. "Naples, you say."

"*Oui.* A lovely villa with a sea view and four bathrooms, him and Giselle alone, can you imagine? *Il est fou,* crazy. Who needs four toilets?

"I have not seen him in a long time. I've been busy, business is good, and Naples is too far and hard to get to; I hate those long flights and going through all that immigration stuff. Too much work."

Really? Joy thought as she continued the conversation. "Francois, I would think that Paris to Naples is only a couple of hours by plane, and they are part of the EU, so there would be no immigration."

"No, no, my Cherie, not Naples, Italy, Naples, Florida. Isn't that near Disneyworld?"

Joy was thrilled to learn which Naples Monsieur Longchamp was residing in. It meant he was a lot closer.

"Yes, Francois, Disney isn't too far from Naples, maybe a couple hours by car. Now, may I have his phone number?"

Francois provided his Papa's phone number and address. He ended the call, but not without one more try.

"So, Mademoiselle Joy, are you sure that you are sure? That there is no room in your heart for Francois? He is a wonderful man, a lover extraordinaire! And his wife doesn't understand him."

She smiled ruefully. "*Bonsoir*, Francois, and thank you for the number."

The rehearsal was on Thursday night, and Joy was as ready as ever. Monsieur Longchamp, now a young seventy-six, moved to New York and agreed to help Joy produce her line. He was bored-silly in Florida and missed the action. Giselle came with him and was invaluable in training the American cutters and tailers Joy hired.

De Beers and Sotheby's came through too. They were more than enthusiastic about seeing that every detail was world-class. Money was no object, but despite that, Joy managed to bring the whole project in below budget, a fact that did not go unnoticed by everyone.

The event was called *Plus que Beau*, Beyond Beautiful. Massive efforts were made to publicize and promote the event. It was a very select and imposing guest list–names that would add panache and celebrity to the auction: international royalty, Hollywood megastars, and billionaires of all sizes and colors.

Registered bidders were to receive the best seats. Pre-qualified bidders would be allowed to handle the jewels after the fashion show. addition to Sotheby's regular security, Ogilvy & Mather hired more than seventy-five additional security officers and convinced New York City's mayor to provide beefed-up building surveillance. Of course, two complimentary tickets for the mayor were part of the deal.

The auction star was the L'incomparable diamond necklace, a one-of-a-kind creation by world-famous Italian-Lebanese jeweler Mouawad. Joy was to wear it, and she spent an inordinate amount of attention creating a frock worthy of the piece. She knew it had to be simple, elegant, and, like the necklace, a showstopper, but in a way that did not distract. The necklace was considered the most valuable in the world, estimated to be in excess of $55 million U.S. dollars. It featured a flawless GIA-graded 407.8-carat fancy deep brownish-yellow shield-step-cut diamond suspended gracefully from a 229.52-carat white diamond necklace intertwined by 18-karat rose gold branchlets.

Joy took her dress's design inspiration from the fifteenth century, adding a modern flare. She chose a cocoa brown silk fabric, knowing that the rich dark brown hue would offset the brilliant yellow stone and the avalanche of diamonds on the branchlets. The dress featured a flattering V-neck bodice, with a plunging neckline allowing the entire necklace to lie flat on Joy's breasts. A two-foot-long trailing cape-detail, flowing naturally from the shoulders, gave a medieval feel, and an A-line skirt gracefully draped to the floor completed the stunning regal design.

There were more than thirty-six original designs to accommodate each of the show's jeweled pieces, one more spectacular than the other. After the rehearsal, Monsieur Longchamp led Joy aside.

"My darling Joy, I am in awe. You have created one masterpiece after another. In all my years in the trade, I have never seen such raw talent turn into *La Magnifique*. Your talent only exceeds your natural beauty, and your spirit and good heart exceed your talent."

Joy blushed hearing this from the Maestro. He continued. "If I had half your talent, Maison de Paris would have been par excellence with the best of the best. I predict, my little darling, that you will become not only recognized but revered compared to the likes of Coco and Giovanni, even Giorgio."

"Oh, Monsieur, you flatter me, but this is not the case. I have much to learn and a long journey ahead of me. But thank you from the bottom of my heart. Thank you for coming all this way to help and support me. But most of all, thank you for believing in me. You are *mon héros*."

When Joy strutted down the runway, the room ignited with energy! A battalion of photographers from every major newspaper, trade journal, and global TV outlet captured the electrifying moment on film.

The evening was a huge success. Bernie planned an after-show party at a SoHo hot spot, The Dragon Lady, for the cast, De Beers executives, and the Ogilvy & Mather, the brains behind the event.

The legion of armed guards collected the numerous pieces as the models walked off the runway, escorting them to a super-secure area where a half dozen or more rigorously vetted buyers gathered to inspect the pieces prior to the next day's auction. The viewing lasted less than forty-five minutes when a detail of guards secured the gems, placed them in their fitted steel boxes, and whisked them off to two awaiting Brink's armored vehicles and a lead SUV. One truck was a decoy; the other would carry the priceless cargo. The chief of security, Shimon Glick, formally with Mossad, Israel's Central Institute for Intelligence and Special Operations , and a decorated war hero of the Israel Defense Forces, was in charge of the transportation. Glick was a master in security matters and, in a last-minute shrewd and audacious precautionary measure, decided to put the jewels in neither of the Brink's trucks but in the lead car with only a driver and a female officer.

Joy retired to her dressing room for a quick change before the SoHo shindig at the Dragon Lady A knock at the door interrupted her.

"Can I come in? Darling? It's your Bernie."

"Yes, come in. I'll just be a few minutes."

"Well, what can I say? You were magnificent! And the schmattes were … sensational."

"Did you really like them? Or are you just saying that?"

"Look, Joy, I don't know one schmatte from the next, but all I can tell you … I know people, and from the reaction of that audience, you have arrived."

"Oh, Bernie, I hope you're right. I put my heart and soul into those designs."

"It showed, my little sweetheart. You will see. Bernie knows. Doesn't he always? Now, get that nose powdered and meet me at the restaurant. George is waiting outside. Don't keep your public waiting."

"Please, Bernie! My public! Don't get carried away."

Joy prepared to exit the dressing room, filled with floral arrangements and bouquets. As she glided by one of the tables, she was struck by a particular exotic bouquet with a mixture of orchids, lilies of the valley, and Juliet roses. She lifted the card with it.

Your beauty remains unparalleled, J.

Joy placed the card down on her dressing table, her fingers lingering on its edge. "There it is again: J," she murmured, her brow furrowing. The sight of that initial jolted her memory, pulling her back to the first time she'd seen a card like this.

At the time, it hadn't just unsettled her, it had left a strange, lingering unease she couldn't shake. Not fear exactly, but something deeper, a primal instinct whispering that she wasn't alone.

Her skin had prickled as though someone was watching her, hovering just out of sight yet far too close for comfort.

Now, as she stared at this new card, that same eerie sensation crawled up her spine. Her mind flickered to the other night, outside her apartment, the night George had dropped her off. The man who had lunged from the shadows, the pungent scent of frankincense and rose water still haunting her memory.

Could this card be connected to that incident? Could J be connected to him?

Joy's hand tightened over the card and then shrugged. *How foolish*, she thought, imagining cloak-and-dagger villains. *It's probably nothing.*

CHAPTER 29

❦

An Eyeful!

The Dragon Lady was this year's favorite after-hours spot among the trendy, hip, and accomplished New York partiers. The building façade came from a movie theater in Chinatown, which was relocated, piece by piece, to a warehouse, formerly a meat-packing facility. An enormous dragon flanked the entrance, and every few seconds, a fire blast roared out from its threatening mouth. A vintage marquee read: "Private Party Tonight." Two gorilla-sized bouncers guarded the door, ensuring only the "invited guests" would be allowed in.

Joy stepped out of the SUV to thunderous applause. A long line of VIP well-wishers had assembled along the red carpet, the very one Bernie had insisted on with the event organizers.

"No carpet, no show," he'd barked. "After all, we're talking about the most beautiful woman in the world here."

She entered the trendy club to a flurry of squealing wanna-bees and news-hungry reporters. Bernie was sure to tip off the media and promised future exclusive interviews with the more important ones. The fever was white-hot. A syncopated beat of non-music music groaned in the background, and groups of people clung to small counter-high cocktail tables as if they were life rafts thrown from the decks of the Titanic. A fire pit danced seemingly synced to the music with blue and gold flames in the front of the room, and servers skimpily clad in Asian garb passed trendy, unidentifiable hors d'oeuvres.

Among the guests were the mayor, half a dozen TV personalities, a boatload of clinging paparazzi, and, waiting quietly off to the side, someone who would change Joy's world forever.

Joy took a seat at one of the high-tops, and a lovely young page, assigned to ensure she wanted for nothing, delivered a tall glass of sparkling water, Joy's drink of preference.

One of the De Beers executives stopped by to make a little small talk before politely excusing himself, leaving Joy alone once more. She didn't mind. In fact, she was perfectly happy sitting by herself, taking in the scene.

All of this, the lights, the crowd, the whispered attention, was about her. And that realization felt like an unfamiliar, even unwelcome, companion, one that had been following her ever since *that* photo appeared in the *Times*.

She mused, *A picture may say a thousand words, but for me, it said "Here is your destiny."*

A tall man stepped out of the din. "Excuse me. Good evening, Miss Nordstrom, may I introduce myself? I'm Jamie Harper-Smyth."

"Good evening," Joy responded.

"I've been a fan of yours for some time now, but until this evening, I have not had the pleasure of meeting you." Jamie was role-playing the "gee golly," cock-eyed, bushy-tailed admirer.

Joy swiveled on her chair to get a better look at the intruder. No, she thought she'd never seen him before, and she would surely remember since this guy was quite an eyeful.

"A fan? That's flattering, but I don't consider myself having fans."

"Oh, oh contraire. You have no idea how many followers you and your career have."

Jamie was suave and sophisticated, and it oozed from every pore in his handsome body; the gee-whiz kid bit was gone, and she saw in front of her someone who was confident, self-sure, and knew what he wanted. Sure, Joy had met many, as Sunshine called them, "Stage Door Johnnies," but this guy was a cut above.

"May I call you Joy? And I would be enormously pleased if you would call me Jamie."

There was no doubt that this sophisticated, debonair guy had caught Joy's attention. Jamie sensed it instantly. After all, his massive experience with women had endowed him with an almost eerie sixth sense, much like a predator scanning for its prey.

The two chatted easily, and Joy was intrigued to learn that Jamie was an accomplished financier. He spoke, without a hint of bragging, about the IPOs he had shepherded to market, a client list that read like a who's who, and the time he spent mentoring young interns.

Joy had no idea about Jamie's heritage, but she sensed there was history behind him, perhaps something unusually interesting tucked away in his past. She concluded there was far more to Jamie Harper-Smyth than his appealing looks, his impeccable wardrobe, and his ridiculously expensive cologne. A tell-tale hint was the impressive ring bearing a family crest that he wore on his right pinky finger.

Just as things were getting even more interesting, Bernie was at her elbow. "Darling, you must come and meet Mr. Ludlow. He runs a major private equity firm, and he and his wife are dying to meet you ... *Potential customers,*" Bernie hummed. He looked at Jamie and said: "Sorry, bud, but this is work."

Jamie grabbed Joy's arm as she turned to leave. "Look, Joy, I'd like to get to know you; how about it?"

Joy took another good look at this polished specimen of a gentleman and thought about what her best friend Cynthia would do ... and then she did it: "That would be nice ... um," Joy struggled to recall his name.

"Jamie. Jamie Harper-Smyth. Tell me your number, and I'll call."

"I don't have a pen."

"I have a perfect memory."

Bernie, becoming more insistent, tugged at Joy's other arm said in typical "Berniese," "Come, *mein kleiner schatz*, my little sweetheart. Uncle Bernie needs you. We have to roast the marshmallows before the fire goes out."

"What?"

"Never mind, just come with me. Uncle Bernie is making magic."

As she walked past Jamie and bid him goodbye, she rattled off her number.

It was late when Joy returned to Christopher Street, alone as usual. She had invited the Campanellas, Davis, and even Noush to the DeBeers event, but none of them accepted the invitation. Mrs. Campanella felt "out of her league," and Davis, well, he never gave a reason but just declined. Joy figured he might.

She couldn't get the stranger, Jamie, or whatever his name was, out of her mind. Was it chemistry? Or was it just her own yearning to find someone?

As she removed her makeup, she caught her image in the mirror and paused, staring intensely into her own eyes. Was this dashing, confident man interested in something more than just "the most beautiful woman in the world"? Did he really see *her*, or just the illusion everyone else was captivated by?

Sliding into bed, Joy reached to turn off the bedside lamp but hesitated, a smile tugging at her lips. *God, he smelled incredible. That cologne was... amazing.* Her grin widened as a mischievous thought crossed her mind. *I'll have to find out what he was wearing and buy some for Davis. God knows, it's a lot better than that Old Spice he wears. And the right scent drives women crazy. He might even get a girlfriend!*

With that, she switched off the light, still smiling as she drifted off to sleep. It had been an evening she would always remember, the launch of her new adventure: World Couture, and who knows, maybe some to share it with. This Jamie fellow had so much going for him, wicked smart, his finger on the pulse of the world of finance, and pretty darn cute.

Sleep crept over Joy, but suddenly, she became fully awake. She remembered: The card ... The one that came with the flowers. What did it say? Something like *we shall soon meet.* It had been signed "J." Was this the mysterious, handsome Jamie Harper-Smyth? And if it was, what a relief; he certainly wasn't a villain lurking in the dark.

CHAPTER 30

Life Marches On

It had been sixteen months since Sotheby's Extravaganza and World Couture had taken the fashion industry by storm.

Bernie had been hard at work applying his business expertise, transforming Joy into a bona fide fashion guru. In an incredible business coup, he engineered World Couture's acquisition by an English design firm. The firm paid millions and agreed to retain Joy as Chief of Design, responsible for all creative decisions. The arrangement suited Joy perfectly since it allowed her to do what she most loved, design, and to be relieved of the burden of running the business. Joy's modeling career, meticulously handled by Bernie, was streamlined to almost exclusively doing "celebrity endorsements" with the occasional odd fashion event to keep her in the game.

Joy continued living at her cozy Greenwich Village apartment and spending quiet evenings with Davis and the now-widowed Mrs. Campanella, enjoying delicious home-cooked dinners. When the three were together, they would once again hear the long, drawn-out story of how Mrs. Campanella lost her husband, a tale she dubbed The Sauce Incident.

"So, he was sticking his nose in my cooking. You know how I hate that. Anyway, I was out picking up a fresh loaf of *pane siciliano*, that bread sprinkled with sesame seeds and made with semolina flour. It was his favorite, and the poor guy never got to have a slice ... it was still warm when I found him.

"The pot was simmering, and my Tony must have decided to sneak an early meatball. The medical report said he put the whole thing in his mouth and tried to swallow it ... and of course, he choked. *Stonato.*"

And, as always, she ended the saga with bittersweet logic: "Well, at least he went without being hungry. And the sauce didn't go to waste. I put in a pound of rigatoni and fed the Rescue Squad who came to get my Tony."

Joy and Davis had to hold back a slight snicker, not wanting to offend Mrs. C.

Joy regretted missing Mr. Campanella's funeral; she had been in Paris, caught in the whirlwind of a high-profile fashion event. Davis, faithful as ever, was there with Noush, and he played the piano, singing a medley of Tony's favorite songs that brought tears to more than a few eyes.

Even Cynthia showed up, to Mrs. Campanella's undisguised dismay. She swept in, dressed head-to-toe in black, a sleek, skin-tight mini-mini dress, six-inch stilettos, scarlet lipstick, and a veil that looked more nightclub than chapel. The priest made the sign of the cross as she exited, a gesture that seemed more exorcism than blessing.

After the service, Mrs. Campanella pulled Davis aside and muttered, "That one looked more like Tony's mistress than his upstairs neighbor.

Joy came to think of Davis and Mrs. Campanella as family. She often spent time in Davis's dark, semi-subterranean apartment whenever she was in town, taking care of Noush and pitching in with chores. His simple, unpretentious world gave her warmth and refuge from the high-pitched rat race of fashion shows, endorsements, and fame. She kept her career stories low-key, despite her success, just to remain one of the "regulars." A no-big-deal friend, like them.

With Cynthia globe-trotting and waving at peasants, Davis was always there, a ready ear, a steady confidant. His calm friendship, mixed with Mrs. Campanella's chaos and cannoli, gave Joy the reality check she sometimes desperately needed.

In recent months, Joy had confided another "big thing" to Davis. She might have met "Mr. Right" and was perhaps standing on the precipice of what she thought could be love.

On one of those rainy evenings, she had finally said it out loud.

"Davis, I think things are getting serious with Jamie."

Davis smiled and leaned back into the old, wrinkled sofa, his expression warm and endearing, the kind of smile that said he was genuinely happy for her.

"Serious?" he teased gently. "Wow. Mr. Right! That's amazing, Joy. You deserve something real, and I'm so excited you might have found it."

Joy tucked her long legs beneath her, straining to see out the small basement window above. Rain fell gently against the pane, a soft rhythm that somehow made everything feel more real.

"Thanks, Davis," she said, her voice soft. "It means a lot that you're happy for me. I didn't think it would happen, not like this, and certainly not with someone like Jamie."

"Someone like Jamie?" Davis asked, curious.

"Well ... what I mean is, he's nothing like anyone I've ever known. Mysterious, a little roguish, alluring, even elusive at times, but also thoughtful. He's always showing up with some small gift or doing something to make me feel comfortable. I've heard the rumors that he's a playboy with a past. Maybe he is. But with me, he seems sincere, like he's outgrown all that.

"Just the other night, I casually mentioned that I hadn't been to the beach for months. The next morning, he arranged for his plane to take us to a little beach house rented for the day, in Bermuda. Just the two of us, and an amazing picnic with all my favorites, set up on the beach on the famous pink sand. It was simple, but ... he listened, and he genuinely wanted to please me." Joy paused and thought deeply. "He makes me feel special."

"Joy, you are special. Very special."

"Stop. You know what I mean. He just is ... different."

"Yeah, I hope he's a lot better than that Ali fellow you told me about. He was a humdinger, four wives and all!"

Joy thought back to Ali, a crown prince of somewhere or another, who pursued her like a tomcat on the prowl. For months, he was relentless, almost obsessive, showering her with gifts she always returned and showing up at every public event where she appeared. He even proposed marriage more than once. Their mutual friend Frederica pushed the match as if she had a stake in it.

"But Joy, Ali is amazing. He will make your dreams come true."

"Honestly, Frederica, how could you possibly think I'd consider him? He's got four wives, for heaven's sake."

"Oh, Joy, that doesn't matter. You'd be number one, and the 'number one' calls the shots. Palaces, jets, unlimited shopping ... don't be a fool."

But there was no chance. Joy had no intention of being anyone's chattel. least of all "wife number five."

And then there was that night at her doorstep when she was almost abducted. She still shuddered when she thought about it. Somehow, she suspected that Ali was behind that. She had read of women who disappeared, never to be seen again, after catching the eye of one of those Middle Eastern princes.

Her recollection was interrupted by Davis's question. "You said he's a Brit."

"Yes, actually, he holds dual citizenship."

"And he has some kind of pedigree?"

"Yes, through marriage, almost a century ago, I take it. Something to do with the Churchills. But he's not hung up on that. He's more into success and power rather than being some kind of blue blood."

"So, he's rich and powerful. Somebody like that usually doesn't make a good soul mate," Davis worried out loud.

"I thought about that too, and to be honest, it has given me pause. Jamie is wealthy and a bit spoiled. That's something I don't like very much. He's used to having his way, and when he doesn't, he kind of ... well, kinda gets upset, maybe even mad."

"That's not too attractive, I would imagine," Davis said, sipping his coffee.

"No, it isn't, but despite that, I can't explain it ... I sort of melt in his company. He has that 'way.'"

"Way? What way?"

"I don't know, that 'I can't live without you' way, I really can't explain it."

Joy was speaking sheer gibberish, which was probably a good sign that she was in love. "Well, dear friend," Davis said. "The fact that you're finding it difficult to articulate what you want to say sounds suspiciously close to 'cock-eyed in love' to me."

"Yeah, maybe. But yet, I'm still not sure. He's the package, everything any girl would want. And he treats me like a goddess."

"So, he's the real deal for you, yes?"

"I'm not sure. He's pretty special, but I wish he were a little more like you, though, easy to talk to and always attentive to things that matter."

Davis never really thought much about more than friendship, mostly because he was solidly cast in the friend zone, a place both he and Joy respected. Sure, he'd considered something more, but time and circumstances never really presented themselves. Rather than dwell on what could be, he was content with what was, a lasting friendship built on showing up, every time, just as they were. And besides, Noush loved her.

A hug good night, a special rub for Noush, and Joy made the journey up those two flights of stairs, a short climb, but one that reminded her just how different their worlds were. And yet, despite those differences, their friendship remained solid and unshakable.

Morning rose, and Joy's respite ended all too soon, and she was on the road again, leaving Davis and Mrs. Campanella to keep the home fires burning. Bernie had a jam-packed schedule for her, starting with a meet-and-greet for Piccadilly Cosmetics, the firm that contracted Joy to be their "face." After that gig, Joy headed to Los Angeles for a slew of meetings, including a visit to Rodeo Drive to scout a potential designer showroom that the British firm, now the owner of World Couture, was considering. The CEO insisted on Joy's approval, which not only flattered her but validated her worth to the company.

Jamie arranged to meet Joy in LA, and his people booked a bungalow at the Beverly Hills Hotel, the hotel of celebrities, the rich and famous, and those choosing discretion. Unlike the main hotel, the bungalows provided the ultimate in luxury and, even more importantly, the gold standard of privacy.

Designed in the Beverly Hills Hotel's signature colors of peachy pinks, apricots, yellows, and greens, all twenty-three bungalows were uniquely furnished and scattered throughout twelve acres of lush, manicured gardens. Many rooms had their own balconies, and some even featured private swimming pools. But most notable was that each room had its own story to tell, some happy, others tragic, and even some infamous.

For instance, Bungalow 14-21, known as "Bachelor," accommodated movie stars and their affairs. Bungalow number 5 was Elizabeth Taylor and Richard Burton's hideaway; local lore had it that they maintained a standing order for two bottles of vodka at breakfast and two more at lunch. A regular was Marilyn Monroe, whose choice was Bungalow number 7, later dubbed "Norma Jean." Even Beatle John Lennon and his wife Yoko Ono stayed in the 1970s in Bungalow number 10. The guest list was endless: Marlene Dietrich, Frank Sinatra, Orson Welles, Charlie Chaplin, and Howard Hughes, who lived in Bungalow 4 for more than thirty years.

Unknown to Joy, Jamie was a frequent and well-known guest at the hotel, and his reputation preceded him. Over the years, he had occupied many bungalows with women of all ages and backgrounds. The staff jokingly referred to any room that Jamie occupied as the "love shack."

Joy arrived first and was escorted to Bungalow 15, a two-room suite in a secluded corner of the lush private hotel gardens. *Wow, this is gorgeous,* Joy thought as the houseman opened the double doors.

Joy proceeded to the terrace and flung open the French doors leading to a stunning garden with a small but tempting private pool.

"Will there be anything else, ma'am?"

"No, thank you."

"Very well then. Where would you like your bags? I can open a luggage rack for you if you like."

"That would be fine; just over there is perfect. Thank you. You have been very kind."

"You're welcome. My name is Josh, and if I can assist you in any way, please call the desk."

Joy opened her purse and pulled out a twenty-dollar bill. As the young man was leaving, he turned and timidly said, "At the risk of stepping out of place, ma'am, but I must say your reputation is understated. You are the most beautiful woman I've ever seen, and believe me, I see plenty of them around here, and I would know."

Joy blushed and graciously replied, "Thank you, Josh, you are most kind." If he only knew how much she hated being singled out.

"Oh, one more thing, ma'am. I'm told that Mr. Harper-Symth will arrive by helicopter around three. The pad is at the north end of the property."

Joy figured that was just like Jamie, he would arrive in a whirlwind.

As she walked through the suite, she noticed that great attention had been paid to the décor. Southern California's soft, warm colors made the room feel welcoming and almost "toasty." The furniture, a superb blend of tailored 1940s Hollywood Regency and European classics, was exquisite. Decorative wallpapers and fabric-covered panels, many with hand-painted designs, accented the artful floor inlays and wall-to-wall carpeting. Pillows abounded, and the lighting added to the romance of the space.

Joy sat on the huge California King and was moved. She thought, *I could do a whole line of clothing inspired by this place. Yeah, maybe I will.*

—— 🐦 ——

Joy relaxed on the sun-kissed terrace as the California sun warmed her body. The surroundings reminded her not of New York, but of Portugal. She recalled her last visit over two years ago at Christmas, when they celebrated her birthday. She was met at the airport by her folks, who brought flowers, as is the European custom.

"Oh, Mama, it's so wonderful to see you!" "*Sim, minha querida filha*. Yes, my darling daughter. It is wonderful to see you too."

"And Papa, you look so good. Are you well?"

"Very well, dear, and even better now that you are here. We have a lot planned for you."

Mother and daughter had embraced and walked arm in arm through the airport toward the baggage area. As they reached the conveyor belt, two giggling teenage girls approached.

"Oh, Miss Northrup, is that really you? You look just like your picture in *Vogue.*"

"It is her," answered the other girl. "May we have your autograph? I'd be so happy to have it."

Within a minute or two, a larger group of "celebrity seekers" surrounded Joy and her family. A couple of paparazzi appeared out of nowhere, and soon more curious Portuguese travelers stopped to see who was causing the commotion. A couple of armed airport *polícia* noticed and scurried to investigate. They broke up the crowd, noticed who was at the center, and went a bit goggle-eyed.

"Allow me, Miss Nordstrom. I'm Sergeant Camarata, and my partner here, Officer Luz, would be happy to escort you. We don't want these locals disturbing your visit."

"No, that won't be necessary," Joy replied.

But, not heeding her declination, the two *policiais*, one grabbing her bags, led her through customs and to the airport exit. Joy and her parents followed closely behind, trying to keep up with their expeditious escort. "May we call you a motor escort?"

"Absolutely not," Joy responded. "We'll be just fine. Thank you for your help."

"No problem, *senhora*. It was our pleasure. You know, you are a *celebridade* here in Portugal. And it was our honor to meet you." The sergeant clicked his heels together and kissed Joy's hand.

On the ride home, Joy felt utterly foolish. "Mama, I'm sorry for such a fuss. Those *policiais* were completely over the top."

Joy's father looked into the rearview mirror and replied, "Well, Joy, maybe you don't realize this, but you are a big deal in Portugal. Many Portuguese are very proud of you and follow you like soccer stars. Mama and I are treated specially when we go to restaurants, and we hear people whisper, '*São os pais da Joy*' … 'That's Joy's parents.'"

"No, not really. Oh, God!"

"Yes, but we don't mind. In fact, Mama gets extra dressed up when we go out, just in case someone recognizes her."

Joy sighed and thought, *Even here!*

The recollection gave her pause. *I must phone Mama.* But before she could pick up the phone, it rang.

"Hello?"

"Hello, Miss Nordstrom, it's Josh, your houseman. I have a delivery for you, would it be all right if I bring it now, or would you like to wait?"

"No, now is fine. And thank you, Josh."

Josh arrived as if he'd been jet-propelled. He rolled in a cart with a mammoth arrangement of orchids and tropical flowers. "If I must say, Miss Nordstrom, it is one of the loveliest bouquets. The delivery guy said these flowers were flown in from Hawaii and that when the florist heard the arrangement was for you, she outdid herself."

Josh placed the vase on the credenza, stepped back, and took another look at the flowers. "Yeah, they are beautiful, but I must say, no, not as beautiful as you."

Josh blushed, realizing he was overstepping once again.

"Thank you. You are too kind."

Joy stepped onto the terrace, where the sun was sinking low, painting the California sky in shades of pink and gold that mirrored the soft hues of the room behind her. She leaned against the railing, the cool evening breeze brushing her face as she gazed at the beautiful gardens. Taking a deep breath, she felt the weight of uncertainty pressing against her chest. Where was all this leading? Was Jamie a fleeting chapter in her story, or could he be the one to rewrite her destiny, a spark that would ignite a lasting transformation and fill her life with the passion and allure she'd always yearned for? She sensed she knew the answer, and it was yes. As the last rays of sunlight faded into a brilliant pink horizon, she closed her eyes and let the question linger unanswered. She understood her fate was yet to be unveiled.

CHAPTER 31

❦

A Lifetime of Me

The helicopter dipped toward the big white H, but the veranda guests barely looked up, convinced they were more important than whoever had arrived. Jamie peered out the window, anticipating his rendezvous with Joy, though his eyes lingered on the manicured grounds below. His thoughts slid back to the night they first made love. For Joy, it had been a profound act of surrender; she wasn't the type to engage in intimacy casually. For her, it was about connection, an emotional fusion, the potential for a lifelong commitment, and an honest, meaningful relationship. She wanted what her parents had: a love built on respect, permanence, and a lifelong bond.

Concepts like that were alien to Jamie. His world revolved entirely around himself. Women, to him, were little more than fleeting diversions, vehicles to scratch a momentary itch, discarded as thoughtlessly as a used condom. And deep down, he knew that if Joy ever discovered who he truly was, his selfishness, his secrets, she would leave him without hesitation.

But Jamie's ego, colossal and unyielding, fed by rampant narcissism, justified everything. Having the most beautiful woman in the world on his arm and in his bed validated his sense of entitlement. He was Jamie, after all. Why shouldn't he have it all?

Joy found herself, slowly but surely, imagining a future with Jamie. She genuinely enjoyed his company, and his lifestyle blended effortlessly with hers, glamorous, star-studded, and undeniably public. Someone with less confidence might have been overwhelmed by her newfound fame, but Jamie wasn't. He moved through her world with ease, never overshadowed, never shrinking. Maybe, just maybe, this was turning into something, something called love. The very thing Joy had always hoped to find.

Jamie was in love, too. He loved it when they arrived at a restaurant or party, and his contemporaries gave him the thumbs up, the unspoken "Way to go, Jamie; you got the trophy ... first prize ... the best of the best." He loved Joy's unparalleled beauty and the power he felt, knowing she was his whenever he wanted. On some level, he even relished his control over their relationship, the ease with which he could end it with barely a second thought. This was who Jamie truly was. Joy was for now, but deep down, he knew there would always be another "next."

Lately, however, he had a nagging feeling. He knew Joy was the kind of woman who valued relationships over things, permanence over fleeting partying, and sincerity over superficial charm. She sought depth. Unlike so many of his nefarious exploits, Joy was no dummy. She was smart and savvy, which meant he had to be on his toes if he wanted to keep her. But keeping her did not include marriage, and if push came to shove Jamie would do all he could to vacate that as a possibility.

Jamie couldn't shake the fear that sooner or later, she might see through the carefully constructed façade he had spent a lifetime perfecting. And when and if that time came, like all narcissists, he had a plan. One that took care Jamie, a hurtful, devious, but effective plan carried with him just in case.

Moments later, a golf cart zipped up to the pad, collecting the one and only Jamie with all the fanfare he believed he deserved.

A soft knock on the door woke Joy from a rare nap. "May I come in?" Joy sprang from the king's side bed and rushed into Jamie's arms. "Of course." A lingering embrace ended as Jamie pulled away to survey the room. He knew it well but did not let on. "Great room, huh?"

"Beautiful, feels like home."

"Well, it's ours for the next few days ... enjoy, sweetheart."

The couple dined in the room, watched old movies, and made love. As the weekend ended, Jamie noticed that Joy was a little circumspect. He'd seen that mood before with many of his paramours; it always came just before the big "Where do we go from here?"

Joy packed her Louis Vuitton roller bag, carefully folding every item. She stopped, looked down, then over to where Jamie sat reading the morning papers.

"Jamie, I was thinking."

Jamie instantly knew what was coming, it wasn't the words but the aura that hung over the room. He just sensed what was next.

"What, Joy?"

"Well, you know how much you mean to me. Ever since I've been in your life, my world has been centered around you. Oh, don't get me wrong, I don't mind that, but sometimes..."

Jamie, now standing behind her, planted a little kiss on her long, graceful neck, just above the heart-shaped birthmark. "Sometimes what?" he asked.

"Sometimes I feel like you love *what* I am more than *who* I am," Joy admitted softly. "And when we make love, it feels more like conquest than intimacy."

Jamie stiffened. "You don't like the way we make love?"

"You're wonderful, Jamie. But do you mean it?"

"Joy, I don't know what you're talking about. Of course I mean it, I worship you; you know that."

Joy smiled. She was savvy enough to know that Jamie's ego was what it was, but she also believed that love could change everything, and she was on her way to making an honest man of him.

"Worship, that's quite a compliment. But seriously, what part of me are you worshiping, my body or my soul? There's a difference."

Jamie didn't want to continue this conversation. It was too close and personal, and besides, it would lead to nothing but disaster ... he knew this from experience.

Jamie was prepared for moments like this, and it was time to implement his plan. It would change the conversation and move the needle. "Stop, Joy, stop. Look, I really do love you. And here, this proves it."

Jamie reached over, opened his briefcase, which hung on the back of a chair, and pulled out a small, worn leather box. It looked almost ancient, as if centuries old.

He reached over and pulled Joy close. "Look, I'm not very good at something like this, never done it before, but I'd like you to have this." Jamie opened the box. It contained a diamond ring.

"It was my great-great-grandmother's engagement ring, and I'd like you to have it. It comes with a lifetime of me." Jamie had practiced that line in case he needed it, and he was particularly pleased to pull it off so authentically.

Joy allowed Jamie to slip the ring onto her finger. Although the gesture was exciting, she was a bit taken aback. Most men would drop to one knee and ask "the question," but his casual "I'd like you to have it" felt less than genuine. Given Jamie's ego, bending the knee, even for the woman he was proposing to, might have been too much to expect. Joy held her hand up high to admire it. "It's amazing, and you said it was your great-great-grandmother's?"

"Yes, in the family forever. And now it's yours to wear, to become a part of my family."

Joy admired the stunning piece, angling it to catch the light. The vintage style was timeless, and for an antique, it was remarkably well-preserved and in amazing condition. The large, table-cut diamond at the center gleamed with understated brilliance, framed by smaller stones that sparkled like tiny stars.

Joy, in almost a whisper, said, "Jamie, I have never seen a ring quite like this." "That's because it's a one-of-a-kind piece, commissioned by my great-great-grandfather from Cartier centuries ago. And now it's yours." "Are you sure, Jamie? You know this will be a life-changing move for you ... for both of us."

For a moment, Jamie hesitated, the weight of his insincerity pressing against the edges of his already fragile conscience. He glanced away, a flicker of shame crossing his face, before he forced himself to remember the ultimate justification for everything: Jamie comes first, what Jamie wants, Jamie gets. He looked back at her.

"Yes," he said, the single word carrying all the conviction he could muster.

CHAPTER 32

Que Serà, Serà

What?" Cynthia couldn't believe her ears. "Shut up! Engaged?"

"Yeah, Cyn, it happened in LA."

"To whom? Not that playboy, what's-his-face... Jamie?"

"He's not a playboy; he's really quite different from what you think."

"Are you kidding? More women have seen his equipment than a dermatologist has seen zits. His reputation is infamous!"

"No, no, Cynthia, he's different now. He loves me, and I think I've finally found the love I've been looking for. He's different from the kind of guy I thought I'd want, but he's exciting and fun, and underneath that bravado, he's a nice guy. At least... I believe he is."

"Is he good in bed?"

"Cyn, why does it always come down to that with you?"

"Well, is there anything else? So, is he? I heard from one of my friends who went out with him that he's... very well-equipped."

"Stop. Can't you be serious for just a moment?"

"I am."

Joy changed the subject. "Besides being right for me, we're going to have a wonderful life together. He's going to give up his 'high life' and settle down."

Cynthia scoffed and thought, *Yeah, sure, just like I would.*

Joy continued, "We spoke of his fabulous family estate in Wales. And maybe even settling down there and having a normal life, maybe even raising some kids. I can continue my career remotely, and he has business and interests all over Europe and the world."

"Sounds like a fairy tale, castle and all."

Joy, not missing the sarcasm, ignored the comment. "And being in Europe, I'll be near my folks. They're getting on now, and Dad isn't that well."

"Oh, I'm sorry to hear about your dad. But seriously, Joy, are you sure? And more importantly, is he? Did you ever think he might be scamming you?"

"Scamming? No. He gave me a fabulous family heirloom ring. It was his great-great-grandmother's engagement ring, a Cartier."

"Now you're talking. How big? Did you get it appraised?"

"Really, Cyn, are you serious ... appraised? That's ridiculous. It's a family piece. It even came in an old box."

Joy glanced at the diamond as it caught the light. It was beautiful, no doubt about that. Maybe even too beautiful, she thought, like something out of a catalog. But it didn't matter, it was his family's, and that's what counted. Or at least, it should.

"Well, good luck, sweetie. Is there a date? I need to make sure I'm available, that is to say, if I'm invited."

"You're invited, don't worry. How could I get married without a maid of honor? As far as the date, I'm not sure when or where. Jamie is so busy all the time and jumps from country to country. But we'll sort it out."

"Right. So where are you now?"

"I just finished up in LA and will head to New York in the morning. I can't wait to tell Mrs. Campanella and Davis. They'll be shocked."

"I'll bet. Who wouldn't be? Everyone will be. I can see the headlines now: The most beautiful woman bags the world's most eligible bachelor."

"Oh, I almost forgot. Don't tell anyone about this. Jamie wants to keep it quiet until he gets home and speaks with his family. You know, these old families, they have all this 'stuff,' traditions and protocol."

"But you're telling your neighbor friends."

"Oh, don't worry, they'll keep it under wraps. I trust them."

"What about your parents and Bernie?"

"God, Bernie. He's going to have a fit when he finds out his 'little cupcake' is tying the knot. But I'll deal with him. I'm going to call my parents too. Jamie would have liked to ask my father's permission, but that was too complicated given his business travel and commitments.

The call ended with Cynthia's heartfelt promise. "Look, babe, I know you're a lot smarter than me. You've built an amazing life and career, so don't throw it all away to live in some fairy tale with Dr. Jekyll and Mr. Hyde. But if you're absolutely certain this is what you want, I've got your back. And if that SOB so much as thinks about breaking your heart, I'll turn that rooster into a hen."

It was late afternoon when George picked up Joy at JFK and drove her directly to Christopher Street.

"Welcome home, Miss Nordstrom."

"Thanks, George."

As she gazed around the old neighborhood, her eyes lingered on the worn sign above her door: 100 Christopher St. The memories flooded back with every crack in the concrete, every chip off the painted doors, long ignored since Mr. Campanella had died. She took a deep breath and could smell the homemade bread made by Joe, the baker, just on the corner. She smiled to herself as she visualized Mrs. Campanella carrying tray after tray of cholesterol-laden delicacies for Davis and her to share. She had always wanted a fairy tale and maybe was now getting one with Jamie, but now she wondered, at what cost?

Her warm, cozy apartment on the second floor, the one that had soothed her after long, hard days and welcomed her after lonely weeks away, would soon be a part of her past. The comfortable furniture that felt like an embrace, a bit battered but loved, would no longer be her sanctuary.

Before she could settle in, there was a thunderous knock on the door.

"Who is it?"

"It's me, Mrs. Campanella!"

Joy hurried to the door, opening it wide. "Come in, come in!"

Mrs. Campanella wrapped her arms around Joy, kissing both her cheeks. "*Così bella!* Look at you, Joy. We've missed you, Davis, Noush, and me. But you're home now."

Joy laughed, holding onto her hand. "I've missed you too. You never change."

"Change? Pah! Look at me. I'm an old goat but never mind that. Look, I brought you something." She handed over a tin, and Joy knew instantly what it was. "Oh no, you didn't!" She opened it to find perfectly arranged pizzelle. "You know I can't resist these."

"Then don't! You look too skinny. Eat one. Now."

Joy took a delicate waffle-shaped cookie, biting into its anise-flavored goodness. "God, these are heavenly. Thank you."

"They were Mr. Campanella's favorite, too." She paused, dabbing at the corner of her eye. "He loved everything, you know. It showed."

"He will be missed, but don't worry, Mrs. C. Davis and I will always care for you."

Joy hesitated, but finally said, "Can you keep a secret?"

Mrs. Campanella tilted her head, curious. "That depends. If it's the kind of secret that could save someone's life, you must tell it. But if it's not, then maybe it's best left unsaid."

Joy laughed nervously. "I got engaged."

Mrs. Campanella's eyes widened. "Engaged? To who?"

"Jamie Harper-Smyth."

"Harper-Smyth? British? Pah! They're cold fish."

Joy smirked. "Not Jamie. Trust me."

"The ring, let me see the ring. I hope it's worthy of you and that this Jamie guy didn't cheap out with a chip or two."

Joy proudly held her hand up high for Mrs. Campanella to see.

"Wow, that's no chip."

"Hardly, it's a family heirloom; it belonged to his great-great-grandmother.

The two women savored the moment, and as Mrs. Campanella spoke of Naples, Italy and her own engagement, Joy felt a pang. She hoped that, years from now, she would look back as lovingly as Mrs. Campanella.

"So, this is big news. Have you told Davis yet?"

"No, not yet; I haven't seen him. I just arrived. I'll go down later and see if he's at home."

"He's always at home unless he's at the gym or burying some poor Marine soul." Mrs. Campanella picked up the tin of cookies and passed it over to Joy. "Here, have another one; you could afford to put on a few pounds…. You're practically a skeleton. In Italy, they'd be force-feeding you."

Joy laughed, taking another cookie, but as she bit into the delicate pizzelle, she realized it didn't taste quite the same. It wasn't just the cookie, it was everything. The sense of comfort, the feeling of being right where she belonged. These were the things she'd be giving up, even if she didn't want to admit it. She glanced at Mrs. Campanella, whose warm smile said she understood more than Joy was ready to say out loud.

It was later, after Mrs. Campanella left and she had settled in, she decided to visit Davis. Joy knocked lightly on Davis's door.

"Davis, it's me, Joy, are you home?"

When he opened the door, his face lit up with his familiar, quiet smile.

"You're back," he said, stepping aside to let her in. Noush was beside herself, her tail wagging out of control like a metronome on overdrive, thumping against the doorframe as she tried to decide between jumping on Joy or circling her in delighted confusion. Joy laughed and crouched down, letting the excited dog smother her face with sloppy kisses.

"Yes, I'm back, for a little while," she replied, suddenly nervous. She hadn't planned how to tell him but knew he had to be told. And yet, she wondered why she should be nervous about telling Davis this or, for that matter, anything. He was her friend unconditionally and always would be. But she had a sinking feeling that, for one reason or another, telling him of her engagement didn't quite feel right.

He poured them both their favorite coffee, the one from Portugal, a ritual as natural as breathing, and finally sensed something. "Something's different."

She always marveled at how Davis had instincts far beyond the average person, like a sixth sense, or more like a finely-tuned radar, picking up signals that others couldn't even sense. It wasn't just intuition; it was a quiet, almost uncanny ability to read people, situations, and even the spaces they inhabited as if he could see the world through layers invisible to everyone else. She often wondered if this was something he was born with or later acquired as he coped with life.

Joy hesitated. Not knowing how to even approach what she wanted to tell him and confused as to why it actually mattered, she decided to just blurt it out. "I got engaged," she said softly.

He paused, his face unreadable for a moment, before nodding. "To Jamie?"

"Yes."

Davis took a sip of coffee. "Then I'm happy for you," he said, and somehow, it sounded entirely genuine, after all, why wouldn't it? He was her friend, not her boyfriend, and they'd always wanted the best for each other, whatever that might be. Yet, there was something heartbreakingly bittersweet in his tone, and Joy thought she caught a flicker of something in his expression, gone before she could name it. She rationalized that, as with many friendships, when one person moves on to choose a partner, the other might feel a sense of loss or even jealousy. It wasn't unusual for friends to worry that a new relationship might change what they shared.

When the friends finally said good night, Joy paused at the door. "You know, Davis, this doesn't change anything. We will always be best friends, and I will always be there for you. I know you will always be there for me, too. You'll see."

Davis lingered for a long moment, then slightly nodded. "Yeah," he said, his voice steady but unreadable. "I guess we'll see."

Joy smiled and gave Davis a sweet peck on the cheek, as was their tradition. But as she stepped into the dimly lit hallway, a strange sense of unease settled over her. Maybe it was exhaustion, the weight of travel, and big decisions catching up with her.

But as she turned back for one last glance, just as Davis's door swung closed, she caught a glimpse of his face. He didn't look sad, but there was something else, something quieter, something she couldn't quite put her finger on.

Slowly, Joy walked the two flights up to 2A. She closed the door behind her, pressed her back against it, and exhaled slowly. The apartment felt familiar yet different. The scent of fresh pizzelle lingered in the air, but even that comfort seemed distant now, like a memory she was already leaving behind.

Maybe Cynthia was right. Maybe Davis was right. Maybe, deep down, she knew it too. Joy decided to take Mrs. Campanella's philosophy:

Que serà, serà.

CHAPTER 33

❦

Pick a Date,
Any Date

It had been a week or so after Joy's return from LA when the caller ID on her phone flashed "Bernie." Joy swallowed hard. She hadn't found the time, or maybe it was the courage, to tell Bernie about Jamie and the engagement. Maybe she would let it go to voicemail? But she knew she had to face the music eventually, and it was her nature never to procrastinate.

"Hello."

"Joy, Cupcake, it's Bernie, your Bernie."

"Of course, I only have one Bernie." *Thank God.*

"So, Cupcake, you're thinking I'm dead?"

There he goes again, talking in riddles like only Bernie could. "Dead?"

"Yeah, dead. After all, why else wouldn't you call me and tell me?"

"Tell you what?"

"Oh, sweetie, don't play games with Uncle Bernie."

Joy realized that somehow, someway, Bernie had found out her little secret. She decided to fess up.

Nonchalantly, Joy responded, "Oh, you mean the engagement?"

"No, I mean that the world is freezing over, the planet has stopped rotating, and all politicians have quit lying ... Of course, I mean the engagement!"

"Well, I was getting around to telling you ..."

Bernie interrupted, "When? After the whole world knows? After it's on the signs in Times Square? Or when the Queen throws a party for everyone but me? Is that when?"

"Come on, Bernie, you're being overly dramatic. And besides, it's a secret."

"Honeybun, there are no secrets, especially from Bernie. So, spill it. I already know the what, but I want the when, who, and why."

"It's Jamie Harper-Smyth."

"Jamie Haprer-Smyth! The one who can't keep his pants on? The billionaire playboy? *That* Jamie Harper-Smyth?"

"Bernie, he's not a playboy anymore. That's the old Jamie. He's changed, and we're going to have a wonderful life."

"Oh yeah? And Uncle Bernie's getting his first communion. Please, it's *me* you're talking to." Bernie paused to reload. "And don't tell me you're quitting and letting that playboy ruin your career."

"Hold on, Bernie. First, you don't own me, nor do you decide if I get married or have a million babies. Further, I'm engaged, not married yet. When and if we decide to have children, it's our business, not yours. Do you understand *that, Cupcake?*"

"Calm down, sweetheart. It's Uncle Bernie, just looking out for you."

Looking out for me, Joy thought. He means himself, as usual. "I think you mean looking out for 'us.'"

"All right, all right. Sure, I have a dog in this race. But I also have strong, enduring feelings for you and concerns about your well-being. Uncle Bernie wants the best for you. I hope you know that."

Joy snapped back, "Look, Uncle Bernie knows that what's best for me is even better for Uncle Bernie."

Joy sighed, pinching the bridge of her nose. Bernie was infuriating, nosy, and relentless, but he cared. That was the thing about Bernie. He always cared too much, which both annoyed and comforted her. It was nice to know someone was in her corner, even if they were swinging wildly with no sense of boundaries. Still, his meddling made her wonder how much she really wanted to deal with everyone else's opinions about her choices, especially now.

The conversation calmed down after the first few cantankerous minutes. Joy filled Bernie in on the details, hoping it would hold him over for a while. But as always, Bernie left her feeling both reassured and a little on edge. She set her phone down and glanced at her growing stack of bridal magazines. Her phone buzzed again; it was Cynthia.

"Joy, it's Cyn."

"Hello, Cyn. How are you, and where are you?"

"I'm good. I'm in Estonia, a town called Tallinn. It's gorgeous. Medieval and lots of men."

"Medieval men?"

"No, jerk, the buildings. They look like a storybook. The place is some kinda UNESCO World Heritage site. You'd love it."

"I'll bet. What are you doing there?"

"Hunting."

"Hunting? I thought you hated guns and killing things."

"Oh, sweetheart, it's not that kind of hunting. I'm hunting for Vikings." Cynthia purred, her voice dripping with mischief. "You know that Prince Charming I married? Well, I'm no longer living in a fairy tale. Turns out he likes wine more than women and spends most nights gazing..."

"Gazing? Star gazing?" Joy teased.

"No, honey, *bowl* gazing. The man couldn't hold his vino. Such a wimp. So, I took my tiara, a Bentley, and a few million and set off for a little hunting in Estonia."

Joy rolled her eyes, laughing despite herself. "You're incorrigible. Do they even know what they're up against?"

"Honey, they don't stand a chance."

Joy changed the subject: "I'm up to my neck with wedding plans. Jamie insists on a small private affair, maybe at some out-of-the-way island with just a few family and friends."

"He probably owns the island."

Joy chuckled. "I don't think so, but with him, you never know."

"I haven't read or heard about the engagement. Is it still a secret?"

"Yeah, at least to the general public. Jamie is trying to figure out when would be the best time and place."

"Why?"

Joy thought, Good question. It puzzled her why Jamie was so adamant about this. He said it had to do with business and timing, but it didn't quite add up in her mind.

"Business, he says."

"Crying out loud, is he marrying you or a balance sheet? What's with him? He better not be stringing you along. You know what will happen to him if he is."

"Cyn, he's just so busy. He loves what he does and is so good at it. He was written up in *The Wall Street Journal* last week, an amazing article. He promises once things settle down, we'll have lots of time to be together and travel."

"Well, he better be careful and treat you right, or old Cyn will get that machete out and keep my promise. Well, honey, I gotta run. Lars is waiting in the hot tub. I gotta rush and undress. Bye-bye."

The phone clicked off, leaving Joy looking at a blank screen. Cynthia's words, though sharp-edged, struck a nerve. Joy sighed, trying to shake the unease. Plans, she reminded herself. There were still so many plans to make.

—— ❧ ——

Jamie arrived back in New York for the weekend. He was exhausted but managed to muster up enough energy to take Joy to the opera. On the way home, Claude drove through the park as Joy rested her head on Jamie's broad shoulders.

"Honey," she began, "I'm picking out invitations tomorrow. Can you come with me?"

Jamie, who was half-dozing, wasn't sure what she said. "What?"

"Can you come tomorrow to pick out invitations?"

"Invitations? To what?"

Joy wasn't sure whether to be hurt or if he was just kidding. *She chose kidding.* "You know, the wedding."

"Oh, of course, the wedding. What time?"

"Well, I have an appointment at Tiffany's at two."

"Two? No, I'm tied up."

Joy thought a moment. "I can change it; what time would work for you?"

Jamie snarled, behavior previously unseen by Joy: "No time; I'm tied up all day, in fact, all this week."

Joy forced a smile, hiding her disappointment. She knew he was busy. His work always came first, but tonight it felt as if their wedding wasn't even on his list of priorities. Was this just how things were going to be?

Jamie, realizing that he had stepped on his own words, made a suggestion: "Look, babe, you know how tied up I am, but why don't you go get some sample invitations, and we could look them over together at home?"

Joy smiled and thought, *That's my man.* "Great idea."

Jamie then added, "Hey, I have another idea. You have such beautiful handwriting; why do you have to deal with Tiffany's? Just get some elegant-looking stationery and handwrite them. I think that would be classy."

"Handwrite them? That'd be a lot of work."

"Yeah, but we're keeping it small, so there shouldn't be too many, and just think how personal that will be. Everybody sends printed invites; ours will be different. And then you don't have to bother anybody at Tiffany's."

It was something in the tone of his voice, even though the idea wasn't a bad one, that felt ... well, not right. What caught her was "bother anybody at Tiffany's."

Joy wanted to please Jamie, but something in his tone lingered, an undercurrent that didn't feel right. Still, she pushed it aside and said, "Well, okay, I'll go by Greenwich Letterpress. They have great stuff, all locally made by artisans."

"Perfect, Joy. You are always perfect, especially the way you look." Jamie leaned over, blew into Joy's hair, and tickled her neck with his tongue. Joy melted into her usually self-complacency, at least when it came to Jamie, who demolished all her defenses with his charm.

"So, honey, we have that figured, now how about the date?" I can't do invitations until we pick the date.

"Of course we can't. But I'm incredibly busy and want to wait until after I close on some of these deals. Then my mind will be clear, and I can sit back and enjoy all this planning. So, for now, why don't you just pick everything out? Since you will be hand-writing them, you can do them anytime."

The car went silent for the rest of their ride home, the soft hum of the engine filling the space between them. Outside, Central Park glowed in the evening light, the bare branches of winter trees casting long shadows on the frosted ground. Jamie scrolled through his phone, oblivious, while Joy stared out the window, her thoughts as tangled as the branches overhead.

Claude dropped them off in front of the townhouse and headed toward the garage as Joy and Jamie climbed the lime-stone staircase, unlocked the massive door, and went in, ending the night with a kiss at the side of his massive four-poster antique bed.

Joy lay awake for a few more minutes, her gaze fixed on the ceiling. They hadn't picked a date or a place. She told herself it was fine; there was still plenty of time. But deep down, she wondered if time was the one thing they didn't have.

CHAPTER 34

———— ❦ ————

Invisible Eyes

It was early for Joy, about six-thirty a.m., as she sat in the dining room of Jamie's townhouse. She was up early because she needed to put some finishing touches on a design line she was preparing to launch next month.

"Good morning, Miss Nordstrom," Lou Ann, the house-keeper, greeted her. "Can I bring you some more coffee or something else?"

The question caught Joy a bit off guard because she was so engrossed in her screen. "Oh, thank you, Lou Ann. I'm fine."

"As you wish, ma'am."

Joy had spent the last few nights at the mansion. She looked around: the antique sideboard, massive Palladian windows, and enormous crystal chandelier that hung above the table. The table sat fourteen, and at each end, a host chair waited to be occupied by the head of the household. It was rumored that these antique chairs once graced the summer villa of Pope Pius XI and was sold in a Milan auction for seven hundred thousand dollars after mysteriously disappearing. Two silver candelabras, placed equidistantly on the long oak dining table, were undoubtedly family heirlooms. The ceiling was painted with a baroque scene of lifelike cherubs and mythological figures.

Some place, she thought. But in her heart of hearts, she preferred having her coffee at the shaky old drop-leaf table that sat in her kitchen on Christopher Street. And, of course, she favored Davis's special blend of coffee over whatever this was despite it being dispensed from a sterling silver coffee pot.

An email notification popped up from the London office of the company that had purchased World Couture from her.

"London. Again," she muttered.

She read with interest the long, detailed message, which required a "return receipt" indicating the message had been received and read.

"Good morning, sweetheart." It was Jamie, ready for his day fighting the fights that made him a billionaire. He leaned over and kissed Joy's neck, his favorite spot, just above her birthmark.

Joy looked up and saw what every woman would die to have: a dashing man, impeccably dressed in a tailored suit, fit to perfection.

She smiled inwardly. *God, he's handsome. So tall and trim and youthful. But even more so, talented and accomplished. The whole package.*

"Good morning to you too."

Jamie noticed that Joy seemed distracted despite the lovely smile and warm snuggle she gave him as he kissed her.

"What's up? Looks like you had some bad news," he asked, sitting down across from her.

"No, not bad news. It's just the London people. They want me to come over for some PR work and attend their board's Christmas Gala."

Jamie feigned delight. "Oh, sounds like real fun. I'll bet you can't wait. You must be thrilled."

"Thrilled isn't quite the word," Joy replied, turning her laptop toward him so he could read the message. "I don't know why they even need me to attend. I sold them the company. Aren't they supposed to be running it now?"

"Joy, don't you get it? They don't want you; they want *'the most beautiful woman in the world.'* Unfortunately, that *is* you, the face of the brand."

Joy was clearly displeased. "This couldn't be a worse time. I've got hard deadlines to finish some design projects, the wedding to plan, and traveling this time of the year is a nightmare. Jetting off to London isn't in the schedule."

Jamie sipped his coffee thoughtfully. "It's just a few days, isn't it?"

"Probably three, maybe four, depending. But it might mean I don't get back until Christmas Eve." Suddenly, she had a thought. "Hey, Jamie, I have a great idea," Joy blurted out suddenly.

"And that is ...?"

"Look, you have lots of business over there. You come with me. And we'll take a couple of extra days, we could make a quick stop in Braga and meet my parents, and then you can bring me up to see Wales. After all, it will be my, no, *our*, home not too long from now."

"Branwen?"

"Branwen? Is that what you call the place? Maybe my folks could join us?"

Jamie smiled to himself. *You know, it's ironic, but the name Branwen is the Welsh goddess of love and beauty.* He hesitated, wondering how he could gracefully get out of the idea. But once Joy hatched a plan, there was no backing out.

"Yeah, let's go to Branwen," he said after a pause, his smile edged with forced optimism. "I can't wait to see it."

"I don't know, Joy, I'm as busy as you are … and …"

Joy hesitated, her annoyance surfacing. "I like the idea. And after all, it's going to be our home."

Sensing Jamie's reluctance, she pressed, "Or is there something you don't want me to see there until it's too late?"

"Too late? What does that mean?" he asked, his brow furrowing.

"Too late, like until after we're married, that too late."

Jamie pulled out his phone and scrolled through his calendar. "I'm not sure…"

Joy's eyebrows shot up. "It's settled. I'm going to London, and then, if you don't want to come with me, I'll go see Branwen by myself. Or better yet, I'll call my friend Cynthia, and she'll come with me."

Jamie felt the trap closing. The last thing he wanted was for Joy to show up in Wales without him, and even worse, with Cynthia, that "crazy broad" capable of who knew what. There were a dozen reasons why that idea stank, and none of them he cared to explain. And besides, the last thing he wanted to do was meet her parents, much less drag them up to Branwen.

He decided to make lemonade out of lemons. "Great idea. I'll make it happen. It'll be just you and me, let's do the parent thing another time, after the first of the year. But we'll be off to Branwen." Silently, he sighed, *And God help me.*

Joy jumped up and gave him a sloppy kiss. "Thanks, honey. I'm so excited." Then she smiled mischievously. "And I'll let my folks know we will see them after the New Year. Let's hope I don't get lost in one of those drafty halls before we even get married."

Jamie laughed, nervously, "I'll make sure to keep a map handy."

Like always, Jamie changed the plans. He explained it to Joy over dinner at their favorite neighborhood restaurant, Corky's.

"Pass the balsamic," Jamie said nonchalantly. "Don't you just love this food? It's my treat occasionally, but it's back to the gym for an extra hour of torture."

Joy, picking at her salad, one that Corky himself had created for the diet-conscious, nodded. "Yeah, it looks great, but I'm sticking to salad. It's delicious and requires less gym time."

Joy glanced around. There were lots of reasons Corky's was their go-to spot. First, it was just a five-minute walk from Jamie's townhouse, perfect for a last-minute meal. It was also charming, with its simple but authentic bistro design, white starched table-cloths with little oil lamps glistening and the ever-present bud vase holding today's fresh flower.

The light was low, and the ambiance radiated friendliness. And, of course, there was the food. Corky was a third-generation restaurateur, trained by his father and grandfather, both French.

But tonight, Joy had this eerie feeling, one she'd had before, like someone was watching them. It had happened a few other times, and once even here at Corky's. Oh, sure, she was used to being stared at. Pretty much everywhere she went, people stared, even gawked. But this felt different. Perhaps it was her "Joynar," as Cynthia called it. Ever since she was a kid, she'd had it, a sort of internal alarm. It warned her when something wasn't right in her immediate area or sometimes when certain people weren't to be trusted. Maybe it was a gut feeling or just an advanced woman's intuition, but whatever it was, it had saved her a few times from making the wrong move or the wrong choice. Cynthia called it "Joynar," but Joy thought it was more a mix of common sense and street smarts.

Seated at their usual corner table, Joy pulled her wrap tighter over her shoulders, as if to prevent invisible eyes from seeing her. Her gaze flicked around the restaurant. But she saw nothing, nothing unusual.

"Cold?" Jamie asked, noticing her pulling her wrap tighter, his voice interrupting her thoughts.

"No," Joy said quickly, her fingers still gripping the edges of her wrap. "Just... thinking."

What Joy was thinking about was that horrible incident in front of her apartment when some stranger had tried to accost her, the night Noush had scared the intruder away. She had never told Jamie about it, probably because it was a non-event once it happened.

Jamie leaned back in his chair, studying her. "About what?"

"Nothing," she replied, forcing a smile that didn't quite reach her eyes. "Work, the wedding, you know."

"Joy, you're a terrible liar. What's really going on?"

"Oh, just one of those days."

The waiter arrived, interrupting them with a practiced smile. "Are we ready for dessert?"

Joy raised her hand and was about to say, "Oh, none for me, but thank you." But before she could speak, out marched Madam Janeen, Corky's mother, holding a tray with the most delicate pear tart.

"Just for you. It's my mother's recipe, one handed down from her mother."

Joy looked at Jamie and then back at Madam Janeen. "It's the gym, bright and early." But the light moment passed as quickly as Madam Janeen returned to her work in the kitchen.

"Okay," Jamie said, leaning forward now. "What's bothering you?"

Picking at the tart on her plate, she hesitated and then asked, "Do you ever get the feeling... like someone's watching you?"

Jamie tilted his head, his expression shifting from curiosity to concern. "What do you mean?"

258

"I don't know. I really can't say. It's just sometimes I get this feeling, like a subliminal message," she said quickly, shaking her head. "It's just … little things. I thought I noticed a man lingering outside the building yesterday. And I got a weird note. It came with flowers at the office, unsigned. Probably nothing, but …"

Jamie, now concerned, took Joy's hand. "You should've told me about this. What did the note say?"

Joy thought back. "Oh, they were red roses, all but one, which was white, and the note …" Joy thought harder. "Something like, *You are mine, Joy. Always.* I didn't want to overreact," she said, shrugging. "It's probably just some fan being overly enthusiastic."

"Fans don't send weird, unsigned notes," Jamie said sharply. "And they don't hang around your building. Does Bernie know about this?"

"Sort of. But you know Bernie. If I tell him too much, he'll have the National Guard at my door and drones flying overhead. He's so dramatic and extreme."

"Yeah, you're probably right about that."

The tension between them hung heavy for a moment. Joy reached for her glass, taking a small sip of wine as she tried to dismiss the unease in her chest.

"I'm probably imagining it," she said finally, her voice softer now. "I've been stressed, Jamie. That's all."

Jamie didn't look convinced.

Joy glanced around the restaurant, half-expecting to see something to validate her concerns. And for a brief moment, she thought she saw someone standing just outside the frosted glass window. A shadow. Then it was gone. But her Joynar told her it hadn't been her imagination.

CHAPTER 35

❦

Duncan Who?

The antique Daimler met the plane just south of Branwen, at a private airport located some six miles from the estate. It was an out-of-the-way airstrip, with little commercial traffic.

Jamie had changed their travel plans at the last minute. So typical of him. They left New York and flew to London via British Airways. Once there, Jamie arranged for a private flight to Wales.

Jamie stepped down the Lear's few steps and stretched out his hand for Joy's. "Careful, Darling."

It was a bitterly cold, December night. The wind ripped across the empty runways like a merciless predator, howling a welcome that felt more like a warning. The deserted tarmac stretched endlessly, devoid of warmth or comfort, surrounded by darkness under a moonless night. Joy shivered and pulled her coat tighter, hoping to keep the cold from seeping into her bones. The wind's eerie whistle was almost like a message that set Joy on edge. Her hopes of a warm and welcoming Wales vanished as she looked around and saw a lot of emptiness.

"Good evening, sir, madam," announced Higgens, the houseman. He had been with the Harper-Smyth family for decades and was as much a part of Branwen as the ancient beams in the great hall or the massive stone lions flanking its entrance. Tall, slim, and seemingly ageless, Higgens belonged to a dying breed, a breed devoted to service. Like his father and his grandfather before him, he was born into the trade and knew no other life. Content and well-cared for, he never even considered other forms of employment.

Jamie extended his hand, shaking Higgens's firmly. "Thanks, Higgens. And this is Miss Nordstrom, Joy."

"Welcome, Miss. May I take your bag?"

Joy smiled and glanced at the car. "I love the car. What is it?"

Jamie smiled nostalgically. "It was my cousins's car, a Daimler. I've kept it all these years. It was part of her estate, and I bought it from her heirs. I never knew her personally, but a lot of folks say we were two peas in a pod. Historians claimed it was once part of the Royal Household and my cousin managed to convince someone to sell it to her when they modernized the fleet. Anyway, it's a collectible."

The gleaming automobile glided effortlessly down the winding Welsh lanes, heading toward the estate. Rolling hills filled with sheep and cattle roamed at will. As they approached the gates, Joy looked out the window and murmured, "So this is my new home?" She had hoped Jamie would say it first, but he never did.

Branwen was an ancient estate that defied imagination, mysterious, majestic, and massive, yet utterly devoid of warmth or hominess. It seemed steeped in myths and shrouded in secrets, a place where every stone and shadow whispered of hidden promises and untold stories. To Joy, it felt like an old mother-in-law turning her nose up at anyone not good enough to marry her son. As the car pulled up to the house, Mrs. Alcot, chief house-keeper, appeared from one of the enormous wooden doors.

"Welcome home, Mr. Harper-Smyth. And welcome, Miss."

"Thank you," Joy replied.

"Look, Joy," Jamie said, "I've got some calls to make. Let Mrs. Alcot show you to your room, then have a look around. I'll catch up with you later." She thought, *My room? Not our room.*

He leaned in, planting a familiar kiss on the long, graceful curve of her neck before disappearing into the dimly lit foyer.

Mrs. Alcot escorted Joy to a room adjoining Jamie's. She called it the Blue Room, though oddly enough, the room wasn't blue. It was more of a misty gray. Joy assumed it might have been blue centuries ago, the color fading over time into what it was now. She then recalled reading that the British aristocracy often did not share sleeping quarters, explaining the separate rooms.

As she unpacked, an uneasy feeling crept into her conscious-ness. Her thoughts drifted back to the flight over. The first-class section had been completely full, every seat occupied. One man had caught her attention. He had walked the aisle near her seat several times, pausing ever so slightly to glance at her.

At first, she brushed it off as a curious fan or celebrity seeker. But this man didn't fit the usual profile. He was rough-looking, dark, and ominous.

Joy shook her head, snapping back to reality. "There I go again, chasing ghosts," she muttered to herself. "It was probably nothing, just my imagination. Cloak-and-dagger delusions." She chuckled softly. "He was probably just a guy with a weak bladder, making frequent trips to the restroom." Ever since Christopher Street, she had been nervous whenever she saw characters like this guy even glancing at her.

Around nine, Joy descended the grand staircase for what Jamie had called a "look-about." The staircase, like everything else in the house, was old, likely part of the original structure, perhaps from the 1600s.

As a designer, Joy was always mindful of fabrics and patterns, and the carpet running up the stairs immediately caught her eye. Woven into it was an intricate design that resembled golden branches twisted together into a rope.

Joy stopped by a large console table and glanced into the ornate mirror hanging above it. She opened her small purse, retrieved her trusty tube of Naked Pink lipstick, and applied a fresh layer. As she leaned closer to the mirror, she caught sight of someone standing behind her. Startled, she turned quickly.

"Oh, hello there. Duncan here, Jamie's best mate," the man said with a charming grin. "Thought I'd pop by and surprise him. He hasn't the foggiest I'm coming. Higgins tipped me off, he's a proper gent, salt of the earth. Always reliable and ready to assist. Known him since I was in short trousers."

Joy took one look at Duncan and thought, God, he's like a double-breasted, British version of Jamie, remarkably handsome, trim, and just as effortlessly charming. He was impeccably dressed and smelled heavenly. Joy couldn't help but notice his hands. His nails were shiny, painted in a clear glossy coat, fresh from a manicure, and his pinky ring was almost exactly like Jamie's: gold, with an embossed family crest.

Before she could say a word, Duncan continued with a confident tone. "Jamie and I go way back, don't you know? Thick as thieves since Eton. Of course, his lot dragged him off to New York for his studies while I stayed behind in London. But we've always kept in touch, as you'd expect, being best mates, and all." Duncan put his hand in his blazer pocket, and continued: "Actually, I've got a little pied-à-terre in New York myself these days. Spend a fair bit of time with Jamie there, when he's not preoccupied with other distractions, naturally."

He glanced at Joy briefly, the look lingering just long enough to make her wonder.

Duncan eventually stopped with the small talk and asked, "And you are ...?"

"I'm Joy, Jamie's fiancée," Joy smiled and replied smoothly.

"Fiancée? As in engaged-to-be married fiancée?" Duncan asked, his tone dripping with surprise.

Joy, too, was taken aback. If this was Jamie's best friend, how could he not know about her, or her about him?

"Yes, fiancée," she said firmly, raising her hand to show him the ring. "See? Engaged."

The look on Duncan's face was hard to describe. It fell somewhere between incredulous and mystified. He seemed to struggle to process the information. Here was this stunning woman, vaguely familiar, perhaps even a celebrity, telling him she was engaged to Jamie, someone he knew as well as himself. They had grown up together, sharing everything, no secrets, no pretenses. Or so he had thought.

Duncan took Joy's hand to examine the ring. "Ah, a beauty, that. Proper bit of antiquity, no doubt. Congrats."

"Thank you," Joy replied. "The ring is a family heirloom, apparently belonging to Jamie's great-great-grandmother. Lady, somebody or other."

"Ah, yes, very Jamie," Duncan said with a knowing smile. "Always one for a bit of heritage. So, Joy," he began, his voice carrying a hint of mockery, "what's it like being engaged to our Jamie? He's ... quite the character, isn't he? Bigger than life ... or at least he thinks so."

Joy hesitated, caught off-guard. "He's ... wonderful. Charming, funny, ambitious, everything I could hope for, really."

"Right. Jamie does have a knack for making people feel special," Duncan said, his tone faintly sardonic. "But tell me, has he shown you his 'adventurous' side yet?"

"Adventurous?" Joy echoed. "What do you mean?

Duncan chuckled softly, turning and strolling toward the window. "Oh, you know ... Jamie's always had a restless spirit. Gets bored silly if things aren't thrilling enough. Loves a bit of excitement and variety." He glanced back at her, his expression unreadable. "When we were younger, it was the usual schoolboy pranks, tying prefects' shoes together, sneaking off to town. But as we grew older, well, let's just say his ... pursuits became a touch more experimental, maybe even a bit untraditional or 'exotic.'"

Joy frowned, sensing an undercurrent to Duncan's words. "Variety? Experimental? Exotic? How so?"

Duncan shrugged casually. "Oh, nothing that everybody else wasn't doing, of course, maybe a tad notched up from the others. Just Jamie being Jamie, always chasing the next exciting thing. Settling for the ordinary was never really his style, you, see?"

Joy forced a laugh though her mind churned. "Well, I like to think I'm not exactly ordinary."

Duncan smiled; his expression was amused. "Oh, of course not, darling, far from it, I'm sure. You're stunning, practically a goddess walking among us mere mortals. Jamie's done well for himself, hasn't he?"

Something in his tone unsettled Joy deeply. A mix of snotty, snobby, and maybe even slightly bitchy. "You don't think he feels that way?"

"Of course he does," Duncan replied quickly, too quickly. "Jamie adores the spotlight and having you on his arm? Well, it's like a crown jewel in his collection, wouldn't you say? Adds a touch of legitimacy if you follow me."

Duncan paused, and looked Joy over, this time closer: "You are the crown jewel, aren't you, Joy?" Again, his words were delivered with a faintly biting edge.

The comment hit Joy in all the wrong places. She forced another smile, her voice tightening. "I'd like to think Jamie values me for more than that."

"Of course, he does, dear, of course, he does. You're lovely." Duncan said smoothly, his tone almost dismissive. "Jamie's many things, but he's no fool. He knows how to keep hold of what matters to him ... for as long as it suits him, anyway.

Joy's pulse quickened. "What exactly are you trying to say, Duncan?"

Duncan's smile softened, and for a fleeting moment, he looked almost regretful. "Nothing at all, Love. Just ... enjoy the ride, Joy. Jamie's never been one for dull moments."

Duncan looked down at his newly polished nails, then met her eyes with a faint smile. "So, you're here for ...?"

"I'm here to see Branwen. It will be our home, Jamie's and mine, after we're married."

"He said that? This is going to be your home?" Duncan asked, his tone tinged with disbelief.

A twinge gripped Joy's stomach as she thought, had he? For a moment, she really wasn't sure he said that exactly.

Joy glanced around, "I must admit, Branwen is a bit over-whelming and living here ... well, it will be something quite different."

"Yes, overwhelming comes to mind, more than you could imagine," Duncan replied knowingly.

Before excusing himself, Duncan glanced at the nearby mirror, casually brushing his hair back into place. "Well then, I'll be off. I'm going to find Jamie, and won't he just love that I've turned up unannounced?"

Joy watched as Duncan disappeared through one of the many doors and down a passageway and muttered to herself, "What a piece of work he is."

Joy's head swirled in thought: *Why wouldn't Jamie ever mention Duncan? And if he's in New York, and they see each other, why haven't I met him? It's strange... maybe Jamie is trying to save me from putting up with this insufferable, self-absorbed, condescending aristocrat.*

She decided to put it aside for now and continue her exploration. Joy soon arrived at the Great Hall. She stopped in her tracks and took in the grandeur.

"The Great Hall ... this must be the soul of the estate," she murmured.

She paused, skimming her fingers across the long runner on an ancient Tudor sideboard. Her gaze wandered up to the towering beams above.

"These beams must have seen centuries of history," she whispered, her attention returning to the tapestry runner beneath her hand. "And this ... still so vivid, as if it was woven yesterday. How does something this old remain so perfectly intact?"

She took a deep breath, suddenly noticing the scent of the room, centuries of wood fires and aging carpets mingling with the undeniable smell of antiquity filled the air. It reminded her of something between a museum and a neglected attic.

Joy smiled faintly, her thoughts wandering. "This old place holds so many secrets ... much like Jamie."

Joy wasn't sure, but she seemed to hear shouting just down the hall. A half-open door allowed light to peek through. Casually, she approached and recognized Jamie's voice. He was arguing with someone, possibly Duncan.

Yes, as they spoke, she knew it was Duncan, and he was in a heated discussion with Jamie.

"So, mate, engaged? Really? That's bloody cheeky, isn't it? What on earth are you playing at? You've got obligations and arrangements already in place, you're accountable, Jamie."

"Let me explain, Dunky," Jamie said, using Duncan's nickname to defuse the tension.

"Oh, this ought to be rich, a proper corker. Go on, I'm all ears," Duncan replied, folding his arms and fixing Jamie with a steely gaze.

"It's nothing, really."

"Nothing? You've given that stunning woman a ring, Jamie, and you call it nothing?" Duncan's voice rose, incredulously.

Joy held her breath. Was she really hearing this? And what did all this mean, obligations, arrangements, accountability? She remained frozen, ears straining as the men continued.

"Well, you see," Jamie began, his tone smug, "this isn't just any woman. She's the most beautiful woman in the world, a proper trophy. Not many blokes could manage to claim something like that. I had to have her."

"You absolute swine," Duncan said, his voice laced with disgust. "Don't you have a shred of decency in you? And the ring? Let me guess, another part of your scheme?"

Jamie grinned, unfazed. "It's a fake. I buy them in bulk, a half-dozen at a time, and spin some charming little yarn about it being my great-great-grandmother's. Works like a charm every time, Dunky."

Duncan was momentarily speechless. "You're having me on. Please tell me this is some twisted joke."

Jamie leaned back, utterly unbothered. "Oh, come off it, Dunky. Don't be so dramatic. A guy needs a bit of fun now and then, it's what keeps life interesting. Surely, you, of all people, should get that?"

Duncan's expression darkened, his voice sharpening. "You're barking mad. And you expect me to go along with this nonsense? To stand there and nod like some lackey?"

"Frankly, Dunky, I couldn't give a toss what you do. It's not your business. Look, like I said, a man needs his diversions. It's what makes me tick, and that's not going to change."

Duncan couldn't believe what he was hearing. Jamie's complete lack of ethics and his cavalier dismissal of relationships left him reeling.

There was a long, charged silence before Duncan spoke again, his voice lower but cutting. "And what, pray tell, do you suppose I should say to my sister? To my family? Hmm? You bloody bastard!"

Jamie and Duncan, now standing across from each other, had stopped talking. Duncan's expression was a mix of disgust and disbelief, while Jamie appeared calm as if calculating how to manage the situation.

Duncan broke the silence first. "So, you're telling me you're perfectly happy to leave Joy standing at the altar? Jilted and utterly humiliated?"

Jamie smirked, leaning casually against the desk. "No, I won't let it get that far. I know she's planning a wedding. I even talked her into handwriting the invitations, saved her from running to Tiffany's. Everyone at Tiffany's knows me, and news would have traveled fast." He laughed, a low, unsettling sound. "I'll postpone the wedding a few times, and eventually, she'll move on. But in the meantime, I've enjoyed myself."

Duncan shook his head in disbelief, letting out a slow, incredulous laugh. "God, you're absolutely heartless. It's astonishing, really." He walked to the bar to pour himself a drink, his hand trembling slightly as he lifted the glass.

Jamie turned to face him; his tone suddenly became sharper. "Look, Duncan, let's stop dancing around. I'll put my cards on the table. You know as well as I do that there's only one person for me. It was decided years ago, back in our Eton days." He chuckled softly. "Like they say, it's written in the stars."

Duncan's jaw tightened as he stared at him. "Written in the stars? Oh, please. More like scribbled in your bloated ego."

Jamie ignored the jab, continuing with an air of entitlement. "It's the way things are. Great families stay with great families, Duncan, despite the warts and mishaps. That's exactly what I intend to do. After I've had my fill, I'll settle down and do the right thing, for us, for the family."

"And what, pray tell, is the 'right thing,' Jamie?" Duncan's voice was clipped, his gaze unwavering. "For you, for me, for the family?"

Jamie's eyes gleamed, almost devilishly, as he delivered his intentions. "Marry your sister, Jane."

Duncan's hand froze mid-air, the glass hovering inches from his lips. He stared at Jamie, his face hardening.

Jamie leaned back smugly. "I know you know I already gave Jane the ring, the real one, and she's on board. Unlike you, she's a realist and knows exactly who I am and what I am. She's willing to take the deal: power, status, and everything that comes with being part of this family, no illusions. In exchange, she gets me, an incorrigible perpetual tomcat with a wandering spirit.

Jamie sat on the Chesterfield sofa and teasingly spread his long, athletic legs, strutting his "stuff," letting a smug grin spread across his face and crudely gesturing "And she can't get enough of 'this,' Dunky, just like you, back in the day as Eton-boys. The only difference is, for me it was adolescent curiosity, and I outgrew it; you didn't."

Jamie's taunting gesture sent a jolt through Duncan, a stark reminder of desires both past and present.

Duncan strolled over to the French doors, his eyes drifting across the sprawling estate and its impeccably manicured grounds. He lingered there for a moment, hands clasped behind his back, before speaking in a voice tinged with quiet reflection.

"You know, Jamie, you were always my favorite. My absolute favorite. At Eton, I let you in, shared parts of myself I'd never shown anyone else. I admired you, even … loved you, if I'm honest. At least, for a time."

He paused, his voice growing softer, almost wistful. "And then, with you and my sister, a proper relationship, well, I was happy for you and her, too. It meant you were going to always be connected to my family and me. "But now … well, now I bloody don't even recognize the man standing before me. Who are you anyway? And how could I or my sister or anyone ever trust you?"

The silence that followed was deafening. Duncan stared at Jamie as though he were a stranger, his eyes full of disbelief and revulsion. Finally, he muttered under his breath, "You're absolutely insufferable. Truly, you're beyond redemption."

Jamie sneered at the rebuke, his voice dripping with spite. "Oh, bugger off, you daft poof."

Joy, standing just outside the door, heard it all. Her breath caught in her throat. No. She must have misheard. Maybe this was some kind of inside joke between old friends, a bit of British sarcasm that didn't translate well. Jamie loved her. He had given her his great-great-grandmother's ring. That had to mean something … didn't it?

The words hit her like a slap. The blood drained from her face. The walls of Branwen seemed to close in, the heavy wooden beams pressing down on her chest. She clung to the stone wall for support, her world closing in on her.

That beautiful ring….

It's a fake. I buy them in bulk. Jamie's words echoed loudly in her head.

Joy was barely able to suppress hysteria. Her pulse raced as she almost could feel her heart breaking.

Was this real? Had she been living in a dream, believing in a future that was nothing more than an elaborate lie?

She swallowed hard, holding back nausea. Her knees wobbled, and for a horrifying second, she thought she might actually collapse right there, outside the door, exposed. If Jamie or Duncan turned toward the doorway, they would see her. And then what? What would she say? She had to get out. Now!

Joy wasn't sure how she managed it, but she stumbled back to her room, her mind clouded with shock and betrayal. The walls of the grand estate seemed to close in on her as the weight of what she had heard sank in. She yearned to be back home, at Christopher Street, with Mrs. Campanella, Davis and the lovable Noush enjoying the comfort food so joyfully served up and the warmth of human kindness.

Once inside her room, she sat at the edge of the bed, her suitcase forgotten for the moment.

Joy replayed the scene again. Jamie's voice was so casual, so utterly unconcerned. She looked down at the ring, the one she admired, the one she dreamed about. Bitterness filled her as she came to grips with the fact that it was nothing more than a cheap prop in Jamie's twisted scheme. How cruel, how calculating, how cunning.

She ripped it off, staring at the worthless piece of glass and metal. She realized that Jamie thought she was just another notch on his belt, a toy to be discarded when he was done.

And this Jane, she thought. *Duncan's sister? What's that all about? Is it conceivable that he is playing her, too? But it sounded like she really didn't care. How bizarre.*

Joy wiped the tears from her eyes and wondered: Who was the real Jamie? A devoted, loving fiancé, or a calculating, heartless deceiver? A master manipulator? A sociopath? Not that it really mattered at this point. Her life with Jamie was over.

Once again, her heart had been broken. It seemed to be a cruel pattern in her life, love slipping through her fingers time and again. Was her beauty a curse? Was it too high of a price to pay? Was it a trick God played on her?

She thought back to the prep school Romeo, her first crush, the one who she first gave her heart to, her first love, the purest kind, never to be another quite like it and only to be taken away by a jealous mother. Then there was Carlos, the brilliant Brown University exchange student, whose eyes sparkled but had mal-intent from the beginning. He was willing to savage her. His character flaws left no room for love or being loved.

Tyler came next, the hockey player who literally saved her from disaster and whose charm she adored and was perhaps the loveliest person she ever knew. He had it all: looks, smarts, and character. She had loved him so much and he had loved her, or so she thought. But he couldn't fully give himself to anyone, broken as he was. "I can't love you because I can't love myself," he'd confessed one night, leaving her to piece her heart together yet again.

Joy remembered the dashing Navy officer who loved his country more than he could love anyone. He broke her heart when he chose to be a warrior and not a lover. And now, Jamie. Charming, successful, larger than life, and, as it turned out, it was only skin deep. His true measure was of an utter cad and despicable.

Her thoughts drifted to the old gypsy she had encountered years ago at her village's piazza. The woman had grasped her tightly, her eyes widening as she studied the heart-shaped birth-mark, the one on Joy's neck. It was a heart in two pieces, a broken heart … foreboding.

"Many will love you; even more will lust after you. But you must be vigilant. Love, when it comes, may be an illusion, a fantasy surrounded by temptations," the gypsy had said in a thick accent. The warning had seemed absurd at the time, was it? But now, sitting in the suffocating silence of Branwen, it felt like a curse. *Am I doomed to be unloved?* She wondered, her hands shaking as she pressed them to her face.

The sharp realization jolted her back to the moment. This wasn't just heartbreak; it was betrayal. Jamie had used her, toyed with her emotions, and made a mockery of her trust.

Her resolve hardened. She couldn't stay here, not a minute longer. Rising from the bed, she grabbed her suitcase and began throwing her belongings into it with renewed determination. Tears blurred her vision, but her movements were quick and purposeful.

I'll figure it out, she thought, her jaw tightening as she zipped her bag. *I have to get out of here!* And she did.

CHAPTER 36

❧

Send in the Clown

London

Tired, distraught, and heartbroken, Joy still boarded the flight to London, the consummate professional, going through the motions. Her corporate partner had scheduled a gala Christmas party at Claridge's, the world-famous hotel that embodied old-school British luxury. For generations, Londoners had said the same thing: "Claridge's is simply the height of luxury, quintessentially British, effortlessly elegant, and absolutely first-class."

Before leaving New York, Joy emailed Cynthia and mentioned she would be at Claridge's a couple of days before Christmas, and unexpectedly, Cyn showed up. "A Christmas surprise," as Cyn put it.

The best friends decided to have drinks in the hotel's famous Fumoir Lounge, one of London's best-kept secrets. This was no ordinary drinks place; it was ultra-exclusive with dark and mysterious vibes. This was the kind of place where secrets were shared, deals made, and legends came to drink. The rich velvet seating, dark wood paneling, and dim lamps set the tone, one of quiet elegance and privacy. Joy, as a supermodel, was made welcome by Maurice, the barroom manager.

"Welcome, mademoiselle. You are most welcome. So pleased, you are a guest with us, and we look forward to serving your every need. And yes, your lady friend is here already, just over there. I arranged for a quiet corner where you ladies can, how do you say ... 'chit-chat,' *oui?*"

Cynthia had been there for at least half an hour and was already enjoying her second cocktail, served in bespoke Lalique crystal glasses.

"Oh my God, Joy. You look ... awful. What the hell is going on?"

"I'm fine ..."

"The hell you are. Now start talking, bitch. I'm ordering a bottle of Grey Goose, and we're getting to the bottom of this."

"Oh, Cyn, you won't believe what's happened."

A few drinks later, Cyn was fully up to speed, and ready to hire Tony the Butcher to castrate Jamie, shoot him, dismember him, and toss him into the meat grinder.

"No need for that. It's over, done, finished." Joy paused. "Cyn, do you really know someone named Tony the Butcher?"

"No, but I know people who do. And let me tell you, more than once I've picked up the phone but, thankfully, reconsidered. I'm so sorry, Joy. You deserve better than this. You are so perfect, and you should be with a perfect guy, not some asshole like Jamie, the aristocratic charlatan."

Joy smiled, despite her melancholia. "Yeah sure, perfect, all right. But there's more."

Cynthia lit up her fourth Newport: "Christ, Joy. More? What more could there be? You got dragged to Wales, a country where even the sheep aren't virgins, and sunny days are as rare as reliable WiFi. To a ghastly mansion with more cracks than an army of plumbers and putting up with a poof best mate who was probably considering wrestling you for that Birkin bag. There's more? PLEASE."

Again, Joy smiled through her funk. What she loved about Cynthia was her ability to succinctly sum up any situation and turn it into something that could be, at the very least, smiled upon.

Cynthia poured another. "OK, what is it?"

"I really can't describe it. It's more of a feeling than a fact. You know how you always say I have Joynar ... you know, like radar."

"Yeah, girl, you do. I've seen it many times."

"Well, I get the feeling that someone, or maybe 'someones,' are following me. Ever since that ordeal on Christopher Street, way back when, I get these feelings that I'm in danger. But then, I'm not. I can't figure it out. Maybe I'm getting paranoid or just jumpy after that attempt."

Cynthia gave Joy a serious look. "So, is this all the time?"

"Oh, no, just on occasion. Like in New York when we were at Corky's or on the plane over to London."

"Hmmm ... What does Bernie think, or Jamie?"

"If Bernie thought this was true, he'd hire the CIA, FBI, Metropol, and his brother-in-law, Melvin, to escort me everywhere I go."

"Well, maybe that's not a bad idea."

"What ... the CIA?"

"No, amigo, security. You know lots of famous people have it. I'd have it if I could, but then again, I'd probably seduce the guard, and while we were doing it, some rogue would pop us off.

But seriously, why don't you have Bernie look into this possibility?"

"Maybe you're right. He is the one who would know what to do. After all, he looks at me as his 'lottery ticket' and would never want to jeopardize that." Joy almost regretted those words as soon as she mouthed them. "But he really cares for me." Joy smiled. "I'm his cupcake."

Joy and Cynthia spent the next day together, catching up and, in Cynthia's case, "window shopping for a right proper Brit with all the right equipment." The prince was long gone, in fact, there were two others after him.

It was the day before Christmas Eve when the hotel Rolls drove Joy to Heathrow Airport. She just wanted to get home. Home to her cozy little unpretentious apartment. Home to Mrs. C., Davis, and the ever tail-wagging, sloppy-kissing Noush.

As the Rolls circled past Piccadilly, Joy's radar flared. A van lingered too close, shadowing them, then slipped back into traffic. She tried to shake it off , *just ghosts, just imagination.* But her Joynar told her otherwise.

CHAPTER 37

The Trap

Joy walked briskly toward the airport lounge, eager to put the painful breakup with Jamie behind her.

The Christmas gala was an elegant event, but one she hardly could remember given her state of mind. Her UK colleagues went overboard honoring her celebrity, providing a one-of-a-kind Russian sable wrap designed by no one less than Fendi. Foreign and domestic press covered the gala and morning papers were plastered with photographs of The Most Beautiful Woman in the world. Joy had done her duty and longed to return to New York. As it worked out, she would be flying the day before her birthday.

First class had been sold out, but she'd managed to snag the last business-class seat. It wasn't ideal, but at least it offered a measurable amount of comfort. As she inched forward in the long security line, her phone buzzed.

Her heart jumped. Could it be Jamie? The thought of hearing his voice made her stomach twist. They were done, and she never wanted to speak to or see him again. She shook her head; how foolish and completely duped she felt. Shame on her for falling for a reprobate like him. And that sharp-tongued Duncan, what was his deal? Was he another one of Jamie's pawns, a willing victim, or both?

She checked the screen, and "Unidentified Caller" flashed. Letting out a sigh of relief, it wasn't Jamie, she answered.

"Hello?"

"Good afternoon, Miss Nordstrom," a pleasant, polished voice began. "This is Sarah from British Air's passenger services. We're reaching out regarding your upcoming flight."

"Oh?" Joy replied cautiously. "What's this about?"

"Well," the caller, a skilled imposter, said smoothly, "I see you've booked one of our flights. I wanted to check if you had any special requests or if there's anything we can do to enhance your travel experience today."

Joy relaxed slightly. The voice was friendly and professional, the kind of service she'd expect from British Air. "Actually," she said, "I did put my name on the waitlist for a first-class upgrade. Is this about that?"

She was hooked. The scammer skillfully steered the conversation to extract her flight details and set the trap.

"I'd be delighted to help you with that, Miss. I just need some information for security purposes. Is that all right with you?"

"Of course." Joy took out her boarding pass and eagerly read off the details.

The caller paused as though confirming something. "Ah, yes. Thank you, Miss Nordstrom. It looks like there might be a first-class seat available for you. Could you please confirm your current seat assignment so I can verify the availability?"

"Oh, sure," Joy said. "I'm in Seat 4A in Business."

"Perfect. I'll change that to Seat 1C in Premium First Class. Would that be acceptable?"

"Very. Thank you! Is there an additional cost?"

"Let me see." The imposter continued, "My, Miss Nordstrom, aren't you the lucky one. You're eligible for this upgrade at no charge."

"Fantastic, the first good thing that's happened to me in a while."

"Perfect," the voice said. "Now, to finalize your upgrade, you'll need to return to the ticket counter. They'll reissue your boarding pass there. You have plenty of time before your flight."

Joy frowned. "Return to the ticket counter? Can't you handle this now?"

"I wish I could, ma'am," the caller said apologetically, "but upgrades require a specially modified boarding pass, and those can only be issued at the counter. If you head there now, they'll process it right away. We'll hold the seat for fifteen minutes. Or, if you'd prefer, I can offer the seat to the next passenger on the list."

Joy was hooked. "No, don't do that. Okay, I'll head there now," Joy said, stepping out of the line and walking toward the ticket counter.

"Wonderful," the caller said. "Thank you, Miss Nordstrom. Have a pleasant flight, and Happy Christmas to you

As the line went dead, Joy tucked her phone into her jacket pocket and started toward the broad corridor. She didn't notice the two men in dark suits stepping away from a nearby kiosk to follow her.

Joy strode purposefully through the terminal, the thought of a first-class upgrade lifting her spirits slightly. She stepped into the bustling crowd of passengers and headed toward the ticket counter. For a moment, she thought she smelled a familiar scent, but before she could place it, two tall men flanked her, their movements sharp and synchronized.

"Miss Nordstrom?" one of them asked, his voice calm but firm.

She stopped, startled. "Yes. Who are you?"

"We're friends," the man said.

"Friends?" she repeated, her pulse quickening.

"Friends of Prince Ali," he clarified, his tone unchanging. "He has invited you to join him."

Alarm bells went off in her head. She tried to step back, but the men tightened their grip on her arms.

"Please cooperate, Miss Nordstrom," the second man said with a chilling smile. "See that wheelchair following us? If you resist, we'll sedate you and wheel you out of here. No one will be the wiser."

Joy's mind raced. She forced herself to remain calm and think. If she let herself be taken, she might never be seen again, or worse, survive. She'd heard stories of models abducted while traveling, especially in the Middle East, who were never found, possibly victims of white slavery.

But she knew she was a survivor. She had survived that unthinkable episode with Carlos, who had planned to drug and violate her. She begged herself, *Stay calm, think ... think.*

Her mind raced. Then she remembered Bernie's special gift, a custom phone equipped with a panic button. Once pressed, it would notify Bernie and local authorities of her location and movements using a powerful GPS signal. It would also emit a silent tracking signal, allowing authorities to pick up the trail. Her mind flashed back to the day Bernie gave her the device:

"Look, Cupcake, your Bernie has a present for you. It's really special and very practical."

"How sweet, Bernie." Joy unwrapped the small box to reveal a cell phone. "A phone? Thanks, Bernie, but I already have one."

"Not this one, kitten. This is the kind all the celebrities have. For those who are, well, how do you say... targets."

A cold chill ran through Joy's body. "Target? Bernie, you're scaring me."

"Don't be scared, kitten. Bernie's here. But the truth is, we're all targets in this meshugana world. The old lady coming down the church steps with six bucks in her bag or the rich kid in the sports car showing off with daddy's money, everyone's a target. Some are bigger and richer than others, but it's all the same."

This reality check wasn't something Joy wanted. The unsought-after fame and notoriety were already a burden. Being a target was just too much.

"Bernie," she said, "I really think this is over the top. Nobody is going to bother me."

"Joy, like it or not, you are *the most beautiful woman in the world*. With that comes a lot of benefits, but also some baggage, and being a target is now part of your territory. And remember that night on your doorstep. Oy vey. That's what I'm talking about."

Joy looked at the phone, then at Bernie, as a wave of realization washed over her. "I suppose you're right."

"Of course, your Bernie is always right. So, if you ever need help, just press the button, and Bernie will send the Mounties after you."

Carefully, Joy slid her hand into her pocket, feeling for the raised "P" button. With her heart pounding, she pressed it hard, praying Bernie would receive the alert.

The men continued to lead her toward an exit, ever vigilant and determined. They knew failure wasn't an option. If they screwed this up, they'd face the prince's wrath, a prospect far more terrifying than any authority. His reputation preceded him; whispers of his ruthlessness and sadistic punishments echoed in hushed tones. There were even rumors that he had enemies drawn and quartered in medieval fashion.

At the exit, a sleek black Mercedes van with dark, tinted windows idled ominously. Joy's mind worked furiously. Were the authorities on their way? Had Bernie's signal reached them? And even if it had, how long would it take for them to find her? Did the device even work outside of the United States?

Just as the men reached for the van door, Joy's phone began to emit a loud, piercing alarm. The sound startled everyone around them, including the abductors.

"What the hell is that?" one of them barked, releasing her arm.

The sound drew the attention of nearby travelers and security personnel. A group of onlookers gathered, their curiosity piqued by the commotion. Joy seized the opportunity, twisting free from the remaining man's grip and stumbling toward the crowd.

"Help! These men are trying to kidnap me!" she shouted, her voice filled with desperation.

The terminal erupted into chaos. Travelers scattered, some pulling out their phones to record the scene while others called for help. Airport security officers rushed toward them, their radios cracking with urgent instructions.

Realizing their plan had fallen apart, the men bolted, abandoning their plan as the escape van screeched away from the curve. They ran in two different directions, disappearing into the chaos of the terminal. Joy collapsed onto the floor, trembling, and praying that this ordeal was finally over.

"Ma'am, are you okay?" a security officer asked, kneeling beside her.

Joy nodded weakly, clutching her bag. "They said they worked for Prince Ali. They've been following me."

The officer reassured her. "You're safe now. We'll handle this."

Her phone buzzed in her pocket. She saw Bernie's name flashing on the screen.

"Bernie," she whispered, tears streaming down her face. "You got my signal."

"We tracked your location," Bernie's steady voice replied. "Stay with the authorities. I've already contacted local law enforcement. You're going to be fine, Joy. I'm coming to get you. Stay put. Bernie's on his way."

As the chaos began to settle, Joy took a deep breath. She had outsmarted her captors, just as she had once outsmarted Carlos and his gang in Providence. Her ordeal was over, and she was safe, waiting to go home, under the protective gaze of Bernie, to the nurturing care of Mrs. Campanella, and the friendship and understanding of Davis, not to mention a few dozen licks from Noush.

CHAPTER 38

———— ❦ ————

Alone and Blue

Ladies and gentlemen, please fasten your seat belts, stow your tray tables, and bring your seats to a fully upright position. We are making our final approach to JFK, where the local time is 5:45 p.m., and the weather is just about 34 degrees. Our navigator says it's looking like we may get a white Christmas later this evening, so bundle up!"

Joy glanced over and saw a sleepy Bernie awakening to the announcement. She smiled. Who would have ever thought he'd be her knight in shining armor? The silly little man with the funny glasses who spoke with a forked tongue. But he was, and she'd forever be grateful. She smiled again, taking a deep, contemplative look, not so much at Bernie but at life, her life. By the grace of God, things could have turned out quite differently if events at the airport had gone the wrong way.

Waiting in the baggage claim area for Joy was George, her SUV driver, who had come to collect her and her luggage. Bernie had arranged everything. He had flown thousands of miles to rescue her, and now he was concerned about her ride home.

As they walked through the reception area, Bernie's phone blared. The ringtone was set to Frank Sinatra's "My Way," a fitting anthem for a man who brokered deals and handled people.

"Europe," he muttered, answering briskly.

"Bernard Rubin?" came a formal voice on the line.

"Yes, speaking."

"This is Inspector Hardcastle from Scotland Yard. We have apprehended the perpetrators. We picked them up a few blocks away from the airport. They were on the run. Apparently, they are citizens of Qatar, here illegally. We contacted their embassy and got their rap sheet. Bad lot, these boys. We are currently holding them at Scotland Yard, Northwest. A formal investigation and charges will be forthcoming, right and proper."

Bernie's face lightened. "That's good news. At least we can feel comfortable that Miss Nordstrom is no longer in danger from these thugs. Keep them locked up. I would appreciate you keeping me advised."

"Of course, Mr. Rubin. We will send all the paperwork immediately to the US authorities and a copy to you."

He ended the call and turned to Joy. "Well, Cupcake, looks like they got the bastards."

Joy nodded, relief washing over her. Perhaps this would end the fear that danger was around every corner.

After a brief hug and a quick goodbye, Bernie was on his way. He had arranged his own transportation and was heading out to see his sister in Brooklyn as a Chanukah surprise.

"Is that all, ma'am, just this roller bag?" George asked.

"Thank you, George, and yes. I always travel light. In my business, they give me clothes when I get there."

George shrugged and grabbed her bag. "Follow me, ma'am. I'm just out here."

The ride was longer than usual as it was Christmas Eve and the city was bustling. Clogged roads and endless lines of traffic made the trip feel interminable.

Joy commented, "This traffic is brutal."

"Yes, ma'am, especially tonight. Seems like there's a broken pipe or something ahead, and the cops are directing traffic around it."

Time seemed to stand still, and Joy grew tired of waiting; she was anxious to get home. Exhausted from her transatlantic flight and the life-threatening ordeal, she just wanted to be in her comfy pajamas.

"Look, George, I'm only a few minutes from here. I think I'll step out and walk," she said.

"But, ma'am, I'd feel bad if I didn't make sure you got home."

"No, George, don't worry. I'll hike it from here. I know the area; I'll be just fine. I only have this little roller bag, and it's no problem. Besides, I might stop at a bodega and pick something up."

"Very well. I can't pull over, but you can jump out since the traffic isn't moving."

Joy dropped a hundred-dollar bill on the front seat. "Something extra, George. Merry Christmas." She exited the SUV into the crisp December evening air. The colored lights twinkled over the thresholds of the old brownstones and townhouses. Like little kids, these portals were all decked out for the holidays, each building with its own personality and stories. She was on her block in a couple of minutes and walked into the corner bodega.

"Hi. Do you have any chicken soup?"

"Over there, lady, next to the cake mixes. We have all kinds."

"Thanks."

Joy picked up two cans and wandered until she found some Ritz crackers, a jar of peanut butter, and a package of chamomile tea, which she hoped would help her sleep. At the checkout, she noticed a rather sickly Christmas tree, the last one on the shelf. It wasn't more than twenty-four inches tall. She thought, Hmm, some Christmas tree. I remember those magical ones at home with Mama and Papa. Oh, how she loved those celebrations, the age-old traditions. How she missed them. Oddly, she thought, I have the world at my feet, and I only want what I don't have.

"I'll take the tree too," she told the preoccupied clerk.

"Sure. Anything else? How about some candy canes, they are half price.'

"No thanks, just these things."

As she waited for the clerk to tally her bill, a headline on a pop culture magazine jumped out at her: "*Will the Most Beautiful Woman in the World Ever Find Love? Read her story and see exclusive pictures.*"

Her picture was prominently displayed. The painful reality of her life flashed before her and was broadcast for the world to see. She was tempted to buy the magazine but then thought, why torture herself with such tripe? She paid her bill and wished the clerk a merry Christmas.

"Yeah, you too, lady, and happy New Year too."

Joy barely made it up the two flights of stairs, too spent, too numb. The door to her apartment opened and seemed to whisper, *welcome home.* She set her purchase on the counter and moved toward the couch; the old one she loved so much. She couldn't decide if this was a close call or just a plain lucky break. Tears came hard, and she buried her face in a pillow, muffling the deep, gut-wrenching sobs in case a neighbor lingered in the hall.

She propped the pitiful little evergreen on her coffee table, and she went into her bedroom and slipped into sweats and a t-shirt, and then went and put her feet up. It was almost 7:45

p.m., and she was just grateful to be home. She closed her eyes and thought about the strange hand that life had dealt her.

She laughed bitterly to herself. *"The 'Most Beautiful Woman in the World,' alone on Christmas Eve.' Now that's a headline!"*

She thought of her mother and father, far away but in her heart, and she was glad she had saved them the agony of meeting Jamie and the "pretend" engagement. How much more mortified she would have been if they'd been part of it.

The phone rang, breaking the silence and her melancholia.

"Hello."

"You're home! Merry Christmas."

"Yes, Davis, I am. Merry Christmas to you."

"I suppose you're going to the Ritz or Four Seasons for dinner or someplace like that? Probably with Jamie and some of the A-list or movie stars."

"No, no. I'm exhausted. I just got in a little while ago. I'm vegging out."

"All by yourself … on Christmas Eve … you're kidding? Where's the dashing Jamie? Not under your tree this year … ha ha."

"No." Joy sniffled into the phone. "It's over, Davis. He turned out to be a terrible person, just stringing me along."

"Oh, no, Joy. No one deserves that, especially someone as sweet as you. What are you doing for the holiday?"

"I'm here, alone with my Charlie Brown reject of a Christmas tree."

"Well, that won't do at all. You march yourself down here to my dungeon. Mrs. Campanella dropped off a pan of homemade lasagna and a shitload of cookies this afternoon. You know her. She said she didn't want me to eat takeout Chinese or, worse, Luigi's horrible pizza on Christmas Eve. Come help me eat it all."

"No, I'm good. I'd make lousy company tonight. And besides, I've had a horrible thing happen."

"Besides the Jamie thing?"

"Yes."

"What do you mean, horrible? Are you all right?"

"I think so, but ..." Joy couldn't help it and began crying into the phone.

"You're crying, I can tell! That settles it. Come down here. I want to know why."

"I'm already in my pajamas, and I don't feel like getting all dolled up."

"PJs are fine," he laughed. "I won't even notice. Come on. You're my best friend, and best friends don't let best friends be alone, especially on Christmas! And besides, I want to know what happened. Is there anything I can do?"

"No, no, it's all over. I'm fine."

"It doesn't sound like it to me. Come on down and have a good cry on your buddy's shoulder."

Davis knew Joy well enough to tell that she was hurting. He decided to make light of it until he could investigate.

"Joy, I need a little help warming up this yummy lasagna. Better yet, maybe we can get Mrs. Campanella to stop lighting those candles for her dearly departed Tony and join us. You do know how to cook, don't you?"

"Well, to be honest, I'm no Julia Child."

"Well, I'm not sure who she is, but it doesn't matter. Just come on down. I'll call Mrs. C. How about nine? Does that work for you?"

Joy ran her fingers through her long, beautiful hair, thinking it must be a mess. Her eyes were probably red from sobbing.

"Oh, I don't know, Davis. I'm a mess."

"Don't worry, I won't even notice. Look, company is company. It's Christmas Eve, so you are coming. See you. Bye."

The line went dead, and Joy sat there staring at her little tree, the phone still in her hand. For the first time that night, she felt the faintest flicker of warmth, even a sense of relief.... She wouldn't be alone this Christmas Eve after all.

CHAPTER 39

———— 🍎 ————

The Last Chapter

Davis hung up. Reluctantly, Joy agreed. She knew Davis was right. He was her best friend, the only living person she ever confided in and trusted. Yes, she could tell Cyn anything, but her advice was always the same, go out and get a man. Apparently, she believed that cured everything.

But Davis was deeper. He was just a regular guy, not as tall or handsome as some of the men she had known. He certainly wasn't rich or powerful, which she had learned came with significant drawbacks. But he was ... well, Davis. Someone she liked talking to and who made her feel safe and comfortable.

She couldn't think of a better person to share her anxiety and fear from the airport confrontation.

Joy slipped on her gym clothes and made the familiar jaunt down the dimly lit flight and half-flight of stairs to the basement apartment. She grabbed the pitiful little tree with its cheesy red bows she had picked earlier to bring. It was a sad little thing, but she knew Davis wouldn't care how it looked. He'd focus on her thoughtfulness.

The door was ajar when she arrived at his landing. Noush knew Joy's footsteps and the familiar scent of her perfume and didn't feel the need to bark at her arrival. Instead, the dog greeted her with a frenzy of tail-wagging and sloppy kisses.

The aroma of Frasier pine filled her senses. The apartment was dark, except for the glow of scented candles emitting a wonderful Christmas fragrance.

"Hello, it's me."

"Hi, there. Merry Christmas. Come in."

"I brought you this little tree. It's pathetic, but at least it's something."

"Right. I'm sure it's perfect. Thanks for bringing it. I never think of getting one, and besides, I can't get them straight on the stand."

Joy sympathized, recalling the only argument she ever saw her parents have was over getting the Christmas tree right. Joy walked over to the sofa, leaned over, and turned on a table lamp, and then another one on the other side of the sofa.

"I hope you're hungry ... come on, let's eat. The lasagna is in the fridge. Mrs. Campanella won't come; she must finish her baking for tomorrow and then she's going to Midnight Mass. She said to pop the pan into the oven at 350 for about thirty minutes, and voila, it's ready to go. So have a go at it, 'Julia.'"

Thirty minutes later, Joy pulled the bubbling golden brown lasagna from the oven and put it on the counter to cool just a bit. Davis searched around and finally found some wine glasses and plates in the depths of his cupboards. He carefully put them on the small coffee table in front of the tired but comfortable leather sofa. Joy noticed but didn't say that one of the dishes was chipped; she thought it was typical of bachelorhood.

Dinner was delightful, homemade and delicious. It featured crusty Tuscan bread from Joe the Baker's, generously slathered with Mrs. C's legendary herb butter, paired perfectly with a bottle of Chianti that Tony had gifted Davis before he passed away. Joy allowed herself to indulge, setting aside her usual disciplined diet, while Davis, with obvious enthusiasm, devoured two man-sized portions of what he dubbed a *culinary masterpiece.*

"So, what's going on?" Davis asked gently, his voice filled with concern.

Joy recounted everything that had happened, from Jamie's vicious betrayal to the incident at Heathrow, her words spilling out as Davis listened intently. When she finished, he wrapped his strong arms around her, offering silent comfort. "You're safe now, Joy. You're home, and I'm here with you. And so is Noush."

For the first time since the incident, Joy felt like everything was going to be OK and decided to talk about something else.

The conversation was light, and the trauma at the airport began to fade like nightmares usually do after a while.

Joy looked at the miserable little Christmas tree sitting on top of the piano and thought of Christmases gone by.

"You know, Davis, I love Christmas; it's my favorite time of the year. I was born on Christmas Eve."

Davis sat up straighter. "That's today.... Today is your birthday?"

"Yeah, it is."

"I've asked you what your birthday is for years now, and you would never tell me."

"I don't like people making a fuss."

"But your friends and family should fuss."

"I know. I heard from my folks and, of course, Bernie and Cynthia."

"And when were you going to tell me ... your favorite downstairs neighbor?"

"I don't know; it just didn't seem important. And after what happened, it didn't seem to matter."

Joy's thought returned to her Christmases past. "When I was growing up, we had wonderful holidays. The Portuguese had rich traditions that centered around family and church. My mom went all out, and my dad would take me to every Christmas market and festival in the surrounding areas."

"Really, nice."

"Yeah, a lot better than the fake and phony stuff they do nowadays. The kind of things that create real traditions, something generations can actually pass down."

Joy wondered. "And how about you? What did you do?"

Davis forced a smile, hesitated, and began: "Well, Joy, unlike you, I didn't have a family or, for that matter, much to celebrate. I was raised in foster care, mostly in group homes. My mom had to give me up, and I never really knew my father. So holidays were filled with other people's charity and pretty much leftovers."

Joy's light-heartedness changed to a sorrowful mode as Davis filled her in on his youth.

"Yeah, so most Christmases were pretty much the same. A hand-me-down sweater, and maybe a package from Toys for Tots,...something you really didn't want. However, a bright spot was that I had a good voice and was often asked to sing. I was invited to events. I met some guy who took an interest in me, and I cut a CD; I was just about eighteen years old at the time. The guy died, and, well, the album really didn't go anywhere, so I joined the Marines. It was the only path I saw, at the time."

"I heard your singing was pretty good."

"You did? How would you know that?"

"Oh, a little bird told me."

Davis added two and two and figured the little bird had to be Mrs. Campanella. "Does that little bird cook a wicked lasagna?"

Joy smiled, that mischievous one she frequently showed with Davis, "I'm not saying ... But you've only let me hear you play piano a little. You are hiding your talents!"

"Now it's my turn to say it didn't seem important. Anyway, I grew up in the Corps. It was the family I never had, buddies who would die for each other, and often did."

"As that's how you got ..." Joy stopped and didn't mention the scars that peeked out from under his shirt."

"Pretty much. But we all suffered, and like the rest of them, I bucked up and moved on."

"Bucked up! I think getting a Navy Cross is way more than bucking up." At that moment, Joy realized she had slipped and said something she wasn't supposed to know.

"Who told you that?"

Joy was caught and figured the best answer was "a little bird."

"I spent a lot of time in the hospital after that, and well, it was life-changing. And here I am."

Joy was touched and moved a bit closer to Davis, taking his hand into hers. "I can't imagine how hard it was ... and how it still might be. But I am, so proud of you and so are millions of Americans. You are a hero and by any measure, someone that earned and has my highest respect."

Davis blushed and pushed it aside. "They are a lot of heroes, but the real ones, the ones that count, aren't here anymore to soak up the glory or admiration."

It was just like Davis to push off any recognition or praise.

Joy walked over to the piano and ran her fingers over the yellowed and well-played keyboard. "Let's focus on the present, not the past...how about you play some Christmas songs for me? I miss being home with my folks. My Mom would play, and we would all sing, come on, let's see what you got ... big shot," she teased.

Reluctantly, Davis moved from the couch, almost tripping on Noush, who had scoffed up crumbs most of the evening, to the rickety piano bench. "What will it be?"

"I don't care, I love them all."

Davis began to play the somewhat out-of-tune piano with "White Christmas." He was amazingly well-trained and played from memory, like a true professional.

They sang together, sitting close on the old bench. Then came "We Wish You a Merry Christmas" and "Greensleeves," followed by "Joy to the World."

When the final note of "Joy to the World" faded, Joy took Davis's hands and looked into his eyes. "You are so talented. And thank you for making me feel so safe. You are a true friend, one of the most important ones in my life. You seem to understand me, and you are always there to hear me out, to stand by me, and yet never ask for anything in return. Do you know how rare that is? You are special."

"And so are you, Joy, very special."

Davis squirmed in his seat. He had been debating something all evening, finally deciding.

"Joy, I have a Christmas present for you."

"You don't! I didn't get you anything. I meant to, but I didn't have a minute to shop. I didn't even know if I'd be here in New York until yesterday. Oh God, this is awful. How embarrassing."

"Don't sweat it. My gift is homemade and didn't cost a dime."

Now Joy was curious: "Homemade," she thought oddly, wondering what it could be. "So, what is it?"

"It's a song. One I wrote for you. I hope you love it as much as I do."

Davis began to play his song. It was a soft, lovely ballad with a beautiful melody. His talented fingers floated over the ivory keys as he softly hummed the first few bars. He began to sing, his trained voice filled with emotion, articulating each word. His eyes filled with tears as he exposed his innermost feelings, words he never dared speak but would sing, words that were so long hidden. In his deep and resonating voice, he began to sing his gift to Joy:

I see you in my heart; I feel you in my soul,
Your love is like the sunlight that makes my spirit whole.
Though dreams may fade to shadows, and stars may leave the sky,
My heart will still be yours until the day I die.

I see you in my heart; I feel you in my soul,
A love I've held in silence, a story never told.
Each day begins in darkness, until I hear your voice,
And then the world feels brighter, you'll always be my choice.

Though fate has drawn a distance, a line I cannot cross,
The thought of you sustains me through every pain and loss.
I see you in my heart; I feel you in my soul,
Forever bound together, a love that keeps me whole.

As the song ended, he worried: *That was it. If she doesn't feel the same, it will be the end. But at least she'll know, finally know.*

Davis turned to Joy. "Was that out of line?"

Joy, deep in thought, said nothing.

Worried by her silence, Davis turned crimson and began to stammer. "I'm so sorry; it *was* out of line. I'm a fool to think you would ever want me. What a fool."

Joy paused, his question lingering in the air like something fragile, something priceless, as if he wasn't sure whether she would catch it or let it shatter. Her thoughts whirled out of control. *What was happening?*

Without thinking or hesitation, she kissed Davis's unsuspecting lips and melted into his arms. From the deepest, darkest corner of her being, an epiphany rose, catching her completely off guard. She had spent her life searching for a love that was real, the kind she had always dreamed of but had never been offered. The kind her mom shared with her dad. The kind that was boundless and with empathy. Instead, she had been surrounded, for the most part, by men who wanted her for her beauty, men who couldn't see past the surface to the woman beneath.

But now, in this quiet moment, everything became clearer. The love she had been searching for, the love she didn't think existed for her, had been right there all along, just downstairs. It wasn't loud or flashy, and it didn't come with empty promises, big bank accounts with egos to match. It was quiet, steady, and true. Davis saw her for exactly who she was and asked for nothing more, no demands, no expectations beyond mutual admiration.

Then, as if to say, "I get you," she took his hand and led him toward his room, just down the dark corridor.

Tears welled in her eyes, but this time, they weren't tears of pain or regret. They were tears of joy, tears of revelation. *How had I been so blind?* she thought. She'd been looking for love in all the wrong places and it had been right under her nose all along, one and a half stories away. *How did I miss this?*

Davis, overwhelmed by emotion, followed Joy's lead. Joy pulled Davis closer, and they fell to the bed.

The two lay next to each other without uttering a word. They kissed again. Davis rose to remove his T-shirt, then the rest, as Joy slipped out of her gym clothing. They lay stark naked, their bodies speaking the truths they couldn't yet say aloud. Davis explored Joy's body, touching her as if she were a rare treasure. And Joy breathed in the scent of a man's man, one whose strong and muscular body was irresistible. She pulled him close, and the weight of his body upon her was a comforting blanket, one she never wanted to let go of. It was then that they made love for the first time. His gentleness, tempered by a self-assured masculinity, the kind every woman craves from her lover, was exactly what she needed and, in many ways, what she had expected from him. After all, he was a Marine, a hero, a man who embodied strength and courage, yet beneath it all was tender and loving. He took her breath away. And when they were done, they knew that they had been taken to someplace very special. They fell asleep in each other's arms, knowing that this was a love that felt lasting, passionate, filled with meaning, and a promising future.

The couple woke to the morning bells of St. Andrew's, just down the street, announcing Christmas Day, a day filled with hope and renewal for so many. The morning light had not quite peeked through the darkness of the night.

Davis awoke first, rising on one elbow, exhilarated yet with lingering doubt. He waited for Joy to stir, her face sleeping peacefully until she woke and turned toward him.

"Good morning." She smiled.

"Good morning to you." Almost apologetically, Davis asked, "Did I wake you?"

"You didn't."

He took a deep breath, gathering courage as he decided to speak from his heart, throwing caution to the wind. Softly, and with a little shake in his voice, he laid his head next to Joy's and said, "I've loved you, from a distance, for a long time now, Joy, but I didn't think I had a chance or the right to ask you to love me. I have serious baggage, the kind that lasts a lifetime. I could never measure up."

Joy listened carefully and moved closer, wrapping her arms around him. It wasn't the polite kind of embrace that said, "See you later." This one said, *You matter, and I'm not letting go.* She looked at his face and deep into his eyes, past the scars of battle that doctors had worked tirelessly to blend into his rugged, manly face, seeing only the strength and kindness that truly was his.

"Measure up? Davis, you are, beyond measure, a beautiful person who has touched my heart in ways I never thought possible. You may not see it in yourself, but I do, and that's all that matters.

"Then we're good?" he asked, his voice barely above a whisper.

"Yes, Davis," she said, her voice warm and certain. "We're more than good."

She pressed her lips to his, tasting him and committing the moment to memory. They lingered there, savoring a moment that felt entirely new and entirely right.

Why hadn't she seen it before? Maybe she hadn't been ready. Maybe she had been chasing love that sparkled and dazzled, love that blinded her to what truly mattered. But Davis, a creative soul, a war hero who gave of himself first, steady, selfless Davis, had always been there, waiting in the quiet shadows. A man who loved her not for *what* she was, but for *who* she was.

She thought back to last night, to the beautiful words he had written for her and his unforgettable voice: "I see you in my heart; I feel you in my soul." They said it all on so many levels. No man had ever come close to saying and meaning anything like that to her.

Was this Christmas magic, or something that had been brewing but unnoticed for so long? But was it lasting? Instinctively, Joy felt in her heart of hearts that it was.

Joy looked out the window and saw in the rapidly disappearing darkness of the new day, Christopher Street lit up like a Christmas card, the welcoming front door stoops, bright lights, and Christmas trees peeking through the old windows. Soon, people would be laughing behind those windows, and children would be peering under their trees to see what Santa Claus had brought. A light snow fell, not enough to cover the street, but enough to make it a white Christmas, just as that navigator on the flight over had predicted. The two lay so close, each pondering the greatest gift one could receive ... the gift of love.

Davis broke the silence and whispered, fearful that saying it out loud would perhaps damage the fragility of it all. "I love you, Joy, are you certain, that this can be for us?"

"Davis, it will be; my heart tells me so. For the first time, I feel something that has eluded me. I promise wholeheartedly that we will make a life journey for the two of us."

She kissed him again as if she could never get enough, pouring everything she felt into that moment. Davis held her face in his strong, steady hands when their lips finally parted as if afraid to let go. With deliberate care, he ran his index finger along her features, studying her like an artist would a model, admiring every line, every curve. He traced her cheekbones, followed the soft slope of her jaw, and lingered gently over her lips as if sketching her beauty.

When he finished tracing the features of the woman he had fallen in love with, the one he had never seen, nor ever would, the one the world called the most beautiful woman in the world, he whispered in quiet awe, "God, you're beautiful? Aren't you?"

Joy's cheeks flushed as she smiled, leaning closer. She realized that Davis had never seen her. Not the way the world had. And yet, he loved her in a way no man ever had, or perhaps ever could.

Joy answered Davis's question. "Beautiful? Some might think so," she whispered. She guided his hand to her heart, holding it there to feel its steady beat. "To the world, my beauty was a trophy, but to you, I was a person, someone with more to offer, more to give. You gave me the gift of being truly seen, without ever even seeing me ... wanted, not collected." Her voice broke on the last word, and she clung to him as though she had finally found what she had been seeking her entire life, the home she had been searching for all along, and the man who mended her heart.

The End

And the Rest of the Story... Miracles Happen

Joy and Davis married and built a life filled with love and laughter and three children. After buying the building and completely renovating it, they split their time between Christopher Street and a comfortable villa in Braga, Portugal. Mrs. Campanella lived in the building until her death at eighty-nine, as their guests.

Joy concentrated on Davis's health, using her fame and connections to open doors for him. Her tireless efforts led her to a small clinic in Switzerland, where doctors diagnosed Davis's blindness as conversion disorder, something the overburdened VA hospitals had never considered. This disorder manifests temporary symptoms, such as blindness or paralysis, without a physical cause. Swiss researchers attributed it to the trauma Davis had endured in dangerous wartime situations.

Davis underwent ten months of extensive treatment, and against all odds, his eyesight returned to 20/20.

Joy also introduced Davis to influential figures in the music industry. Captivated by his talent, they dubbed him the second coming of Frank Sinatra. With her encouragement, Davis began a long and successful career as a singer and songwriter. Nine years later, his work reached its pinnacle when he won both a Grammy and Academy Award for writing and singing the Best Original Song for a blockbuster film entitled *Love is Blind*.

The couple thrived. Joy's design business flourished, and Davis's career brought him a level of fame that nearly matched hers. Together, they were unstoppable.

But the most inexplicable phenomenon came after the birth of their first child. The tiny birthmark on Joy's neck, the one shaped like a broken heart, seemed to change, no longer broken, it had formed into a complete, unified heart.

And the Rest of the Characters:

- **Bernie:** Seeing that Joy was all set, Bernie moved on and found a new "Cupcake" with a rock star client who called herself *Hot Mess*, and who struggled becoming fluid in "Berniese."

- **Cynthia (Cyn):** To date, she's been married four times, each husband younger than the last. After her father's death, she inherited the family business and the vast fortune that came with it. Last seen in Monaco, she was seeking "Mr. Next."

- **Travis:** After finishing prep school in California, he attended Harvard and married Bunny, his mother's best friend's daughter. Together, they have four kids.

- **Kevin:** Kevin stayed in the Navy, rising to the rank of Commander. Tragically, he was killed in action during a mission in Afghanistan. He was posthumously awarded the Silver Star for bravery. He never married. Joy mourned Kevin's sacrifice, a quiet reminder that love and life are fragile, and even the bravest are not spared.

- **Luke:** After graduating from Brown University, Luke was drafted into the NHL and became a celebrity player with a massive fan following. Women swooned over him, but Luke lived his life in quiet denial, never acting on the secret he kept close to his heart. Joy always held a dear spot in her heart for Luke, wondering if Luke's greatest vulnerability was not on the ice, but within himself. He never declared himself and probably never could.

- **"D":** D returned to Italy to continue as a world-famous fashion photographer, Icon. He spent his entire life chasing women, never granting his mother her only wish. "Beabellissimo, settle down and get married; make me some grandchildren."

- **Jamie Harper-Smyth:** Jamie lived *La Dolce Vita*, never changing his hedonistic ways. He married Jane, Duncan's sister, but they lived apart most of the time. Jamie never lost his looks, his money, or his charm, but he lost his soul years ago.